THE BURIED MAN

Norman Stahl and Don Horan

THE BURIED MAN

McGraw–Hill Book Company

New York   St. Louis   San Francisco

Toronto   Hamburg   Mexico

1 2 3 4 5 6 7 8 9 D O C D O C 8 7 6 5

ISBN 0-07-060699-4

LIBRARY OF CONGRESS CATALOGING IN PUBLICATION DATA

Stahl, Norman.
  The buried man.
  I. Horan, Don.   II. Title.
PS3569.T313B8   1985   813'.54   84-26094
ISBN 0-07-060699-4

Book design by Kathryn Parise

THE BURIED MAN

1

Stanislaw Kuzianik struggled at last to the top of the tall ridge and looked down into the rich farmlands of the long, narrow valley. There was still much cold to come to Poland, but here in the south the spring sun and the long climb had worked up a sweat beneath his down jacket. He knew that if he removed the jacket he would soon be shivering—his dying heart didn't seem to send the blood hotly enough anymore. While he was sleeping in the open last night, even the coat and the heavy blanket that he carried in his backpack had not kept him from feeling he was packed in ice.

Despite his great size and strength, this climb after the morning's lengthy cross-country walk had left him breathless and set his legs trembling. Thirty-seven years old and almost finished, he thought. Bitterness welled up in him, but he choked it back and willed with an enormous force that his heart should not stop as long as one Russian soldier remained in Poland.

Kuzianik sank down with his back against a rock and waited to recapture his breath. The climb down into the valley would be easier, he knew, but he did not want the men waiting below to see how spent he was. Removing his cap, he tiredly rubbed a big hand through his roughly cut hair. He thought he must look like a lost gypsy, and the small metal mirror he pulled out of a shirt pocket confirmed this suspicion. His broad, full mustache hadn't been trimmed in weeks, his hair tumbled past his brows, and his wide, dark eyes were ringed with fatigue. Although he had shaved by a stream on the previous day, his powerful chin was already well stubbled. A strong temptation to sleep suddenly came upon him, but he responded to it as he always did by shaking his head clear and redoubling his vigilance.

Kuzianik scanned the way he had just come, looking for patrols or for travelers who might be something more. There was nobody in sight.

Then he turned and checked the valley into which he would, in minutes, descend. His people had done their job well. The knot of villagers at the edge of the looping, gently flowing river were to all appearances a group of local burghers on a Sunday picnic. Having wives and small children with them was a good touch.

There was one automobile, a shiny black sedan, which no doubt belonged to Zentok, the mayor. Zentok had probably made several trips to bring the children and older women. The rest must have walked from the town of Ulcidow, three miles away.

Having been raised in farm country, Kuzianik savored the smells of freshly plowed land that came up to him. He knew how content the few small figures working in the distant fields must be, and he envied their peaceful, toil-filled days. The only sound beyond the birds and insects was the slow, muffled drone of a stubby crop-dusting plane, skimming faraway fields in dry runs to block out its spray patterns.

Kuzianik was halfway down the ridge when his people spotted him. Several started to run forward, but he impatiently waved them back. If anybody was watching from afar, he didn't want attention called to himself.

When he came to them the men, most middle-aged and, judging from their Sunday dress, well established, embraced him. There were tears in many eyes, which embarrassed Kuzianik, but at the same time he knew that he must depend on such devotion to carry him through.

The women and children who came forward out of curiosity

were turned back to their picnic, and the men motioned Kuzianik to a long table flanked by benches.

When they were seated, Mayor Zentok, a stocky old man with a shaved head, introduced himself and the men whose names Kuzianik already carried in his head: Wiscotzil, Buldaz, Smurawski, Vosmik and Kajka.

"Is the town secure?" Kuzianik asked.

"Yes. The police are with us. There are no soldiers. The people will know nothing until it's time. There are three men from outside, though. Agriculture men from the Central, they say."

"Do you believe that?"

Zentok shrugged. "They're young, beefy outdoor types. Their truck looks legitimate. And God knows they are always sending someone to tell us how to do the farming we've been doing for a thousand years."

"Are they being watched?"

"I have one man on them constantly," Zentok said.

One man would not be enough if these men were professionals, Kuzianik knew. But the mayor and his friends were not warriors, and he didn't want them to be.

The man introduced as Wiscotzil, fair and thin with darting eyes that had not missed Kuzianik's tiredness, spoke. "You're too important to be risking your health living like a shepherd. You could have been driven here, or even flown."

"Vehicles have a way of becoming coffins. Where traffic is thin I go on foot and avoid their checkpoints. I've gotten so I can hide behind a blade of grass."

"I hear you send out decoys when you travel."

"I'm sure you hear many things."

Mayor Zentok could not control his impatience. "When will it be, Stanislaw? For God's sake, tell us when."

The others muttered and leaned forward with him.

Kuzianik smiled and patted the mayor's arm. "That's not for you to know. Not until it happens. I've told you a hundred times in my messages that I don't want anyone even tempted to pick up a gun—that's for others in other places. You're not to break out a flag or dance in the streets or even smile. Those who fight will die. You people are just as important. You will be the government in this area after we succeed. And if *all* the men with guns die, you will still be in place for the next rising. The new Poland must not be run by soldiers."

"How many of us are there around the country? We hear different numbers."

"We'll know that only when it begins. If the men we've trained do their jobs, if those arming and advising us keep their promises, it could be tens of thousands."

Zentok gasped. "Surely you're being optimistic."

"He's talking about foreign armies," Wiscotzil said softly.

The magnitude of what lay before them silenced the men for the moment. Zentok signaled to the women, and the table was quickly covered with food and wine.

"Let's get something into our stomachs before we go on," the mayor said. "Sour bellies make sour plans."

The rich sausage and farm bread mixed with the wine to lift all their spirits. The women ate sitting on blankets and kept their distance, but the children would not stay back, whooping happily about and beneath the table. One of them, a blue-eyed boy of no more than two, scrambled into Kuzianik's lap. Wiscotzil started to signal to the child's mother, but Kuzianik stopped him.

He stood the boy on his lap and laughed with him.

"What's your name, big fellow?"

"Josip," the child said. "Look." He pointed a chubby finger at the sky. The bright red crop-dusting plane, still on its dry run, was now lower and closer. The distant stutter of its engine had grown to an insistent whine as the pilot rolled into a graceful, climbing bank to avoid a stand of trees at the end of a field.

"Do you know what that is, Josip?" Kuzianik asked.

Josip nodded and waved at the plane.

"Would you like to fly in one of those one day? Be the pilot?" Another nod from Josip and much laughing.

The plane skimmed off for another practice run, and the men turned to their business. After a time, their voices took on that low, urgent tone men usually reserve for conversations concerning a great love.

"It will work, Stanislaw. It's bound to," Zentok said.

"The idea is wonderful," said Vosmik. "A people's government in place from the lowest levels the moment we proclaim the revolution. Let the turmoil be theirs. We will know what to do from the first."

"Yes," said Smurawski. "No need to wait for soldiers on the run to issue confused and contradictory orders. We can take the initiative until you're consolidated. There will be no vacuum of power."

Kuzianik was pleased at how quickly they had grasped the concept. "Exactly. The people won't have to wait for guns in their hands before they become a part of it. They will switch allegiances and leaders at a moment's notice. The weapons of delay and noncompliance that we can command at every level will be worth whole divisions."

"You surely couldn't have worked this out by yourself, Kuzianik," Wiscotzil said. "Not for all your powers."

"Of course not. We have brilliant people in exile."

Wiscotzil frowned. "A government in exile is all very nice, but they can't manufacture mines and machine guns. How deeply are the Americans in with us?"

"Very deep, I hope, or we have no more chance than before." Kuzianik made no attempt to answer the question further. "There are more than fifty important leaders in this area who will act with you as part of a network across the country. You'll learn their code names and passwords. You'll receive radio equipment very soon— compact equipment, small enough to hide in a hatbox."

They worked for a long time, memorizing information and asking many questions.

"Why are you looking so sour, Wiscotzil?" Zentok asked.

"For one thing, I don't think we know enough. And, for another, the fire in that sausage is eating a hole in my belly." He pulled himself painfully to his feet. "I'm going to curl up in the car for a while." Wiscotzil scooped up a yellow blanket and walked off.

"Anyone else feel that they don't know enough?" Kuzianik asked.

They all shook their heads and assured him that it was only Wiscotzil's stomach making him cranky.

It was little Josip who finally broke their concentration on work. He tugged at Kuzianik's shirt and pointed excitedly across the valley.

The crop-dusting plane, now less than thirty feet off the ground, was coming straight at them. The engine, ordinarily throttled back to a slow, lazy hum while the pilot made his runs, roared at full power.

"Where's he going?" Vosmik said. "There are no fields in this line."

Kuzianik looked behind him to see if there was some orchard or planted field that he hadn't noticed. His eyes focused on the mayor's car, parked perhaps two hundred feet away. Wiscotzil was in the front seat, not resting but peering intently through the windshield at the approaching plane. The yellow blanket he had taken was spread over the roof of the car.

The plane had now covered half the distance to where they sat. The women and children shielded their eyes and watched the approaching plane grow larger. Abruptly, a wide, boiling fan of yellowish mist burst from the spray tubes beneath the airplane's wings. Trailing out behind, it seemed to reach down hungrily for the ground.

Kuzianik knew what it was with terrifying certainty. "Run. Run. Don't let the mist touch you." He reached for Josip, but the little boy dashed away, darting in frightened circles. By the time he caught him and scooped him under his arm, he saw that the others had made a mistake as fatal as it was understandable. They were running straight from the plane.

Costly experience had taught combat soldiers that the only way to escape napalm was to run perpendicularly to a plane's path of flight. The yellow gas moved more slowly than napalm, but still there was no hope for those running straight ahead. Kuzianik bellowed for them to change direction, but the desperate cries of the women and children drowned him out.

The plane was now almost upon them, and he knew that even

a change of direction would not be enough when the pilot made second and third runs.

Suddenly, Kuzianik thought of the car. He tightened his grip on the squirming child and sprinted for the shiny black sanctuary.

Wiscotzil was unable to drive off, for Kuzianik had the mayor's keys in his own hand. Kuzianik ran on, swearing as he felt his failing heart slow the blood he so frantically needed to drive him forward.

The plane flashed by but the yellow cloud, trailing out behind it in a straight line, had not yet sunk to the ground. He still had seconds, but no more.

Wiscotzil's pale face grew large in the window of the car, and at last Kuzianik was there. He could feel the cloud reaching for him. His grasping hand found the door handle and tugged. Locked. He motioned wildly for Wiscotzil to lift the latch, but the man did not move. Kuzianik willed his heart to keep beating as he fumbled for the small, powerful pistol in his leg holster. He thumbed off the safety and placed the muzzle against the glass opposite Wiscotzil's temple.

Wiscotzil pulled up the lock button with a shaking hand and slowly opened the door. Instantly, Kuzianik slammed the butt of his pistol into the man's forehead, splitting the skin in a long, ragged gash and knocking him back across the passenger's seat. Then Kuzianik seized him by the belt and flung him out of the car as though he had been a disobedient dog.

The door had barely slammed shut before the yellow cloud settled over the car. All the windows had been rolled up tightly and the vents were closed. Wiscotzil had known how to stay alive.

The running people had by now been swallowed up in the settling mist. They stopped in confusion and began to beat at the air as if trying to clear away cigar smoke. Some of the men wrapped women and children in their coats, but the mist had already enveloped them and been inhaled.

Three times more the banking, twisting plane made runs at tree-top height. It was just finishing the job now, laying down the yellow cloud more thickly.

Great sobs burst from Kuzianik's throat as he stifled his raging desire to rush the car to the terrified group at the center of the meadow. But that would only warn the pilot that something had gone wrong with the plan, and could not in any case save anyone.

By the time the plane flew off, the yellow fog had dissipated, but its work was done. The people in the meadow were dropping, one by one, in a silent, heartbreaking scene.

Then an awful apparition rose at the side window of the car. Josip screamed hysterically. The nightmare face of Wiscotzil showed something far more terrible than the blood streaming from the split forehead. His mouth gaped horribly, the tongue thrusting straight out as he vainly sought air. A thick froth of bubbling, bloody mucus pumped from his nose and throat. His eyes rolled insanely. His limbs jerked uncontrollably.

If Kuzianik had not known that this was exactly what Wiscotzil had done to the people in the meadow, he might have ended the man's agony with a bullet. Instead, he watched with a terrible satisfaction.

Wiscotzil struck the side window a great blow with his fist, cracking the glass but not shattering it. Then he fell to the ground, vomiting and jerking in bone-cracking convulsions that spun his body on the grass like some mortally wounded beetle.

Kuzianik realized it would do no good to go to his friends and watch them die in the same way. Besides, security forces would be closing in now to clean up the area. Within hours, this would once again be a quiet, peaceful meadow. They were masters at that.

He soothed the quivering Josip and started the car with the mayor's keys. Were the roads blocked yet? He couldn't stay with the car, but he knew a place where the terrain broke into gullies and thick brush. If he could reach there and go on foot they would never take him.

The car bounced across the meadow past the pitiful forms of his fallen comrades, many still writhing. Within moments, he found the road back to town. It was the last place he wanted to go, but there was no other choice.

At a spot where the road narrowed between walls of rock to the width of a single car, Kuzianik skidded around a curve and saw three men. They were double-timing toward him, their automatic weapons cradled against their chests in the easy manner of veteran soldiers. The three agricultural experts, he thought.

For a fatal moment the men relaxed, believing him to be their friend Wiscotzil returning. But then they saw that the car was not stopping, but accelerating. A glance told them that they could not avoid it in the narrow gorge, they could only try to stop it. They stood coolly and began to level their guns, but there was time for only one short, misdirected burst from the man in front before the car was upon them.

The radiator slammed squarely into the chest of the lead man and carried him back into the second. They went down, the car passing over them. Kuzianik could feel them dragging between the chassis and the road. Then the third man was hit and flipped up over the hood. His head cracked bloodily against the slanting windshield, and he slid away to the side. There was one final lurch as a rear wheel bounced over a body, and the road ahead was clear.

Kuzianik pulled into the outskirts of town and delivered the frightened Josip to a wide-eyed woman. Then he swung the car around and sped along a circling road for a half hour to the spot he wanted. He jumped from the car while it still had momentum, and it plunged out of sight into a deep, brush-filled ravine.

Later, as he moved cautiously cross-country under cover of thick foliage, his mind was already reformulating the leadership roster to replace the men lying dead behind him.

2

Father Smead was frightened of Father Glasgow. Even when Smead was being good he found himself looking behind him for the fearsome stare of his pastor. And today Smead was not being good.

The old priest pulled the battered blue Pinto of Our Lady of Jasna Gora into the driveway of a small stucco house and crossed quickly to the side door.

Alfred Smead was a tiny ball of a man whose only salient feature was the amount of white hair that sprang from everywhere on his head. From scalp and forehead, cheek, ear, nose and eyebrows, he seemed to be sending forth stuffing like a burst Morris chair.

Smead's knock, as usual, brought no response. A waste. The man inside, he knew, wanted him to be seen going in the front door. Frequent visits by the parish priest meant status in these old Polish districts. Smead swore under his breath and went out to the sidewalk.

A man in a sleeveless undershirt leaned from an upper window of the house next door. "Everything okay, Father Smead?"

Nothing as nosy as a nosy Polack. "Yes, Mr. Juzelski. I'm after Mr. Dizak."

"He's not sick, Dizak?"

"No."

"I wouldn't ask, but you're here a lot."

"Am I?"

"Well, you're on the block a lot. Four houses all the time, two others once in a while. And I see your car parked on some of the other streets, too. I bet you make more house calls than any priest in the valley."

"God's workers don't punch time clocks, Mr. Juzelski." *And neither do you, you shiftless bohunk.* "I hear you're drinking too much again."

Juzelski looked pained. "It's my sciatica, Father. Hurts awful."

"Try doing something for your soul, Mr. Juzelski. That's what's really hurting you. Maybe I should stop by a couple of times a week." Smead needed money so desperately he was even willing to sit with this pig.

"Yeah," smirked Juzelski, "while you're in the neighborhood." He pulled down the window.

Dry hole anyway, Smead thought. Boozers don't have enough to make an hour worthwhile.

He walked to the sidewalk and checked up and down the block. Father Glasgow would be stuck back at the church as long as Smead had the car. But then again, with Glasgow, you could never be sure.

Waiting for Dizak to answer his knock, the old priest had time to notice that the first warm stretch of April had brought a haze of green to the trees of Lost Hessian. Flowers blazed in the small front yards. This love of colorful gardens was one of the few good traits the Polacks had, he thought. Even the terrible Steven Glasgow gardened resolutely alongside the rectory. A sudden breeze brought a breath of pure freshness from the Pennsylvania hills and made Smead doubly dread the stifling smells of the dark and airless room to which the door now opened.

Dizak, a hulking, muscular figure in his sixties, talked steadily for half an hour. Five more minutes, Smead decided. As the man in the musty bathrobe rambled on, the priest glanced at the wallet on the sideboard. Good. They would not have to hunt for it this time. He could see the edges of several bills peeking out. Smead was sure one of them was a ten.

Dizak's story had not changed for the past three years.

"You'll speak to her then, Father?"

"Of course, Karl."

"I know she hasn't been well, but you must make clear to her that Holy Mother Church gives wives certain duties."

"Yes, I understand."

"There's that look of yours again. I can't stand that look, Father. Ah, but you're a priest. You don't feel the needs of a man."

At these words Smead decided to take an extra five dollars from Dizak. In the days before his priesthood, he had tumbled more girls than the old bastard had hairs left on his head. "Christ be thanked for that," Smead said.

"Danya still has wonderful breasts, Father. She's thirteen years younger than I am. Her legs are so soft. And she was always wet. As wet as a fifteen-year-old."

Smead squirmed uncomfortably. "These things were given to you as God's gift. They brought you your lovely children and your grandchild. Now the days of bearing fruit are over. God wishes you to begin thinking of a higher world. Mercifully, our bodies begin to grow away from the cares of the flesh. That, too, is God's gift."

"It's no gift to me," Dizak said. "My wants are still the same. But that damned disease makes her crazy. She won't let me near her. You've got to talk to her, Father."

"I will."

"She just lies up there with all those damned holy pictures and statues of Our Virgin Lady around her. But let me tell you, the same fingers that are feeling those rosary beads have other skills, if you'll excuse me. And there were times, not too long ago, when she'd forget those statues and take me with her lips."

Dizak looked toward the stairs. Tears suddenly filled his eyes. "Doc Wallinski says she'll just keep getting worse. Pretty soon she won't even know who I am, he says." He turned to Smead, his voice very soft. "I want my wife, Father. I want to be with her again. Make her understand, will you?"

"I can only try," Smead said.

Dizak's eyes turned cold. "Look, I need help! And you owe me. All the time you suck away my money and give me nothing."

"I give you my prayers, Karl. Day after day."

"Screw prayers. I just want to be inside my wife again." Dizak looked toward the wallet on the sideboard. "Fifty dollars. It will starve me, but I'll give you fifty dollars if you can get her to lie with me again."

Smead knew that for fifty dollars he would hold the woman down while Dizak mounted her. "Our gifts to God can only purchase grace," he said. "But I'll try."

Smead parked the car two blocks away from Sam Sandusky's Star of Poland Candy and Stationery. He thought of the seventy-one dollars in his pocket and worried about the neighborhood, one to which the good people of Lost Hessian gave wide berth. It had been settled by mean, wiry men who had been swept out of their mines to the south by illness, age or bad times. Their wild offspring, sullen, unread and uncaring, roamed the streets in packs, a never-ending source of trouble. The neighborhood was known as the Den. A priest was never out of place in it, because a day seldom went by without some victims needing comfort.

The Star of Poland was a grimy throwback to those candy stores that once seemed to stand on every corner in America's cities. A faded roll-down awning covered a scarred wooden newsstand that was pulled from the store to the sidewalk every morning. Upon this sat never fewer than three all-day loungers.

The owner, Sam Sandusky, as scarred, pitted and durable as his newsstand, had never been seen by Smead except behind his greasy, marble-topped counter. Sam's silent wife, Marie, who seemed to be a somewhat smaller slab of her husband, arranged the stock and waited on the customers, who were few enough, since the real business of the Star of Poland was booking bets.

Sam's eyes were not as friendly as they had been a month before.

"Hello, Alfred," he said. "I been missin' ya. God been keepin' ya busy?"

"His work is never done, Sam."

"Should be worth a few bucks overtime, huh?"

Smead lowered his voice a notch. "I have something for you. Can I see you alone for a minute?"

At the side of the store, two young miners were reading the odds on a sports page opened on the counter. Sandusky pulled the paper away from them. "You been starin' at that for forty minutes. This ain't the Christian Science Readin' Room. Now take the odds or take a hike. I got things on the fire."

"What's this crap about three to two on the Phillies? This is Valenzuela we're talkin' here, Sammy."

"And this is Carlton I'm talkin', pally. At home. That fat bean-eater's been doin' it with mirrors. Schmidty's gonna be takin' him downtown all night. Next year you'll be askin', Fernando who?"

"I'm not bettin' next year, I'm bettin' now."

"Not so's you'd notice. Come on, Al. We'll talk in the back."

As Sandusky led Smead toward his rooms at the back, one of the men called after the priest. "What's God say about Stevie's fastball, Father? Worth a little action?" Smead burned inside. There was a time when a place like this would have cleared out if a priest arrived.

Marie Sandusky was in the kitchen when Sam led Smead in. She answered the priest's attempt at a grin with a stone-faced nod. He knew her scowls were not for the money he owed her husband. Marie was a woman who never missed Mass, and her open contempt for his gambling habit made him nervous.

"Coffee, Marie," Sam said. She put down a brimming cup without offering one to Smead. "I need a hundred twenty-five, Al. At least."

"Seventy-one's every nickel I've got."

Sam looked very unhappy. "How long can I carry you when you keep dribblin' me these nickels and dimes? Ain'tcha got any relative who might feel sorry for the tough life ya live?"

"I think seventy-one's pretty good, Sam. Better than most times."

"But it's four hundred and twelve you're into me for. Okay, gimme the seventy-one."

Smead hesitated. "Can you make it fifty-six?"

"What?"

"Sunday is Valenzuela's day. They won't get a loud foul off him. I can feel it all over, Sam. Let me go fifteen on him, okay?"

Sam snorted. "You couldn't read Valenzuela if the Pope sent you a friggin' mailgram."

Smead pushed the money toward Sandusky. "Look, twice as much as usual. I got a source now."

Marie spoke so seldom that Smead jumped at the sound of her voice. "The Dizaks are behind on their mortgage again. I'm on the shrubs committee with Mr. Juzelski."

At any other time Sam would have told Marie to shut up. This time he was quiet.

"You don't think for a minute that this money has anything to do with the Dizaks, Mrs. Sandusky?"

She made a face and went out to the front of the store.

"That's a terrible thing she's hinting about me, Sam. If that kind of rumor got around there'd be trouble. And I don't mean just for me. I hope you'll speak to her about that."

Sandusky poured some whiskey into his coffee. "Hey, there's a thought. Maybe Father Glasgow would be happy to get one of his priests square with the world and save a lot of Polack chatter."

"Put the squeeze on him, and he'll break your arm!" The words had burst out of Smead before he had a chance to think, but Sandusky knew he was right. He took the priest's money with a nod.

Marie suddenly appeared and cleared away the empty coffee cup. Her look was pure poison.

"Marie," Sam said. "if you ever put a dime in the basket of that church, I'll kick your ass."

Smead hurried out, aware that Marie was a half-step behind him, herding him along like an old, bad-tempered sheep dog.

As he walked by the newsstand loungers and headed down the long street, Smead did not see Marie go over to the stationery rack. She angrily removed an envelope and a sheet of paper, the first taken from the dusty old stand in more than a year.

3

Of the thousand things that he hated, Father Steven Glasgow hated the church basement most. It was the room that best embodied the fetid, sunless prison that was his world. Here, under a relentless flourescent glare that turned every face ugly, stupid or evil, he forced himself through countless grueling hours with people he would not have nodded to in some other life. And since he had begun to care, it was, in many ways, worse.

Now he felt pity not only for Edward Sadowski, the boy whose flowering rainbow of a black eye held his gaze, but for the boys who had done it. He was, despite himself, an emotional punching bag, something that every small-parish priest seemed doomed to become. The glowing anger he felt at himself spread, as always, beyond him. The boys on the wooden folding chairs, most of them young terrors from the Den, squirmed under the menace of his eye and voice.

The only tenderness that the silent and wide-eyed boys could see in Father Glasgow was the way his big, square hands cradled the face of Edward Sadowski. The voice, deep and gravelly, was not really loud, but they could feel it threatening them with every syllable.

"Okay, how many of you guys were in on this?" No answer. He turned. "How many, Sadowski?"

"Not remember. I take care myself." The boy's Polish accent was so comically thick that even those most afraid of Glasgow laughed. Sadowski had been in the country for less than a year.

"Oh, so that's it. Sadowski talks funny. Well, why don't you take a sock at your grandfathers then? Most of *them* talk funny, too. Or how about me? Sometimes I talk a little funny myself. Still have some trouble with w's and v's when I'm wound up. Hear that? I just did it. My name was Glasgowicz twenty-five years ago, you know."

A younger boy from the better part of town stood up. "Sadowski's a crook, Father. If it ain't nailed down, he'll get it. He stole my bike. I caught a kid from Allentown riding it, and he said he bought it from Sadowski for sixteen bucks."

"He got my skates while I was playin' softball in the park," another boy said. "Celia Brozik saw him."

"Sooner or later he'll kill somebody," said someone else. "Always carries a tire iron, Father. Someday, *whack*! Thirty years."

Glasgow turned to Sadowski. "That right?"

"He crazy, Father." But Sadowski was grinning because everyone thought he might kill someone.

All Steven Glasgow wanted was to be done with the waiting that had begun so long ago in Poland. The patience of his first years in the priesthood had been rubbed away in a series of airless basements like this one, on a string of small, equally stupid problems.

There had been a time when he thought he could bear the life. As he came to care for his people and sense the timeless grace of the Church, it was, at moments, pleasant, seductive. But now the new thing inside was tearing at him. And even as he looked to escape, his concern for Edward Sadowski was just one more bar in a prison that grew more bars each day.

Seated on a folding chair behind Glasgow, Father Alfred Smead watched and listened. From the first bitter day that this fierce pastor had been moved in above him, Smead had resented him. Although Our Lady of Jasna Gora was a run-down parish, hardly a choice assignment within the diocese, Glasgow had been appointed its pastor only sixteen years after his ordination, a dizzying speed in the eastern United States. More so since the parish was relatively large, with twelve hundred families on its rolls and three hundred others who attended now and then. And when young Father Bolter had been added to assist him, it became clear the chancery realized that Glasgow was bringing new growth to the stagnant parish.

Still, Smead found Glasgow a welcome change from the previous pastor, old Father Gibbons. Still active in his early eighties, Gibbons had been a shuffling, stuttering symbol of one of the worst problems of the modern church.

After Glasgow's arrival at Our Lady of Jasna Gora, old Gibbons's dreaded curfew was lifted immediately, and a radio was placed in the rectory dining room. There it played for most of the working day, bringing in ball scores and racing results, much to Smead's delight.

Glasgow wrote all his own sermons and helped Smead with his when the curate's writing efforts were too feeble even by his usual low standard. The early masses and most lucrative weddings and baptisms were shared with great fairness. In fact, that fairness was almost too much for Father Smead, who would have liked to beat up on the new boy, twenty-seven-year-old Father Bolter, so recently ordained that the oil was still wet on his palms. Yet, all in all, Glasgow could not have been more caring of Smead if he had been his closest friend.

Whenever Smead caught Glasgow's glance and tried to smile, Glasgow responded with a small wink and nod. But somehow Smead knew that his image had never reached the back of Glasgow's big, black eyes. It was all reflex. The reflex, Smead thought, of a truly accomplished actor.

Rumor had it that Glasgow himself had chosen his pastoral assignment at Our Lady of Jasna Gora. Odd, Smead thought. If he had been fair-haired enough to be given a choice, why had he not picked a better parish? One with a school and a fat collection roll and golf courses whose plush clubhouses served free drinks to priests in Izod shirts.

It wasn't as though Glasgow didn't know Our Lady of Jasna Gora. Following his ordination in the early sixties, he had been its curate for almost three years. Why he had chosen to return, Father Smead could not guess. At times it seemed that Glasgow was asking himself the same question.

Smead saw the caged wolf in his pastor more and more now. The man had been born to run free. While he had kept his restless prowling under control in his first years in the parish, now it was barely contained. Was he just wearing out? No, Steven Glasgow was much too strong for that. Smead had a gambler's hunch he knew what it was.

4

It was the kind of party Alfred Smead should have enjoyed. The Broziks were as close to gentry as Lost Hessian had, and the food and liquor were first-rate. Nearly fifty people were crowded into the big Victorian house on the hill to celebrate the christening of Martin Brozik III, a tiny, white-robed jewel who now squalled loudly from his place of honor, a basket at the center of the living room. The jokes were good, the laughter was loud. But on a small TV that Father Smead had turned on in the Broziks' kitchen, Valenzuela's screwball was being jumped on and Carlton was throwing rifle bullets past the fuddled Dodger batters. And Smead had parish money down on the wrong side.

Returning to the living room for one more Scotch, Smead spotted his pastor though the crowd. That was a surprise. It was well known throughout the parish that Steven Glasgow was not one of those Allentown cocktail priests. He might, to be polite, have stopped in to an affair like this for a half hour if he had performed the christening. But he had not. Glasgow had given the job and its hundred-dollar stipend to Smead. (And if Valenzuela didn't start hitting the corners he was going to need it badly.)

Glasgow had even gotten a haircut. The handsome black curls had been trimmed, Smead noticed, not as usual by the heavy hand of Mrs. Sullivan, the housekeeper, but by one of the young experts at the local hairstyling salon.

Could it be for Gustav Kuzianik? Since Gustav's son, Stanislaw, had risen to lead the radical movement in Poland, the old man's reflected fame had brought him a step higher in the social order. People now elbowed each other to invite the loud, rude peasant into their homes. He was sure to put some spark into a party and assure a big turnout. The old man, for all his untaught ways, had a lively mind, a cutting tongue and a sharp taste for a good fight. Smead could see that Gustav's son came by his rabble-rousing ways through good Polish genes.

The word was out that old Kuzianik had been asked to drop by the Broziks'. This might explain the presence of some of the town's politicians.

Although news of Solidarity's near total demise in Poland had slipped to the back pages of the newspapers, Glasgow had continued to follow the story with sharp interest. He studied it in the news magazines and silenced the rectory chatter when anything about it came over the radio or television. Smead knew that Glasgow and Gustav Kuzianik had clashed on the issue before. Perhaps the pastor's presence meant that he wished to renew the battle. When there was a crowd to hear his words, he seldom missed the opportunity to bring up the topic and keep it going. Now, with the rise of the younger Kuzianik to the leadership of the Iron Fist movement, there could be a shoot-out if old Kuzianik came.

Given the pastor's unpopular views, it was a marvel to Smead that he was allowed in the room, much less admired and sought out. He saw Glasgow leaning against the baby grand piano, almost hidden by the circle of people around him. Smead waved a greeting, then headed back to the kitchen to check on the hated Carlton's mastery of the Dodgers.

Steven Glasgow had long ago learned to handle these social events with barely ten percent of his conscious mind, able to survive by constantly changing groups and topics of tedium.

A woman leaned close to his ear. "Father, a lot of us in town are thinking of having you present our views about getting nuns back into the old dress and keeping them there."

"We have no nuns in Lost Hessian, Mrs. Darter."

"My father is truly shocked. He went through almost an entire life not even thinking that those saintly women might have legs and breasts. Now, there they are."

"They're not exactly sporting miniskirts and plunging necklines." Glasgow smiled.

"But they're *there*. The parts that children shouldn't think about on a holy woman."

"Mrs. Darter, even with the Immaculate Conception, our Holy Mother was not spared those parts. She bore a child normally and nursed it."

"Nuns, we hope, will not be bearing children," her husband said. Glasgow turned to face the man.

"Maybe you were more saintly as a child than I was, Mr. Darter. But I recall that my friends and I spent great amounts of time wondering whether or not Sister Assunta had a cute behind or if Sister Maria had a bosom, beneath that black balloon, that equaled Rita Hayworth's. It might have been better to see right off that they were really sort of lumpy."

If Alfred Smead or Father Bolter had spoken the same words, Glasgow knew, they would have been run out of the parish. But he had these people in his spell. They giggled and their eyes said he was special, that the regular rules didn't quite hold with him. His accent, so like an English actor who had been in Hollywood for a long time, somehow put him above it all.

"But, Father," another woman said, "you're strong. You must think of those poor priests who aren't. They're in such close contact every day with these women. If they were to become . . . inflamed by an ankle or a knee . . . or a nice head of hair . . ."

"Mrs. Weil," Glasgow interrupted, "priests walk the streets every day of their lives. They can't help but see what is walking alongside them, what is written on the walls and peeking out of movie fronts and magazine covers. I'm afraid ankles and knees have lost their power, even on us."

"All right," she said, "but say a priest, a bad one, did become . . . inflamed. There's an awful lot of crannies in those old churches and rectories. If those two met . . . alone for a moment when both were. . . ."

"For Christ's sake, Lydia," her husband sputtered as he pulled the drink from her hand. "Sorry about my language, Father, but I'm afraid she's drunk."

"I'm not drunk," the woman pouted. "I'm just interested."

They're all interested, Glasgow thought. The more a sex life is supposed not to exist, the more people wonder whether it might. He eased the woman's discomfort. "I think we priests spend so much time wearing dresses, Mrs. Weil, that it takes the nuns' minds off our charms."

The woman smiled. "You look better in a cassock than Bill does in those six-hundred-dollar Paul Stuart suits he buys in New York."

She looked as though she meant it, Glasgow thought. Her husband, smiling thinly, led her away with a firm grip on her elbow.

Mrs. Martin Brozik I sailed up to Glasgow, grandson in arms. "Don't you think that baptism brings a special beauty to a child, Father?"

"I think genes have a lot more to do with it, Mrs. Brozik."

He kissed the baby and closed the tiny hand around a silver dollar someone had brought him from Las Vegas. "I've blessed that for him," he said. "Tell him to try it in the slots at the Stardust."

The front door flew back so hard that it boomed off its stop. Gustav Kuzianik came from a world where the homes of relatives on festive days were entered with the least ceremony and the most gusto. It was hard to tell whether the biggest roar came from Kuzianik and the entourage of old cronies he never walked without these days, or the guests in the room as they caught sight of the great man's father.

"One more fighting Pole is born and freedom smiles," Kuzianik bawled. He stomped across the room and thrust a bottle of Polish vodka into the hands of the baby's father. "That's for little Martin, not you. Three drops in a bottle of milk every day. It will put the fire in him that otherwise would be lost because that woman you married will not nurse him. Worried about losing the shape of her bust, they tell me. Bah. In our day, she'd have been more afraid of losing the shape of her nose."

Kuzianik's entourage laughed heartily, and the old man glared at the red-faced mother. Then he spotted the baby with its grandmother and Father Glasgow. Kuzianik was seventy years old and the tallest man in the room by several inches. He was bald, with snapping brown eyes and a great, flaring brush of iron-gray mustache. Even with the wild limp he had picked up when his leg had been crushed between two sheets of plate at the Bethlehem mill, he moved with vigor and grace as he crossed to the child.

Gustav Kuzianik peered at the wrinkled face as though sizing up a future enemy. "Not too bad to look at. His mother has good cheeks, I'll give her that. He'll have them, too. And he's missed that silly chin of yours, Martin." Kuzianik tapped the baby's groin so briskly that the grandmother squeaked. "But it's what's down here that's going to count. Will he be one of these American-born dishrags, or will he carry the brave, hard stones of Poland under his belly?" Kuzianik's accent was strong, but every word came hot and clear. He looked hard at the pastor of Our Lady of Jasna Gora. "What do you think, Father Glasgow? Is this a Polish eagle?"

"This is an American eagle, Gustav."

"No such thing!" Kuzianik shouted. "There is also no such thing as a large whiskey, but I shall now try to find one."

The old man settled himself on a sofa among his court, captured a nearly full bottle of Seagrams V.O., and quickly turned Lost Hessian into a Polish village.

"What word of Stanislaw? Where's he hiding, Gustav?"

Kuzianik laughed. "Careful, now. I see there's a reporter in the room."

"We're all friends here. It goes no further."

"In any group of friends these days, at least half are KGB. I can tell you this, though. My son is still in Poland and in close contact with the former leaders of Solidarity. He's in a part of the country where even the army won't go, much less the police. Stanislaw Kuzianik will not be found."

"Some say he betrayed Solidarity."

Kuzianik flared. "It is the Russians who say that, because it suits their purpose. They want the workers to stay true to Solidarity because they control it. Even if it came back full strength, it would be no more than it was. A bunch of brave idiots making just enough trouble to keep their stomachs filled, with never a thought to getting the Russian boot off the neck of Poland."

"You're being too hard, Gustav."

"No. Solidarity was a good start, maybe, but now it is time for Stanislaw's way: the Iron Fist. Not just a plain union for bread, but a union for freedom. Not just men who hold back their work, but men who hold back their hearts. Men who have learned from good teachers that the only labor that can be freely given to those holding back freedom must be given with rifles and bombs as tools. Those are some of my son's own words."

"I know, Gustav. I read the piece in *Newsweek*."

"I saw it on the board at the post office."

"There were four stories about him in the *Times* last week. A friend who lives in New York called me."

"If the Russians catch him, it will be the end."

"Would they put him in prison, Gustav?"

"Never," Kuzianik said. "The leaders of Solidarity are brave men. They prove that every day they defy the government. But compared to Stanislaw, they are a bunch of kittens. Their aims are feeble. Solidarity wants to share power. The Iron Fist wants it all. Every lick-ass Polish soldier or policeman who has ever served the Bear wants my son dead. The man who fails to shoot him on sight will be shot himself."

"According to Moscow, the main work is being done by Americans dropped into Poland by air. They can't think of any other way that the Iron Fist could grow so fast."

Kuzianik snorted. "The Iron Fist grows quickly because it only recruits the best. Men who don't need time to think and nurse their fears."

"What about weapons, Gustav? The *Washington Post* says that the CIA is stocking them all over the country."

"I wish Stanislaw were here to talk to you about that one. If this goat's ass of a government had sent one day's supply of what it sends to El Salvador, he'd have the Russians pushed back to Minsk by now."

"The President can't just stand by. He'll send guns. Maybe planes and men."

"Stop dreaming," Kuzianik said. "It has to come from the inside. The Polish army. That's where the best men are coming from. High officers. Veteran noncoms. That's one thing the papers have guessed right. There are plenty of Iron Fist buttons hidden behind uniform collars."

A reporter from the Lost Hessian *Blade* spoke up. "Mr. Kuzianik, there was a report from London this morning, not confirmed, that Stanislaw is coming to visit America at the request of the President. It would mean a real switch in this government's hands-off policy. Would you care to comment?"

Playfully, Kuzianik laid a finger against his ear. "I hear a great many things from my son, Mr. Green. You can't expect me to keep them all in this poor old head." The group chuckled. Kuzianik lowered his voice. "But I'll tell you this, and you can quote me if you'd like. I bought a new tie last week. And my wife says it would go well with one of those fancy tiepins the President is always giving away."

More laughter.

"That's not a straight answer," the man from the paper said.

The old man shrugged. "This I *will* tell you, though. If my son can grab this President by the front of his shirt and speak to him face to face for ten minutes, we'll soon be using Russian blood to scrub Poland clean."

In the kitchen, Father Alfred Smead heard the spirited applause from the living room just as the Phils pushed over another run. There was a tap at the side door. Glumly, he opened it, one eye still on the TV.

"Father Smead, how are we doing?"

"Five nothing in the eighth. Schmidt's on third. One out."

"Not so good, huh?"

"Terrible. Come in, Michael. You, too, Claudette. Glad you could make it."

"Wouldn't miss World War III for anything," the woman said. "And you don't have to tell us if Kuzianik and his gang have arrived. We heard them clear around the block."

Michael Stassin and Claudette West might be cousins, Smead thought, but the Lord had certainly made no attempt to even up the good looks in the family. Stassin, almost six feet four and egg-bald, had a jaw and brows so heavy that they bordered on deformity. Only his mild ways and gentle, rather high-pitched voice kept him from being frightening. When he had bought control of Appalachian Hardware years earlier, the town's children had nick-named him Frankie, after Frankenstein. But that passed and his easygoing good humor and strong, honest ways in business made him a popular local figure.

Claudette, on the other hand, was a beauty. Even with the shadow of her recent sorrow not yet fully lifted from her face, a great brightness shone out of her. Her eyes were a startling gray, long rather than wide, and almost oriental in their tilt. They had put Smead in their power the first time he had seen her, six months ago. Hardly thirty, she was a full fifteen years younger than her cousin. She was trim and athletic where he was bulky and clumsy, ruddy and clear-skinned where he was sallow and pockmarked. Even if they'd lived in the same house instead of many miles apart, there would have been no thought that they were romantically involved. Stassin had brought Claudette to Lost Hessian only to help her through the bitter months following the loss of her husband. And, Smead noticed, Stassin's steady kindness seemed to be working. Claudette now went weeks at a time without the deep slumps that had made her cousin fear for her life in the first days after her arrival. Bringing her from Cleveland, Stassin said, was the best thing he had ever done.

In the living room, Father Glasgow was so engaged with Gustav Kuzianik that neither he nor any of the others noticed when Claudette and Stassin entered the room.

"Gustav, it's no good saying that the Russians might as well have marched into Poland themselves. The fact is they didn't."

"They didn't have to. They had their stooges. What's the difference?"

"The difference is that these stooges of yours are, beyond the politics, our brothers. What do you think the Russians would have done with Solidarity's leaders? They'd all be serving twenty-five years right now."

"How do you know they won't soon be serving twenty-five years, Father?"

"Solidarity will rise again when its leaders decide that one Pole must never make war on another."

"They never talked war."

"Economic war, Gustav. I admit that it took Stanislaw to bring up the subject of a shooting war."

"When Stanislaw wins his battle, Solidarity wins, too."

"Then you'll have the Russians for certain," Glasgow said. "The Polish soldiers showed us that they won't fight back. It's better, they know, to have three-quarters of a country than no country at all."

"Three-quarters of a country *is* no country at all."

"Your son is talking about murder. That's all that war is."

Kuzianik nodded. "Yes. I remember you saying that often in the Vietnam days."

"I held five funerals for our young men. Do you know what that took out of me, Gustav? How could I be quiet? How can I be quiet now when half the people in this town have someone to lose over there?"

"What about what there is to gain, Father? We never get their foot off our neck for very long, I admit, but we do keep biting at their ankle and waiting for the throat. Isn't that what a man should be about?"

"The defense of his soul is what a man should be about."

"By heaven, Father Glasgow, I think I would be afraid to ask you to pray for Stanislaw."

The room became quiet. Such things were not said lightly in

this company. Glasgow never blinked. "I pray that Stanislaw is given the strength to work God's will," he said.

Gustav Kuzianik smiled. "As long as the matter is in God's hands and not yours, I feel a bit better. And, now, Father, I'm going to fill my glass again and talk to the baby. He makes more sense."

Having just watched the Phillies' center fielder end the game with a running catch that left the tying runs on base, Father Smead was in no mood to join in any of the half-dozen heated verbal battles that had been swirling around the living room for the past hour. Instead, he settled into a corner with a double Dewars to watch and eavesdrop. Long years at affairs like this had trained his ear to reach out to any group while filtering out the surrounding babble.

Where was Glasgow in all this? Smead wondered. His voice should have been filling the room as it had earlier. The priest finally picked him out sitting on the piano bench with Claudette West. He was smiling, a man perfectly at ease.

Smead enjoyed seeing Glasgow's smile. It was hearty and open and more beautiful for being so rarely seen. The women of the parish who had it turned on them did not forget it quickly. They showed that in the collection envelopes and by the way they flocked onto special committees.

The piano bench on which Claudette and Glasgow were seated was backed into a corner of the room, hiding them from the waist down. But when Smead slipped from his chair to pull at his shoe-lace, he was able to see them clearly from below. Their hands, resting on the piano bench, were less than two inches apart. Smead slowed his fumbling, his glance well disguised by the passing legs of the many guests. But watch as he would, those hands, which could have touched with the merest movement of a finger, never budged.

Smead straightened up. Just a hunch, he thought, like the one he'd had on Valenzuela. Still, he would bet on the bean-eater again.

5

Marshal Vorenko took the salute of the sentry and propelled his fireplug body into the cold night lying upon Kremlin Square. He wore nothing over his uniform tunic, so that five rows of medals jingled with every vigorous step. He had made sure that his two visitors, now struggling to keep up with him despite their far longer legs, had not been near their overcoats when he plunged outdoors. Nothing like a little freezing to hurry a meeting along, and Vorenko wanted this decision to be made quickly. Besides, he liked to be out in the open square with as few ears as possible in attendance.

"I hear your Moscow flu is especially virulent this year," said General Janowicz, a sour, gray man who commanded the Polish forces of the Warsaw Pact armies.

"It breeds best in warm rooms," replied Vorenko.

There was a low, appreciative chuckle from young Colonel Mikhailyev of the KGB. He knew the marshal well and had wisely worn a cardigan beneath his suit jacket.

"The germ warfare people are silly fooling with the likes of anthrax," Vorenko continued. "Believe me, the threat of Moscow flu would cause NATO to throw down its arms in terror."

The huge, illuminated red stars that topped the Kremlin wall were like halos in the night mist. Vorenko had always thought them an abomination, mocking the serene majesty of the stunning gate towers.

"Janowicz," Vorenko said, "my staff has prepared an excellent summary of your views and your plans to carry them forward. I have studied them carefully, and I commend you on their scope and thoroughness."

"I am honored, Marshal, coming from such a great tactician as you."

"I am such a great tactician that, after five years of applying a considerable part of the world's largest military machine, I am unable to control a squabbling rabble in bedsheets who kill us with weapons forged in the Boer War. And that, General, is the reason why my answer to you is no."

Janowicz was visibly shaken. "Surely the marshal understands the gravity. . . ."

"This time it's organized from outside," Mikhailyev broke in. "There are arms in the country. They're training for attacks of major units under strict military discipline."

Janowicz picked up again. "It's almost certainly an overall strategic plan made in the Pentagon. A government is being organized right down to the local levels. They're not planning long-term guerrilla activity, sir. It's a full-scale war they're after."

Vorenko picked up the pace, and their shoes rang more loudly on the cobbles. He was glad to hear that his visitors' breath was already beginning to break. "So you would lead an all-out attack against an army that hasn't yet taken the field and whose center is unknown."

"Only a show of overwhelming force will break them up," Janowicz said. "Put Hungary, Czechoslovakia and Poland together and we didn't lose three hundred men."

"I'm sure you neglected to mention Afghanistan, General, out of a tender regard for my feelings. There we lose three hundred men on a distressingly regular basis."

"We'll beat them, sir. Eventually."

"No, we will not. And we should all give thanks for the lesson the Afghans are teaching us. An enemy who will quickly concede the cities and establish a government, however primitive, in the mountains and plains, can hold us off indefinitely and wait for help. And mark this: If there were enough in Afghanistan to cause the United States to make the same material commitment that we made to the North Vietnamese, we might have a Saigon of our own."

Even with his cardigan and his jacket collar turned up, Mikhailyev was starting to shiver. "Then you accept a war at their time and their place. And with all their weapons waiting."

Vorenko stopped and turned so abruptly that the hurrying Mikhailyev bounced off the broad chest. "Don't you understand, Colonel, that the United States already *has* its principal weapon in place?"

"Sir?"

"The weapon is *money*. They know how stretched we are. Have you any idea what Afghanistan is costing us every day? Gasoline, bombs, bullets, food, casualties. To say nothing of propping up their entire corrupt army, government and economy. And bear in mind that in Afghanistan there is no loss of production vital to Russian interests to add to the drain, as there would be in Poland."

"The real cost of any army," sniffed General Janowicz, "comes when it doesn't fight."

"If you'll excuse me, General Janowicz, you now sound like some of the asses who work for me. The fact is that our famous system that can turn out tanks and planes quicker than anyone in the world is far, far less able to turn out hard currency to pay for them. Commitments to our allies everywhere, the cost of the war we already have, plus the cost of this new war that you propose we start, would lead to economic drains unacceptable to the Soviet government."

"But Marshall, you're giving away Poland," Janowicz said.

"You're giving away Europe," said Mikhailyev.

Vorenko rested his eyes and soul on the five silver domes of the Arkhangelsky Cathedral shining magnificently through the wispy fog. "We will give away nothing and pay nothing," he said quietly. "But only if we can eliminate Kuzianik."

"We keep missing him," Janowicz said stiffly, "but we are turning the pressure up."

"What I want you to do, General, is turn the pressure off, and

I mean immediately. We know all about your little yellow bug spray incident outside Ulcidow. It's a miracle it didn't make the front page of the *Washington Post*."

"Merely a terrible accident with a powerful pesticide, Marshal. The town's people understood that socialist technology must not be held up to ridicule. They'll say nothing."

"If Kuzianik had died, General Janowicz, you might at this moment be conducting the defense of Warsaw."

Mikhailyev's breath came in clouds, and he couldn't quite control the chatter of his teeth. "There are other ways to handle the matter, Comrade Marshal. We have things in place."

"Bear in mind that it must not happen on socialist soil and it must be from what seems natural causes. Accident or disappearance will not do at all."

"Kuzianik will soon be in the United States. We know where he'll be peeing at any given moment."

"Excellent, Colonel. Just be sure there isn't a CIA man hiding in the bowl." Vorenko laughed for the first time during the meeting. "And make sure that you don't end up in that bowl yourself." He pretended he had just noticed that they wore no coats. "You two have made an awful mistake coming out like that. You'll be lucky if you don't end up in bed. Go now, both of you. I want to take the air alone."

The marshal watched the two men half run back to the warmth of their rooms. At the age of seventeen, wearing no more than he wore now, while attempting to move forward with his unit against some dug-in German tanks before Stalingrad, he had found his boots hopelessly frozen into the mud. Slipping out of them, he had completed the attack in his socks. He wondered how today's heroes, who fought their battles over telephones with deceit and betrayal to replace courage, would have fared back then.

For a long time, Marshal Vorenko strolled in the square, unwinding from the long day. He had always felt oddly protected here in the ring of beautiful, brooding cathedrals, as if God, long ago deserted by Vorenko and his government, continued to watch over Russia with a strange and sullen love.

So much beauty here, he thought. So much history. And so many relentless enemies arrayed against it. Did they never rest? Did they never long for peace?

Finally, the cold settled in him and he wearily walked to his bed.

6

Claudette West wanted Julia Dean out of her house. When Julia had driven up and removed her armful of sample books from the trunk, Claudette's first impulse had been not to answer the door. But then, she thought, you never knew when she'd be back.

Claudette had taken this house on the thickly wooded hillside, fully twenty-five miles outside Lost Hessian and well off the road, to avoid the likes of Julia. Michael Stassin had warned her from the beginning that newcomers were snooped at almost as much as they were looked down upon, so she was going to have to work hard to get the privacy she wanted. Claudette swore at herself for having mentioned at last week's Ladies Sodality meeting that she was trying to find the right material for some new slipcovers. If only she'd recalled that Julia Dean owned a fabric shop in Lost Hessian! When Claudette promised to drop in on Julia as soon as she could, Julia knew she had better drive out with her samples very quickly if she was going to see the house and get all her questions answered.

Of course, Claudette realized, some care had to be taken. A little too much brusqueness and Julia might turn the town against her. Then even the good offices of Michael Stassin could not fit her back into the town and church.

Claudette had been very careful to accept Julia's advice on what fabrics to buy and had not hesitated when these proved to be the most costly. Julia's request for a complete tour of the house had been granted with as nice a smile as could be mustered, and not so much as a change of tone could be heard when the visitor opened and peered into the medicine cabinet.

"My, my," said Julia, so quick-moving that one had little sense of what she looked like at rest, "you are the cleanest outsider who's ever come to Lost Hessian. I admit we're a little crazed about it, we Losters, but if a person's house isn't clean—and I mean the parts you can't see as well as the parts you can—well, then, their heart isn't clean, you know. And you're so organized! Clutter can look as bad as dirt. I know, Claudette—clutter is my weakness. Just look: every bottle in place, every cap on. I am absolutely mad with jealousy."

Julia flitted into the hall and jerked open a closet door. "I knew it. Perfect. Jackets here, trousers there. Sweaters stacked just so." She closed the door and turned to Claudette. "Isn't it kind of funny for you to be holding onto those old clothes of your husband's? Mary Beskill hasn't thrown away a thing of Jack's either. Left his study just the way it was when he died. Like they did with . . . Lenin I think it was." She took Claudette's hand. "Can we go get ourselves some hot coffee now? I just hate people who do business and then run out the door."

Julia waited until their second cup before she got down to her real business. "You don't know how much we in the town admire your courage, dear. To lose a wonderful young husband in the prime of his manhood, and then just pull up stakes from the family that was all the support you had and start a whole new life." It was a lovely performance. Julia actually seemed close to tears.

"It hurt too much to stay in Cleveland," Claudette began. "David and I had grown up together there. I knew him every minute of my life. Then, when he was gone, the house, our friends, every-thing, everyone was a memory that cut me up. Michael Stassin was the only family I'd ever really been close to. My parents died when I was very young, and Michael was the one who looked after me . . . put me through school. When he left Cleveland to come here, I missed him very much. I think he sensed that. So, after David died, I wrote and told him I just had to get away. He asked me to come here and work part-time for him at the hardware company. He even arranged the sale of my house in Cleveland and bought this one for me."

Julia seemed thrilled. "Now, see, I'm a real detective. Without a soul ever telling me any of that I was able to guess just the way it happened."

"I thought perhaps Michael had talked about it."

Julia laughed out loud. "Michael? Good heavens, no. Before we got to know him through the church, we used to call him the Sphinx. You could never find out . . . he'd never tell you even one tiny thing. He still won't, for that matter."

"Michael's not easy to know," Claudette said.

"I just don't know how I'd behave if I lost my Sidney. Even now, when he's getting kind of saggy and wrinkly and his vital drives are getting likewise. I heard you say once that your husband died during an operation. Was it cancer? It takes so many young people."

"As a matter of fact, it was tonsils. He'd get awful sore throats all the time in the winter. I told him he should listen to what the doctors had been telling him since he was a kid and have the tonsils out, but he hated the thought of being cut. Maybe fear had something to do with what happened. His heart stopped while he was under the anesthetic. They tried everything but couldn't get it started again."

"Oh, my dear," Julia winced, "you must feel so guilty."

"A jury decided the anesthesiologist was at fault. I got an award. Not much, but I just couldn't go on fighting. With that money, some insurance David had and what I got for the house in Cleveland, I can get along on the small salary Michael is able to pay me."

Julia leaned closer. "I'm sure you could have gotten hundreds of thousands for loss of services if you'd pressed it."

"I beg your pardon?"

"*Loss of services*, Claudette. It's an extra award you get to make up for your spouse's not being able to do it to you anymore."

"Oh."

"I know the agony you must feel not having that young, strong man in your bed every night. Do you have any picture albums, dear? I'd love to see what David was like and some of the things you did together."

Claudette glanced at the kitchen clock over Julia's shoulder. A trickle of sweat ran down between her breasts. Julia had been there nearly two hours. Now, she had less than ten minutes to get rid of her. Or maybe Julia's visit wasn't just chance. "I'm afraid I threw the albums out, Julia. All they did was make me cry. I did keep one picture, though. I'll get it for you."

The framed photo that Claudette handed Julia showed a young man with long blond hair whose plain, pleasant face smiled as though he had a million years of happiness before him.

Julia surprised Claudette by shedding a real tear. "Oh, darling, he was *beautiful*. How you must miss him! I'd give up heaven to meet someone like him." She hugged Claudette. "It was certainly God's blessing that you had no children. It's so hard to marry again when there are young children. And you *must* begin looking for another nice young man. You might think that it hasn't been long enough and that your friends will think it wrong that you're looking to put someone new in your bed—in a state of marriage, I mean—before poor David's spot on the mattress is cold, but that's not the case, dear. What's wrong is to hang on to someone who can't take you in his arms anymore. A woman's very well-being depends on having a good lover. If you only knew what Sidney's soggy prostate is doing to my health!"

"I haven't thought about any of that for a long time," Claudette said.

"I'm sure you haven't. What kind of monster would you be if that were all that was on your mind? But you are ready, my dear. You're starting to laugh again and talk to people. I watched you with Father Glasgow at the Broziks' christening. I swear there were some young men and some not so young women there who were positively jealous at the way you two were getting along."

Claudette smiled. "Father Glasgow knows how to bring you out of yourself."

"If all the priests were like him, we'd need a cathedral in every town. Why, you can hardly get into Our Lady of Jasna Gora when he's saying Mass. Even the teenagers are mad about him. It just stuns me to think of my Ina in a church youth group." Julia's voice dropped to a more intimate level. "Honestly now, Claudette, don't you think it's just a *waste* for a gorgeous man like Father Glasgow to be a priest?"

Claudette stood up and spoke stiffly. "I certainly wouldn't call what he does for the people of this town a waste of anything."

"You know what I mean, dear."

Claudette thought she had heard the soft crunch of wheels on gravel down the road. Julia had parked her car in the front. It would be seen only at the last moment by someone driving up the gravel road from the highway. Claudette hoped that her voice would not shake from the desire to shout Julia Dean out of the house. She sorted quickly through the order forms she had signed earlier, then screwed up her face. "My goodness, I must have been carried away by how pretty those fabrics were. Look how much I bought. And those prices! I know you have to pay for the best, Julia, but I'm on a very strict budget. You'd better let me see that sample book again."

Julia was gathering up her things in an instant. "What you are having, my dear, is what we selling people call the buyer's blues. It happens every time you buy something you really want. Believe me, if you change one thing in that order, you'll never forgive yourself. Tell you what: I'll throw in some nice trim. Come to the shop later and pick it out." She looked at her watch. "Oh, my, I was due back twenty minutes ago. Where did the time go?" She pecked Claudette on the cheek. "No time for long goodbyes, dear." Julia snatched the sample book from her hands and all but ran out the front door.

As Julia's car disappeared behind the trees, Claudette listened for the sound of braking and wheels sliding on gravel that would mean Julia had met another car coming up the road. But there was nothing, and after a while the throaty roar of the woman's badly muffled Buick could be heard out on the highway.

Slowly, the tension ran out of Claudette. She turned weakly to clean the coffee cups.

"Oh, sweet Jesus," she said as she saw the rough-clad figure standing just inside the kitchen door at the rear.

"Boy, have you got the wrong guy," the man laughed as he threw aside his greasy cap.

He was upon her before she could stir, pinning her arms at her sides with a strength against which she could not budge. Then, Steven Glasgow covered her parted lips with his broad mouth and kissed her as if to draw her very life into him.

He started to pull her toward the bedroom, but she laughed and drew him down the hallway toward another, smaller bedroom. "I locked this door because I didn't want you prowling into it if I was around back. Lucky. I thought Julia Dean was going to break it down to get a look."

She unlocked the door and pushed him inside. Strung along the back wall above the bed was a banner reading "Happy Birthday, Steven" in letters thirty inches high. Crepe-paper streamers radiated from the center of the ceiling, and a brightly wrapped package sat at the foot of the bed. Just in front of the turned-back covers was a tray holding a small but elaborately decorated birthday cake, a knife and a bottle of champagne.

Glasgow felt a lump in his throat. The love that he could never speak grew still larger. "Thank you, darling. It was very thoughtful."

She made him sit on the edge of the bed and gave him the package. Inside he found a photo album of expensive leather. It was packed with pictures of him, of her, and, less often, of the two of them together. They had been arranged in chronological order. Underneath many, Claudette had written a comment in white ink on the dark album paper. The first of the photos was an official black and white glossy that the parish gave out at baptisms and first communions as a memento of the occasion. In it, Glasgow looked as solemn as the Pope. Next to the picture she had written, "Even then she knew."

"Where did you get them?" he laughed.

"Guile. Long lenses. Even theft. You know how people are always pushing their pictures into your hands for a look?"

"Sure."

"Well, I simply slip out the vintage Glasgows."

"I'll be damned."

They came to several pictures in which they appeared together. In most, Claudette seemed off balance and oddly positioned. She explained. "At all those dinners and weddings I became very good at sensing when someone was about to click some shots of you. Then I'd just happen to stumble in."

"Reprehensible." He turned to another photo. "Hey, what's this?"

It was a picture Claudette had taken herself. It showed Glasgow holding a child seconds after he realized it had wet his arm. The caption read, "Ignacz Grinski baptizes Stefan Glasgowicz." He laughed and moved on. When he had seen all the pictures he put the album down and hugged her to him.

"Time for some cake and champagne," she said.

"Fine."

"Shouldn't we take off our clothes so we don't have to worry about crumbs and spills?"

"Why not? All the etiquette books recommend it."

With Claudette kissing and fondling him all the while, undressing took a deliciously long time.

Later, they lay facing, her leg thrown over his hip, his arm beneath her head and her face just inches from his. He wanted to stay forever, he wanted to leave forever. He felt he had betrayed his life and that he had found it. A part of him, a part he fought back as hard as he could, wanted Julia Dean to walk through the door and scream to the world what she was seeing.

She ran her hand down his white, neatly muscled flank. "And what prayer did you say, Father, to make that car disappear?"

"I just coasted into the woods—near the old garbage heap. I was about forty yards back in the trees. When Julia left, she just zoomed right by me."

"How nice."

"If I'd spotted her car five seconds later, I would have been explaining why I was making a parish call in overalls."

"Maybe staying in uniform is safer."

"I don't think so. There are five hundred faded blue Pintos in this county but not that many priests."

"I know. At least not this kind." She kissed him slowly.

"I hope Julia's not going to be a problem."

"I don't think so. Of course, you could be really sure by not coming back."

There it was, another opening. She kept giving them to him. Making it easy. He only had to say, "That's just it. I can't come back." Then he could dress and leave and return to the life he had chosen for himself long ago as the only one possible. But the thought that she would want him to go scared him badly. "You want me, don't you, Claudette?" Just like a high school kid would say it, but the words forced their way out.

She placed her hands on the softness between his legs. She had not done that before. "Yes, I *do* want you." They lay very still. "Are you sorry this started? If we hadn't begun, we'd never have missed it."

"Of course I'm sorry. You've brought joy into a life that wasn't designed to have any."

"What about that higher joy you guys always tell us about when things are going badly."

"There are more happy priests on golf courses than there are in heaven," he said.

"We can always blame this on Michael Stassin. He never takes care of his cars. No oil, no water, no checkups. It was inevitable that sooner or later he'd break down at church and you'd have to take me home."

"If it hadn't been raining so hard, my sweet, I'd have let you walk. I knew trouble when I saw it."

"I didn't think you guys noticed women."

"We not only notice, but at the times when we're least supposed to. For instance, I fell for your legs at the Sodality dance. The rest of you when you were teaching the Sacred Heart girls tumbling."

"Did I lead you on?"

"I just knew you were the most charming talker I'd ever met. And good talk's in very short supply in a priest's life."

"You know, I've wanted you, somewhere in the back of my mind, since the first day Michael took me to eleven o'clock Mass to hear you. I didn't make any specific plans, of course. Not until I'd asked you in for coffee after our drive."

He laughed sourly. "God, how ready I must have been."

"We were both ready. I was beginning to miss David's smile less and his body more." She saw him wince. "I'm sorry. I said that to make you jealous, and it's not fair. I have no right to you, Steve. And, believe me, I understand there are things you can't *do* . . . and things you can't . . ."

He went on for her. "Things I can't *say*. Thanks for knowing that."

"Darling, I know what you're going through, and it hurts me—terribly. It's not very pleasant knowing that one day you might suddenly realize that this thing in the sky is a million times bigger and brighter than I could ever be."

She pushed him on his back and rolled on top of him. "So if you're going to leave me, Steven, I want you to say it right now. I'll be sad, but I promise I won't be angry." She took his face in her hands. "But if you stay, I'll never again make it easy for you to go."

She lay upon him so lightly that he could have slept the night without knowing she was there. But all the strength he could muster was not enough to allow him to slide from beneath her.

7

Dr. Zamlet Gorslev hated the cold, sunless spring in Poland. Although there was ice in the Moscow River well into April, the thick winter clouds burned off weeks sooner there than they did here on the bleak plains around Radom.

The heater in his Zil limousine was, of course, not working. To call a car so old and battered a limousine was a joke. Especially since his low rank in the KGB did not entitle him to a chauffeur.

Gorslev felt for the bottle of Khvanchkara that he kept in the pocket of his overcoat. It was still a bit early in the morning for a swig, but he knew the day would not grow too much older before he pulled the cork. Middle-aged doctors needed help these days. He wondered whether he would end up a rotten-livered swiller like so many of the others in his section.

Like many physicians, Zamlet Gorslev glumly noted the gradual deterioration of his own health. The jolting of the Zil in the potholes of the neglected road brought short, hot stabs of pain from his kidney stones. After Solidarity and martial law, nothing much was being repaired in Poland these days.

Another jolt, another stab. The pain radiated toward his upper back. Heart? Gorslev worried about his heart. The intense brushing up on that organ and its problems required by his current assignment had depressed him and alerted him to his own new symptoms.

Then there was the arthritis. Still not so bad in his hands as it was in the knees, but coming. That worried him even more than the heart, because if he couldn't keep on playing the piano, he couldn't see much point in living.

He hated his work. His apartment was second-rate and headed downhill. His body was sagging, his face as plain as a turnip. His only good feature, his large blue eyes, were hidden by glasses so thick that he might as well have been peering through two overcoat buttons. Women, always scarce, were almost impossible to entice into his bed anymore. He hated sports and cared little for chess, so there remained only the piano.

Gorslev flexed his fingers, pulled on a pair of fraying wool gloves, knitted many years ago by his last mistress, and swore again at the Polish dampness.

He knew he was getting close to the Volus Tractor Works long before the tall stacks of the vast industrial complex came into view. Hand-sewn flags and painted signs flaunted the clenched hand and spiked-glove symbol of the Iron Fist. They were scattered on fences, in trees and on the walls of buildings. He even saw a flag or two on several houses. Bold, he thought.

Why did people want so much? He remembered his youth in the Ukraine during the Stalin thirties, when a badly made sentence in a student composition could be read as treason and an entire family shipped away. Even today, a Pole's life was freer than a Russian's. Why did Poles expect more than their models were able to grant themselves?

The Volus complex, huge and only a shade grayer than the sky that framed it, came into view. The morning shift was well under way, and Gorslev could see the rows of empty buses that had brought the workers. The vehicles were lined up behind a heavy, barbed-wire-topped steel fence that ran for miles around the buildings.

Less than two hundred yards from the well-guarded main gate he saw a sign bearing a likeness of Stanislaw Kuzianik and the Iron Fist symbol. The sign had no doubt been set in place the night before. He was certain that such things were pulled down every day and that patrols with dogs brought great danger to the unknown artists. He supposed that there were as many men tearing down signs and scrubbing away fiery slogans as there were building tractors in the factory. But this was the former workplace of Stanislaw Kuzianik himself, the hotbed and birthplace of the Iron Fist. At Volus, painters could not be easily contained.

Since a great deal of the work at the complex involved making tracked vehicles for the army, his entry pass was checked by a soldier who looked at it with far more care and coldness than would have been the case had Gorslev merely passed over his KGB papers. But to the soldier he was just a Russian doctor being granted a courtesy visit by the heads of the factory.

Gorslev was given directions to the medical building and allowed to proceed there in the Zil, since the small van that was used to shuttle visitors around the complex was, as usual, long past due on its return from the last drop-off.

As he drove by the empty buses he had spotted from far down the road, Gorslev was surprised to see the drivers either reading behind the wheel or talking and smoking in groups. Incredible. Production had fallen fifty percent, yet these able-bodied men were lounging away an entire day. This certainly could not happen without the knowledge of the Volus managers. Apparently, even with constant pressure from the party, they were afraid to buck the countless Iron Fist slowdowns. Yes, Gorslev thought sadly, his trip here was badly needed.

Unlike some industrial complexes he had visited in East Germany, where the top men hardly gave him a moment of their busy day, three of the Volus plant's highest managers, red stars neatly in place on their lapels, greeted their guest from Moscow at the door to the medical building.

The beaming managing director reeled off three Polish names that fell at once out of Gorslev's mind. It was made plain that the number one man, a dapper figure with very bad teeth and a very good barber, would do all the talking. The others would smile and agree where needed.

The director shooed a worried-looking man out of an office and moved his group inside. Afer they were seated, he offered decent cigars and addressed his guest in English.

"My Russian is very poor, Doctor Gorslev, but I am told that your English is excellent. May we speak this way?"

"Of course, Comrade Director. In fact, I prefer it. There are so many medical journals from England and America. I study their language a good deal so that I can keep up." Gorslev smiled. "You might say 'I dig it, Jack.' " He was proud of his command of idiom and thought a touch of lightness might loosen up the meeting. It didn't.

The director, it was obvious, had rehearsed with care. "I want to assure you and the medical authorities in both Moscow and Warsaw that the Volus plant has put the health of its workers on the same top priority that we have given a rapid return to high production."

"We have complete confidence that what you say is so, Comrade."

The director pressed on. "You must realize, though, Doctor Gorslev, that this complex was designed long before many of the chemical dangers now being discovered were even thought about."

"Of course."

"Our ventilation system was intended to move the largest volume of air through the largest work space at a very high rate."

"I'm sure that seemed proper at the time," Gorslev said.

"When we first received some inkling of the purpose of your visit, it did occur to me that Borowski here, who was in charge of the ventilation design, might have given some thought to the importance of keeping certain fumes from spreading when such a system is in use. I recall mentioning it to him more than once—isn't that so, Borowski?" The man nodded in misery. "I wish I had thought to put it on paper," the director continued, "but Borowski is usually very good about such things."

"We have too much on paper now," Gorslev said with a calming smile.

"And where would we find the men and the money to bring about such changes? Perhaps that's what Borowski had in mind. It's unfair to condemn a man for dealing with the hardships of the world as he knows them to be."

Gorslev felt the urge to slip in the needle. "I can't say where you would find the money, Comrade Director, but you might find the men sitting on their behinds in those buses you have parked outside."

The director paled. "A motion study is now being done in that very area."

Before the director could stop stuttering, Gorslev went on. "Please be assured, Comrade, that you have not been singled out. The Warsaw Medical Directorate has invited me and several of my colleagues from the Soviet Union to look into this disturbing pattern of liver and lung cancer where workers have been exposed to inhaled benzene fumes over a long period of time. Your building number four, making plastic fuel lines for most of the country's tanks and tractors, has been filling the air with by-product gases, one of which is a benzene derivative. Borowski's ventilating system has been busily spreading it to known areas that will give us a nice, controlled study. I will examine the medical records of your workers, past and present, and compare their times of exposure to the fumes with numbers and types of cancers. My findings will be pooled with those of others, and we'll soon have our answer."

"If what you fear is so, will there be . . . punishments?"

Gorslev shrugged. "Who can say?" He could smell a bargain coming.

"Comrade Doctor, it occurs to me that we have a problem here. The state of Poland protects the health records of its workers with great care. The West has its uses for them. I am not at all sure that the cooperation I have been asked to extend to you includes access to our files. Perhaps, if you have a week or two, I could clear it through. . . ."

"I have a day or two at most," Gorslev said.

"But how can I spare the help that you'll need? We employ thirty-three thousand workers here. Because of the troubled times they malinger. We see more than two thousand medical complaints a day."

"Comrade Director, suppose we keep this off the record. Let me into your files. Alone. Within a short time, I can get as much from a good sampling as I can from looking at every dossier you have. If I find something wrong with the system, I can report that the problem was worker carelessness. I can say that you . . . and Comrade Borowski . . . were prudent in every way. After all, it's the findings and the workers' health we care about. Then, you can make whatever changes you think necessary . . . in your own way and in your own time."

The director brightened. "A fine idea, Doctor. We will cut through the paperwork and let you begin immediately." He snapped his fingers at Borowski, who handed him a large loose-leaf notebook. "This fully indexes and explains our medical filing system. It will enable you to locate whatever you want. I'll have a room set aside."

"The book is in Russian, I see."

"Yes. We keep just this one. There have been . . . others like you, from time to time. Come, Doctor, I'll take you down to the files myself."

"Good," Gorslev said. "And remember, Comrade, I'd like to work alone."

Gorslev spent the next two hours making it look as though he had gone through a thousand files. The bulging briefcase he carried was stuffed with spurious notes he had been scribbling for a week in preparation. Scattered about and crumpled into wastebaskets, they would tell the director, who was sure to drop by several times, that the job was being done as described.

The armloads of files they had brought to him from the crammed drawers were covered with dust. They raised havoc with his allergy as he dumped them out on the desk, the floor and every flat surface in the large room.

He covered a corkboard with pinned-up chest X-rays. But he clipped only one to the light box the director had brought him. It was that of a former Volus worker, Stanislaw Kuzianik.

Gorslev had long ago seen an odd thing in himself. He thought of the people he was helping to kill as patients. He looked forward to "meeting" each man, getting to know him by his medical records and forming a bond as strong as if he'd shaken the man's hand and had him to his home. Since the fate of the poor fellow had already been determined by powers far above him, Gorslev felt no guilt at all. Indeed, if the man had known how much care his unknown doctor had taken to make his demise as quick and painless as it could be, he might have been grateful. To be sure, quick and painless were not always easy to achieve. It had once taken a year and a half for a radioactive substance in a telephone earpiece to do its work. But he had, from what he knew of his case, high hopes for Stanislaw Kuzianik.

Gorslev polished his eyeglasses and settled down to study the file of the Iron Fist's young leader with a pleasure usually reserved for reading the thick American newspapers on a quiet Sunday.

Kuzianik, he noted, was six feet four inches tall and weighed two hundred and fifteen pounds. He was thirty-seven years old. The photograph, taken five years earlier, showed an intense, good-looking man with a long, craggy face. There was a touch of gray in his tightly curled hair and in his flaring mustache. Even in the three-inch photograph Gorslev could feel the power of the man. He had always tried not to have favorites, but he immediately felt something special for Kuzianik.

He put a corkscrew to the Khvanchkara and poured a generous glass. It was the best of the Georgian red wines and his only luxury. Taken slowly, it always opened his mind.

As Gorslev had foreseen, the key to Kuzianik's health was found in an attack of rheumatic fever he'd had long ago. Kuzianik had caught the disease at ten, an age when such an infection was intense. What a shame. A man who should have lived to be ninety.

Kuzianik had been treated in the first flush of socialist medicine for the masses, so his records were complete and thorough. The young Kuzianik had developed his carditis in the first week, always a sign of a severe case. As the streptococci attacked his heart, a holosystolic apical murmur developed, a sign of relative or actual mitral regurgitation. There was also a diastolic murmur along the left sternal border at the third and fourth interspaces due to aortic regurgitation. Kuzianik's heart was leaking blood backward in a bad way.

Gorslev studied the X-rays with great care and awe. Looking at a heart like this was like staring into a man's soul. Kuzianik's heart was swollen by years of battling against its damage. It was like the man himself, growing larger and fighting harder as the odds rose against it.

He noted the lesions—rheumatic pancarditis. All layers were

involved—endocardium, myocardium and pericardium. The most serious damage was verrucuous valvulitis. The healing with fibrous thickening and adhesion of the valve commisures and chordae tendinae was the cause of the valvular regurgitation. The deformity seemed worse in the mitral than the aortic valve. Poor Kuzianik had been spared very little.

There were signs of progressive valvular calcification and sclerosis: The breakdown was still going on. If they merely waited eight, maybe ten years, he thought. Then he remembered the fiery signs along the road.

Gorslev had almost finished his second glass of Khvanchkara when he found his opening. Three years earlier, Kuzianik had suffered a transient cerebral ischemic attack—a small stroke most likely caused by a blood clot released from one of the scarred heart valves. What fools these factory doctors were! With all the detailed childhood records on hand, they should have had him on blood thinner years ago.

Following the stroke, Kuzianik had not been able to stand for three days and had shown a general weakness of left-side functions. Speech and mental processes were not impaired. There had been a rapid return of strength and function with no therapy, and Kuzianik, strictly against the advice of his doctor, was back at his welding machine within a month. Now, at last, they had put him on blood thinners. It had been Heparin at first, with a switch later to Coumadin. Gorslev liked Coumadin. It depressed syntheses of coagulating factors in the liver and had a smooth, long-lasting response.

Kuzianik's first dosage of thinner had been in the fifty milligram range. Right for a man of his great size. The maintenance dose was set for twelve milligrams over four days. That seemed high to Gorslev and he frowned darkly and threw down the rest of his wine. Doctors who prescribed large doses of anything were a pet peeve of his. Especially when it was right here in Kuzianik's file that he was lax in the extreme about taking his prothambrin tests to determine the proper Coumadin dosage. Didn't they know that Coumadin was a warfarin compound? Warfarin was among the most effective rat controls ever used. Rats didn't perceive it as a poison, ate it with bait and soon bled to death from internal hemorrhaging in the lungs, bladder and intestines.

If other doctors didn't think about it, Zamlet Gorslev surely did. He immediately began to run some calculations on dosages.

8

The old man before the grimy reception desk of the General McClellan Hotel, an ancient frame building perched at the edge of the Den, was so short and slight he might, but for the rosy cheeks and springing step, have been suffering from some wasting disease. A west Irish look of guileless, reckless cheer was stamped into his deeply lined face and a good part of his brogue was still intact, though made a little less distinct by a set of oversized false teeth. His hair, still dark, remained thick and was combed with a lotion into a sweep not much seen since the nineteen fifties. His sprightly and elegant manner, in some contrast to the clean but worn street clothes he wore, did not sit well with the desk man, whose name was given on the plastic sign at his elbow as George Gambrusco.

"Peter Keene, huh? Hope you didn't come to Hessian 'cause you think the handouts are better than where you're from. This here's a low tax state. They'll starve you out real quick."

"Wouldn't try to fool an old fella, would you, George? Back in White River Junction, Vermont, they said you boys had a state lottery that went into some pretty nice nursing homes for the gaffers. I'm not ready for one just yet, but might as well set up and get ready, eh?"

Gambrusco grunted. "Fifty bucks a week, always in advance. No cookin' and no hookers. They steal the bulbs and towels."

Keene rumaged in a canvas duffel that looked as though it had been stored outdoors between uses. He came out with a fistful of greasy bills, mostly singles, and began counting them out on the register book. "I've got better things to do with my money than hookers, boyo. The games are what I like. And the ponies. Any place around here I can get down?" He counted out an extra three singles and pushed them toward the desk man. "Here's a bit for helping me settle in."

Gambrusco's round, oily face relaxed a bit as he slid the money into a shirt pocket crowded with more pens and pencils than he could use in five years. "Sam Sandusky's your man. Straight out the front door four blocks and hang a left. Three blocks on your right is a candy store, the Star of Poland. Not much to look at, but you can get down on anything and it's fast pay. You can go a hundred fifty, two hundred credit and then Sammy gets tough. He's got an arm-breaker named Ivan Dinkova. You won't like him."

"Very kind of you to share your knowledge, George. What about a church?"

"Our Lady of Jasna Gora. Dead on the other side of town. A good half hour's walk." He looked down at Peter Keene's spindly legs. "Maybe more for you."

"I was just wondering if they got in the way of a bet."

"No problems. Pastor's a guy named Glasgow. Supposed to be hot shit. Always organizin' somethin' and shootin' his mouth off. Kind of a peacenik, I think." Gambrusco rummaged through a cardboard box filled with keys. "You retired?"

"Not completely. I'm doing a bit of . . . consulting, you might say."

"Must pay pretty lousy," Gambrusco said with a glance at Keene's clothes. He tossed him a key. "Two twenty-six. The toilet tank takes forever to fill up. Don't mess with the float. And don't grab the maid's ass. She's not stuff and she don't like it."

"How's the TV?"

"Color stinks. Run it on black and white."

Peter Keene found the room cleaner and more cheerful than he would have imagined, with light pouring through two large windows that had been left open to admit a fresh, cool breeze.

He emptied his duffel onto the bed, moved his clerical clothing and equipment to one side, then made his silent devotions kneeling. Afterward, tired by the bus trip from Allentown, he lay down on the bed to collect himself.

Father Keene was worried by the look of his old friend the bishop. Colin McCarthy's face had seemed gray, and his nails were tinged with blue. He was older than Keene, having already been a pastor when he had helped bring Keene, a young boy yearning for the priesthood, from the small village in Kerry where they had both grown up.

McCarthy had moved up quickly in the church, but Peter Keene, his mind wandering far more in this world than the next, had not moved up at all. Still, the two had remained close for over thirty-five years because both were truly inspired blarney swappers. And while Keene did not achieve stature, there was always a job of special interest for the asking in Bishop McCarthy's diocese.

The bishop's car had taken Keene to the bus terminal.

"I think they'd like to put me out to pasture, Peter," he had said. "They hear this steam-engine wheeze and suspect—quite correctly, I might add—that my ankles are swelling beneath my robes. They have Danny O'Connell all primed to move in on me. You'll hate him."

"I imagine they'll be looking to put me away too when you go."

"Believe me, Peter, you're too old and undisciplined to go to some parish where the pastor will have you doing the five o'clock masses and running the Every Member Canvass."

Keene smiled wryly. "Then please try harder to take care of yourself, Colin."

"How fortunate for you, Peter, that I became important enough to rescue you from everyday cares."

"Rescue *me*? If it wasn't for me telling you all these years who was sharpening the knives at the chancery, we'd be playing chinese checkers at the old priest's home."

The bishop smiled. "I must admit you were born to snoop."

"Lucky for you again. There are a dozen good priests in this diocese that you might have had to bounce out but for me. You'd be saying five o'clocks yourself."

"Don't be vain, Father. Vanity leads to boasting, and that leads to too many ears. It's always been a wonder to me how that nonstop mouth of yours has remained so discreet about our small efforts."

"*My* small efforts, Colin."

"Well, my small idea, then."

"And a good one it was. If we went after the bad boys with the rule book, even as lax as it's gotten, the Holy Father would be running the big store all alone after a while."

"True. But you mustn't get too gentle in your old age. There are, as I hope you have found out by now, some that we have to nail. The church must never be embarrassed because we were soft instead of wise."

The two old men, easy together and feeling the sadness of a fine thing that must soon end, had laughed at their private jokes and rolled back the years until the car had pulled up behind the waiting bus. The driver of the bishop's car, who did not approve of Father Keene's special place with the old man, got out from behind his glass partition and stiffly held the rear door open.

"I'll try to perform as you have suggested in every detail, Your Excellency," Keene said loudly as he stepped from the car.

"God go with you, Father Keene."

The hotel bed was soft, and Keene's heavy eyes told him it was time for his nap. Before he drifted off, he glanced at the pictures he had photocopied out of some old church periodicals so he would know at once the object of his off-the-record investigation. Then he reread the letter from Sam Sandusky's wife and folded it into his crumbling wallet. If Father Alfred Smead could be saved, it would not be returned to the diocesan files.

9

Dermontov had a fierce headache and, though there wasn't a shred of scientific evidence to support it, he was sure that the low voltage pulsing through the wire mesh in the walls at headquarters, meant to thwart electronic listening, would make the pain worse. He had drunk far too much at the Crystal Café the night before, taken in by the lively five-piece band and the lovely girl with the thick ankles. The manager of the place, aware of Dermontov's station, had let him sleep it off on the couch in his office and had even seen to it that his clothes were brushed and pressed for the morning.

To help clear his head, he took the long walk from Kutuzovsky Prospekt to Dzerzhinsky Square. He loved Moscow in its thin April sunshine, and his strong, ex–soccer player's legs ate up the distance.

As he walked he thought about how badly he wanted young Landev to be gone. Young? He laughed to himself. Landev was forty, barely eight years younger than he was. But Landev was very young to have been given access to Level Four security.

Dermontov did not like these lengthy indoctrinations. Not only did it take a month out of current projects, but it was very likely that the "intern" was there from above to size up the teacher. In this case, perhaps to replace him. He had heard rumblings that

Landev had some very important friends and was rising rapidly. But then you always heard that.

Landev, coatless despite the deep morning chill, was waiting for him at the base of the great black statue of Ivan Dzerzhinsky. The first head of the Soviet secret police scowled in his stony, never-ending vigil in front of the massive headquarters of the Komitet Gossudarstvennoi Bezopasnosti.

Waiting in the cold was a move you might expect from Landev: If you were a few minutes late, you would be the cause of discomfort for him and slide ever so slightly into his debt.

"Sorry I'm a bit late, Comrade," Dermontov said as he came up to the pasty-faced, wide-waisted Landev. "You should have gone to my office. My secretary would have brewed you a nice glass of tea."

That was another game they played. Dermontov always offered tea and Landev always refused it, saying he was eager to get to work.

"I don't like to indulge myself during business, as you know. I'd just as soon get right to it."

Landev knew by now that Dermontov would make him sit in his office for twenty minutes, hands in lap, while the teacher disposed of his tea. If Dermontov had held less than the Order of Lenin and the Order of the Red Banner, he might not have put up with it.

The room to which they eventually retired was well guarded even by KGB standards. Two uniformed guards, hand picked and always from different units, stood at the door. They were not allowed to talk to one another while on their six-hour tours and during that time did not eat, drink or urinate. They checked in Dermontov and Landev by their magnetic I.D. cards and fingerprints.

"So, Comrade Landev," Dermontov said after they were seated at a round table that held a microfilm reader and a control console, "welcome to the world of buried men."

When Landev produced a pencil and notebook, Dermontov took them from his hands and dropped them into a wastebasket. "No notes ever go out of this room."

"Sorry."

"Buried men are a remarkable concept. The program was started in the early thirties and began to yield its great rewards in the late forties. It gave us the key data of the bomb, and the principal people were never caught or even suspected. In fact, one has a building in Washington named after him. Standard agents like Klaus Fuchs gave practically nothing by comparison. When Igor Gouzenko turned on us in Canada, one of the men who debriefed him was a buried man. He got our really important people clear before the trap was closed."

"What makes the difference? Training?"

"No. Patience. The patience only a system that has time on its side could practice."

"That's something I never have enough of," Landev said.

Dermontov did not show that he had caught the slight dig at his stately pace, but he resolved to find a way to get some subtly nasty words into his pupil's promotion file.

Dermontov continued. "There are, at present, just short of twelve thousand buried men living around the world. The records of every one of them are in this room. Only four men in the building are allowed access to the file. The grave ill health of Comrade Bushkin, who is one of them, has created an open spot that you have been chosen to fill. Something of an honor, I would say."

"An earned honor, I'd like to think," Landev said.

Earned by being engaged to the right brass hat's slack-breasted daughter, Dermontov had heard.

"It's a very inexpensive operation, because the people support themselves. Most of them even pay for the cost of an active assignment if it's not too grand."

"How cozy."

"The basic concept is to succeed by trust, not stealth. Where most agents lie as low as they can, it is the job of a buried man to move as high as possible in the community. Often these people wait a lifetime and are never called upon. Sometimes we are in contact with them and they don't even realize it is us. The thing is, we don't want them piddling away their cover on things we have hundreds of others to handle. Ideally, we want them to forget that they're with us. We want them to think of themselves as businessmen and legislators and soldiers, all fired with the ambition to make important friends and rise to high places in their communities."

"Isn't that chancy? When the time comes for your buried man, isn't he likely to feel he's one of *them* more than one of *us*?"

"Dear Landev, you have put your finger right on the problem. One day, our buried man is asked to betray all those he has lived among for years. He has standing, success, maybe even wealth. But now he must kill the man he has become."

"Still, Comrade Dermontov, he might very well be able to do his job and go on just as he was. Same family, same friends, same bank account."

"But let thirty years cool the fire of commitment and give him a pretty, loving American wife and a beloved son doing well at Cornell. Yes, he might go on, but his moral tissue would have taken a great bleeding wound that might never heal."

"What would become of him if he just ignored the call? Would it be something for wet affairs?"

"Not likely. But if it were a really important assignment and he knew more than we liked when he said no, he might suddenly have a cramp while swimming across a wide, cold lake."

"Do many refuse?"

"Only our director knows that. What I do know is that the rate of failure—indeed suicide—takes a great jump with men buried for twenty years or more."

"Then care in recruiting is the key."

"Precisely." Dermontov turned and flipped some switches at the control console. "Now let's take a look at some of these men. We deal with them as seven-digit numbers as a rule. If you need to know more, you can call up all the information available on that microfilm reader. Please take a seat at the keyboard."

After Landev had arranged himself in front of the large screen, Dermontov dimmed the room lights and took a bound book out of a padlocked briefcase.

"You can use the system in many ways. This directory lists our buried men by location and area of penetration. For example, say you were looking for a man who could get next to the President of the United States regarding the nuclear freeze movement. Let's see what you would do."

Landev looked up the Washington, D.C., code and matched it with the nuclear affairs number. Four seven-digit numbers appeared on the screen.

"Select one and punch it in," Dermontov said.

When Landev hit the final key, the pleasant face of a middle-aged woman appeared on the left side of the screen. On the right, script rolled slowly, giving her name and the details of her life.

"You can freeze the screen on whatever material you want by pressing that blue button," Dermontov said. "But, in general, you can see that she's been buried for almost eighteen years. She's held, let's see, seven jobs in various nuclear agencies. None of the jobs has been very big, but she has met nearly seventy top men who often invite her to their offices and parties. She has slept with the best of them. You see, there are the names. She is a woman, and the pressure to put more of them in high places is very strong in the United States. She is also of the right party. Chances are good that she will eventually be appointed to an important nuclear agency, perhaps very soon. She might even be made its head."

"According to this, she has lent herself to some peace movements. Was that wise? Wouldn't it make her suspect?"

"Peace movements, yes, but nothing too rabid. And what could be a better cover in one of the most liberal cities on earth? I doubt that she could be approved for any appointment without liberal support."

"Suppose the job she gets is a small one, after all?" Landev said.

"As far as we're concerned, there are no small jobs in nuclear matters. Even if she only goes onto a fact-finding committee, she is there to convince others. Her vote or the vote she changes could swing the balance in a report to the President or the Secretary of State. Think of it, Comrade. It is possible this woman could save us from having to develop twenty billion dollars' worth of missile defenses."

Landev was clearly impressed. "That would be worth a long wait."

With prompting from Dermontov, the younger man turned up file after file, each bringing out a point that added to his knowledge of the system.

Another face appeared on the screen. Landev leaned closer to study the file. "An unusual cover, Comrade. Are there many like him?"

"At one time there were. Not so many anymore."

The two watched as details of the buried man's life rolled slowly by.

"I see he's European," Landev said.

"That's what makes this file interesting. It shows control at its best. An agent brought up and trained here in our system, then fitted neatly into place in theirs—without a seam."

"European, yet he speaks flawless English. That's lucky."

"Not lucky at all. His father was a professor of languages at the university. We search for those things."

Landev continued studying the moving script. "Look at this: letters to the district from his teachers. Misspellings and all."

"Nothing is passed by. You see that the teachers complained about the fist fights he kept getting into."

"And got drubbed it would seem. Those medical reports with the letters are tough stuff. Fractured cheekbone. Broken nose. Stitches in the eyebrow."

"They were thinking of taking him out of the school for some special discipline. But here's what they found when they looked into the matter." Dermontov skipped ahead on the reader to a document in Polish that had a Russian translation in the rolling text. "It seems he was having these fights, always with boys much older and larger than himself, because they were making fun of the government and the party. He turned them in, and it cost him."

"What about his parents?"

The reader whirred at Dermontov's command, revealing the information. "The father was a troublemaker. Good record in the resistance, but later he turned against the party. The job on the young man was the work of our schools. When they get the right boy early, they work wonders. His father was on his way to some pretty nasty duty when we changed our plans for him—and his son."

"You make plans early," Landev said.

"It was a fine bet. We knew the boy was with us heart and soul; that he was bright, brave and ready to fight for what he had been told was good. And fight without regard for convenience or pain. We also knew that it was only a matter of time before the father would try to get them out of the country. By making it easy for him to do that, we had our agent delivered to the United States by a messenger beyond reproach."

"You mean the father never knew what was going on?"

"No more than the boy did. As far as the parents knew, he was enrolled in a special accelerated program of studies for gifted youngsters, which, of course, he was. At this stage it's conditioning, ideology, a sense of who the enemy is. He is not asked to give us his life until we're certain he's ready for it."

"And then you picked the right spot for him."

Dermontov nodded. "His psychiatric profile showed that he has a vast need to be true. Once he commits himself to something he cannot bring himself to turn from it."

"A perfect agent," Landev said. "But it doesn't seem likely that he'll ever get a chance to prove himself. A shame."

The screen brought up a final block of script under the heading *Current Alert*. It was in a cipher that Dermontov was not cleared to break. The script ended with a red triangle.

"Well, I'll be damned," Dermontov said. "Perhaps not such a shame after all."

"What does it mean?"

"Only two things for sure. It's fresh, because it wasn't there when I reviewed this group of files last week, and it's a top priority assignment."

Landev pointed to the screen. "What's that triangle at the bottom?"

"It means a Red Flag operation. Wet affairs."

With new interest they ran the file back to its start and studied the strong, sad face of Father Steven Glasgow, looking for clues that would tell them what they were wondering. Would the system work again? Would their machine function?

10

Steven Glasgow decided he would stay at Claudette's no longer than an hour that evening. And for nothing physical. Just a cup of coffee, a little chat, a parting kiss—a nice midweek surprise.

As he drove up the gravel road he was not careful, even tapped a playful honk on the horn. He didn't have his collar on but was otherwise dressed in the black outfit of an off-duty priest. A short call on any parishioner was certainly above board.

He knew the car parked near the front door at once. The yellow sports car was one of a kind in Lost Hessian. It belonged to the young dentist James Yancey, and Glasgow had seen half of the county's eligible young women in its passenger seat. And several who were not so eligible. He pulled up behind the Corvette and waited for Claudette to appear at the door. When she didn't come after a couple of minutes, he knew he could almost surely back out to the road without anyone knowing he had been there. That would be the wisest move, because the less he was seen here by people of the town, the better.

With that firmly in mind he turned off the lights and engine and marched up the front steps.

The night was warm, and the door looking into the living room was open. Light classical music floated out of the stereo's speakers.

Through the screen he could see Claudette on the couch. She was holding a drink, wearing a nice dress that he knew she didn't wear just around the house, and laughing in the clear, open-hearted way that had drawn him to her the first time they had met.

James Yancey was seated on the couch, too. Glasgow doubted if there would have been room to seat even a very small person between them.

The dentist had been a basketball star at Temple, and his tall body was well kept and hard. His blond hair was always pleasantly out of control, in such a mannered way that it was likely some hair stylist had a good deal to do with it.

Claudette and Yancey were not talking, but apparently savoring something amusing that had been said.

Glasgow found himself rapping on the frame of the door much harder than he intended. He was annoyed that they did not seem more startled.

"Yes?" Claudette asked, making no move to rise.

"It's Father Glasgow," he called in his best parish-rounds voice.

He had thought to walk through the open door without a sound or word and to read the joy in her eyes when she saw him. There had been nothing else on his mind for the last twenty-five miles. To have to defer to Yancey shattered him.

"I told you that was a horn out there," the dentist said.

Claudette stood and came to the door, still not able to see through the screen to where Glasgow stood in the night. The priest watched Yancey's eyes follow her every move.

Yancey didn't rise as Claudette let Glasgow in. The tall man left no doubt that he considered the priest's visit an intrusion and hoped his stay would be a short one.

"Nothing wrong, is there, Father?" Claudette asked with a worried look.

She was either doing a fine job of acting or she was not very glad to see him here, Glasgow thought.

"Hi, Father. Good to see you," Yancey said.

Glasgow was so ill at ease he almost stammered. "Hello, Doctor Yancey. Sorry to barge in, Claudette. Pretty thoughtless of me, I guess. Thing is, I was coming home from way out and the drive just got to me. I could hardly keep my eyes open. Thought a good cup of black coffee might keep me going into town."

"Black coffee coming up," Claudette said. "You two follow me into the kitchen so I can have some company while I'm brewing."

Yancey pulled himself up as though he were on his way to be hanged and made a point of taking his almost-full drink along with him. His eyes and manner told Glasgow it was more than his first drink, and perhaps more than his second.

"Where do you know Jim—Doctor Yancey—from, Father?"

"Let's just make it Steve here, Claudette."

"And make it Jim for me," Yancey said. "Actually, I met Steve when he asked me to do a bit of clinic work for some of his kids' clubs. Worked out terrific. I hooked a few big families. More than made up for some free fillings and yanks."

"Glad to hear it," Glasgow said, struggling to look pleasant.

"Sugar, sugar, sugar," said Claudette, searching over the counters.

"Right here," said Yancey, opening a cabinet. Glasgow tried to challenge Claudette with his eyes, but she never seemed to be looking at him. One thing was certain: Yancey had been here before.

Why hadn't she mentioned it? Because it wasn't important enough explained it fine, but nothing inside him bought that. Why in hell *should* she mention it? What claim did he have on her? She had told him she loved him, but of course that was a miracle that could not last. She couldn't—shouldn't—wait for him when that wait, as far as she knew, could be forever.

All this, which should have been racing through his mind night and day from the first moment he had come to Claudette's bed, somehow had never occurred to him. Now, the presence of this cocky, insolent young ass had brought it all home in the space of time it took to make a cup of instant coffee.

Glasgow tried to keep his tone light. "I suppose you two met in the dentist chair." He hated himself for saying such a stupid thing, but the need to know now consumed him.

"Steve," Yancey said, "let me tell you that looking down a woman's mouth could stop a romance faster than a carload of saltpeter."

A romance, he'd said. Or was it just a way of speaking?

"Jim, please," Claudette said.

"Come on, Claudette. I can tell Steve is one of those modern priests who won't take offense." He grinned. "I'm not even sure I'd leave you in the same room with him."

Yancey's tone suggested he thought he could leave her in the same room for a thousand years and nothing would happen.

Later they sat about the small, round kitchen table. Claudette had left her drink to join Glasgow in coffee. Yancey continued to pull at his whiskey. The cup trembled slightly in Glasgow's hand as he raged at Yancey's inability to see him as a rival.

"As a matter of fact, we didn't even meet in Lost Hessian," Claudette said, picking up the thread. "I was in Philadelphia last month clearing up a few personal matters, and who did I run into but Jim."

"Yeah," Yancey continued, "I was there for a seminar on wisdom tooth surgery. I managed to sleep though most of the first day. Then, when I spotted Claudette wandering past in the street, it was like the big guy in the sky had a hand in it. You can bet I didn't waste much time." Yancey grinned again, wider this time. "Incidentally, Steve, I wouldn't come to me for any wisdom tooth work 'cause that was the last those old farts in Philly saw of me."

Claudette spoke over Yancey's hearty laugh. "Jim was good enough to spend the entire day and evening with me. Even gave me a ride home."

Glasgow remembered she had told him about meeting a friend in Philadelphia. Not in detail or at length, but she had mentioned it. What she had not mentioned was that her friend was a man. And, of course, he had not thought to ask or suspect.

He had no rights and had not asked for any. But now he could have killed them both with his bare, sweating hands.

Glasgow found himself nursing the coffee, then asking for a second cup. Yancey made a great show of pouring himself another long drink, making it plain that he was the invited guest and was being patient with the one who had intruded.

The small talk continued, and Yancey was clever with it. When a topic came up that might have been of substance, the dentist always turned them back to the trivial so that the time dragged and Glasgow's presence seemed to be pulling down the evening.

"I've taken too much of your time," Glasgow said finally. "Thank you both so much. I've got to run along now."

"You're sure as hell not going to fall asleep at the wheel," Yancey said. "You've got at least four cups of black in you."

"I'll probably be kicking the slats out of the old cradle tonight."

Yancey's grin, which had become annoying, erupted again. "That's one of the problems with your job, Father. There's no one to help you kick those slats."

Glasgow had a sudden urge to put his arm around Claudette and say, *"That's what you think, asshole,"* like some miffed schoolboy. Instead, he smiled politely at the dentist's remark.

"It was nice having you drop by, Steve," Claudette said. "Don't hesitate to do it any time the road gets too long."

"I won't."

His every nerve rebelled at leaving them alone. He had no way of knowing how many times Yancey had been there or what they did when they were alone. But, if it killed him, he would never ask her. He tried to assure himself that nothing at all was happening between them, but his trust in Claudette had lost its lovely shine forever.

Claudette walked him to the blue Pinto. Now, Glasgow thought, she would have a chance to give him some sign that everything was all right. He felt he was owed some small explanation and looked for it eagerly. A lifted eyebrow, a pursed lip would be enough. He would see it even in the dim light.

But there was nothing. No extra pressure in her handshake. No quick caress of his shoulder.

"Goodbye, Steve," she said, and it had the sound of the last words he would ever hear from her.

His mind knew well that the slightest grounds for suspicion by Yancey would have been deadly for both of them and that Claudette was doing the smartest thing. And his mind also knew that the vision of Yancey in her bed loomed a thousand times larger than was sensible. But the heart of a once-trusting lover is the last heart in the world able to deal with such things, and as he drove out and the light from her front door vanished from his rearview mirror, that heart fell into a bottomless black hole.

11

A dozen tall flag-bearers marched, the stars and stripes snapping against the bright blue sky. Behind them the polished gold of the tubas and bugles threw back flashes of the brilliant sun. Stamping ahead, making the most of their moment before the brass band took up again, the Junior Fife and Drum Corps of the Peter Pilsudski Post of the American Legion made a brave hash of "Hell on the Wabash."

Steven Glasgow well knew the bred-in joy of a Pole, however far from native flag and soil, in joining into loud, intense groups. He supposed that Lost Hessian had more clubs, societies, youth corps and ten-man unions than any other town its size in the state. And he loved his flock for it. Their sense of being one, the way they flew hot and ready to defend ideals that were elsewhere held as ancient as legends of Arthur moved him strongly.

Only in Lost Hessian did Flag Day call for a school holiday. Here it brought forth great gusts of speeches, martial displays and enough yards of Old Glory to have clothed every man, woman and child in town.

The precise marchers now wheeled smartly onto the great lawn at the rear of the church, formed neat ranks and came to a stop before their pastor with a last shrill blast of fife and drum. Glasgow stood at the top of the high, broad steps leading to the sacristy.

The priests who had spoken on this day in years past had used a sound system, but Glasgow's strong, deep voice rolled to the last ranks without assistance.

"Sit, please," he called.

The marchers collapsed to the lawn with a happy sigh. The nonmarchers, mostly old people and young children, had been sitting in wait for more than an hour, and Glasgow now beheld an expanse of faces and flapping flags that would have set the heart of any office-seeker racing.

"My friends, let me begin by asking you a funny question. Did you feel you were carrying those lovely flags forward . . . or that they were carrying you? If you were charging up a hill under fire instead of marching down a sunny street, would you have followed that banner to the top, or would it have followed you? Not so easy to answer, is it?"

Glasgow was always surprised at how well his words fit together. The doctrine locked in his heart fit well with the one that spoke out of the cassock.

He had never once felt that he betrayed these people. As hard as his own teachers had worked to keep the notion of a Supreme Being out of his mind and heart, he worked to instill that same notion in this flock of his. Emptied of God himself, he plainly saw the strength and comfort ancient faiths could bring to troubled lifetimes; he taught the doctrines with all his great strength and talent; he administered the sacraments true to the strictest detail, his mind locked to the words on his lips—seldom the case, he knew, with Smead or Bolter. If there really was a God, no sin could be put on Steven Glasgow for what he withheld. But today was business.

"The point I want to leave with you in these few minutes is that our proud flag is only a sad rag without proud deeds to uphold it. Old Glory doesn't have a bit of glory sewn into it. Its glory comes from us who love it.

"Flag Day has always meant more to me than even the Fourth of July. The Fourth gets all tangled up with wars and battles, and they are the least worthy thing a country can ever do."

Glasgow was careful to direct these words to where Gustav Kuzianik sat. He got a small, angry toss of the hand in response.

"At best, in its endless murders, war sends us to help our brothers and sisters everywhere. What we did in the last world war was not without honor."

Kuzianik had been drinking. It was in his voice when he called out, "We helped the Russians slaughter Poles in thirty-nine. We helped the Russians put Poles in chains in forty-five. We help keep Poles in chains now. Where is the honor, priest?"

Glasgow went on. "You support my point, Gustav. There is never justice in bloodshed."

"They have solved that against the Afghans," Kuzianik shouted. "Poison gas draws no blood."

There was muffled agreement from the older Poles, but enough of the young people shushed Kuzianik to allow Glasgow to continue. Still, the spell had been broken. Glasgow's listeners would now be keeping score of the points he made in these views so different from their own. Some would no doubt recall the article in the *Blade* that was a thinly veiled attack on those who used the pulpit, in Lost Hessian and elsewhere, to speak against their own country.

It was no great effort for him to shift gears. The gentle rumblings of Jesus were so close to the message that would one day save the world that he hardly needed to separate the appeals of his two ministries.

For twenty minutes he found subtle ways to tell the people before him to love their country, but not to serve it. Glasgow didn't feel he was saving the life of some Soviet soldier ten years down the line, or that he was stripping the young men before him of the instincts that might one day save their lives. He deeply cared for the children of his town. As a young curate at Our Lady of Jasna Gora in the early days of Vietnam, he had wept in the rectory after the funerals of parish boys who had died in the terror-filled rice paddies. And though he knew the cause of the North Viets to be the true one, he had cursed them to himself and felt his hands yearning to be at them.

As he spoke, he felt no regrets for the ideas he planted in those who trusted him. The new world of which he dreamed would lift them high above where they could ever hope to be in their country as it was now. They would know a fairness, a caring, an uplift of the spirit that no amount of church magic could bring them. Steven Glasgow only regretted the smallness of his efforts.

Had any man ever given so much of a blazing heart for so long to so little effect? His teachers had foreseen his pain. They had told him what the waiting would do, how the sense of waste would rise to tear his flesh like no CIA thug ever could.

And now the manhood that Claudette would not let sleep was also rising against him.

Hardly hearing his own words, he searched the faces raised to the sunshine, frightened at how badly he longed to see her now. For a moment he felt that if he had found that sweet gaze he would have stripped off his collar where he stood, rushed to her through the wondering crowd and carried her off. And why not?

Why not? It was the first time that his need had shaken the long-set defenses. Shocked, he drove his mind from it. He had to finish speaking before he lost the thread and stood dumb before the silent crowd.

"The way to be proud of that great flag, the way never to stop being proud of it, is for all of us to put ourselves in its folds. Its every thread is one of us. And if one thread is soiled by doing harm to a creature or creed of God, our flag is that much less lovely, that much less brave. To sin in the name of our flag may be the greatest sin of all because it invites the gentle and blameless to share and revel in that sin."

Glasgow pointed to the flag that flapped nearest him. "On this glorious day, let us vow to give our lives for this banner, not on some bloody field chosen by some bloody leader, but on the one chosen by God—our own loving hearts."

For a moment, the only sound was that of the many bright flags crackling in the wind. Then ringing yells led the crowd into wild applause that quickly brought them to their feet.

Glasgow was annoyed with them, as a father would be with a favorite child who had missed the point during a stern lecture, hearing only the loving voice. It angered him that they could be so moved by such half-thought, deep-purple claptrap as he had just spoken. He felt real shame that he had not worked harder on the speech, telling himself that he was saving his real effort until the Fourth. He had let Claudette distract him and Kuzianik had put him off stride. What small chance there was to reach some vulnerable minds had been lost.

Without waiting for the applause to end, he led them into a brief prayer, then motioned the brass band into action. It seemed hours while they tore "Stars and Stripes Forever" to shreds and mangled "God Bless America" in a way that would have reduced Kate Smith to tears.

He did not descend into the happy crowd but stood at the top of the steps, accepting handshakes and greetings for the shortest possible time before stepping back into the dark, cool peace of the sacristy and bolting the door behind him.

His head ached with the new, restless thought that strained against the walls of this narrow prison. He had always managed to remain above the gray gas of priestly depression, but now he felt it rise about him.

He entered the church and slowly crossed to the altar. The building had been designed after a famous church in Poland, with windows held small and high to keep out the winters on the medieval plains. At midday, light would flood the altar, but now, with the approach of late afternoon, crushing gloom gathered, against which even the banks of votive candles behind the rail made little headway.

In all his years as a priest, Steven Glasgow had never knelt alone before an altar of the image he was supposed to serve. He did so now.

He gazed at the tabernacle and wondered how the merest of the people who came to this spot were able to ask for help and feel they had gotten it, while he, a thousand times more knowing of the mysteries they implored, had that feeling denied to him. The false Glasgow, the venal Smead, the callow Bolter, all of whom would have been spat upon by any god with sense, were the bringers of light to fifteen hundred families. With ease they brought a peace to others that they would never know themselves.

He said a prayer in Latin, pressing it like the tip of a knife against a milky membrane through which he sometimes thought he saw something being formed. Why was he waiting here, scarcely breathing? What was the whisper he sometimes came so close to hearing?

The mind could lie so sweetly. He recalled comforting a grieving mother through the long night of her child's sickness. The gut-wrenching power of the desperate woman's praying had caught him up. He clutched her hands in his own and felt the fire of her faith pass into him. For hours that seemed moments, they had stormed heaven that heavy, rain-filled August evening, never looking down at the still child, certain between them that their link to the Above had turned back the Dark Force. Finally, just before dawn, he had bent forward and seen a great black fly sitting upon the clouded iris of the dead child's open eye.

Steven Glasgow broke off his prayer and snapped to his feet. When he turned to the darkened church, he found himself in the steady gaze of a man sitting several rows back in a center pew. Very likely he had been there for some time. Glasgow nodded to the man and started for the sacristy.

"Steve," the man said.

The voice stirred a dim memory. Glasgow turned. Through the darkness, the man's face was so pale it seemed to glow. He wore long, uncombed hair and a thick beard.

"Do I know you?"

"You did once."

Glasgow walked down the aisle to the pew. The man who rose before him was a full head taller. Glasgow stared at the gaunt, tired face.

"Great saints. Ben. *Ben*."

As they embraced, laughing, Glasgow felt shock at the sharpness of the ribs and shoulder blades beneath his friend's flowered sports shirt.

"Hey," he said, "aren't you the guy who was afraid that rectory food would get him jammed in the confession box?"

"It's been a long time since I was in a rectory, Steve."

"Then you're out?"

"Hell, no. I'm in. Nobody's been more in since they rolled back the stone. Thought it might be better if I dropped up in civvies."

"Up? From where?"

"El Salvador. With the Maryknollers. Mind if we sit?"

"Come see what a rectory's like again. I'll dig up a steak."

"Right here's fine, Steve. My plane leaves in a few hours, and I've got a couple of other stops to make."

Father Bennett Eagles fell to the seat as though his legs, once unlocked at the knees, had no power to sustain him. Glasgow guessed that he was fighting some chronic disease of the tropics.

At Mother of Lourdes Seminary, Bennett Eagles had been determined to hear the laughter of God. He was not to be put off with one of those sickly, pleased-with-Himself smirks on religious statues and paintings. Eagles wanted a hearty roar that shook the clouds and told the world that love wasn't all sorrows and sore knees for Him and His children.

He breathed in the doctrine as though it were clear, sweet air. Then he bent and challenged that same doctrine before his teachers until the most patient among them was ready to strangle him. But in the end, the love and good nature that bubbled out of him won every heart, Glasgow's among them. He and Eagles had ended up as roommates, the idea being that the sober Glasgow might quiet Eagles's saucy, wide-ranging mind. In fact, things had gone the other way. What little laughter there had been in Glasgow's life, what little mischief, had taken place in the company of Ben Eagles. And Glasgow had been the only one to see the other side of this clown of God.

Eagles's mind sucked ideas out of books like a vacuum cleaner. While others smuggled in packs of Lucky Strikes and candy bars, he smuggled in reading material. At a time when the church leaned not even slightly to the left, most of what Eagles absorbed was wild-eyed socialist cant even by Glasgow's relaxed standard.

Long into the night Eagles would recite the plight of the poor and oppressed to Glasgow, who, half-fearing a hook put out by someone, hung back for a long while. In the end, he let himself seem to come around. He threw his own thoughts into the late-night assaults on the grand Silence and, with his own expert training, was able to control, refine and direct Eagles's thinking.

Glasgow had reveled in seeing the man's good mind become a

sharper tool in the cause. For the first time—and last—he felt real pride in the life he had taken up. Bennett Eagles's face had seemed to radiate the freshness of the first dawn. Skin so white and clear that it had to be shielded from even the mild sun of springtime by a wide-brimmed hat. A smile behind cupid's bow lips almost too pretty for workaday use. Eyes so wide, clear and baby-blue that Glasgow was certain they could never be made to look upon evil.

It was all in ruins now. The flaxen hair had turned almost white. The cruel sun of the tropics had clawed and crumpled the fine skin, splotching it with red and circling the yellowed eyes with something very like scar tissue.

"I never did need a mirror when you were around, Steve."

"I'm sorry. You stare at old friends you've missed. Like a drink after a long dry spell."

Eagles chuckled. "Well, you've learned a bit of charm, anyway."

"Just a bit."

"I've heard about you. You've got a big rep. Monsignorsville soon is the word."

"I'd just as soon not have it, Ben. It's a downer for too many of the other guys. I had an old pastor who said, 'One man gets the purple and fifty get the blues.'"

They laughed. Eagles seemed to relax a bit. "I heard your speech."

"That's no way to spend a day off."

"I saw what you were loading on them, Steve. I liked it. It's good to know you haven't changed."

"I hope it didn't stick out too much."

Eagles smiled. "They never knew what hit them. They love you. Once I thought I'd have that touch. Never quite managed." He paused. "Steve, the people need you."

The people, Glasgow thought. How many times had he heard that word in the training classes in Poland. "The people need me here, Ben."

Eagles snorted. "These aren't people. They're fat, dumb cattle who hear the clank of the slaughter tools and smell the roasting fires without realizing they're on the menu. They're using the church to pray for mid-sized cars. Jesus, Steve, go where people are still alive. It'll knock some of that rectory gravy out of you." He lit a cigarette and threw his long, bony legs over the pew in front of him.

"Gonna tell me why you're here, Ben?"

"You won't like it."

"What's it going to cost me?"

"Ever hearing yourself called the Right Reverend Monsignor Glasgow."

"I told you before I can do without that."

"But you could go all the way, Steve. You've got the stuff."

"What is it they say about getting to be a bishop? You'll never again eat a bad meal—or know the whole truth."

Eagles edged closer. "Okay, this is it. We're at a balance point. The Church is as the world is. We can make fun of this old outfit we serve, but with all its creaks it's still the largest unified organ of moral thought and action that's left. Maybe it can't command these days, but by God, Steve, it can push and tilt like nothing you ever saw. The rebels couldn't last a year down there if we weren't with them. Not if Honduras let through a thousand tanks. Believe me, worldwide the people's movements have never been closer to having it all. Greece, France, Portugal came in on their own. Every year there are more of us. For every Afghanistan there are two or three who come in by vote."

"And a little bit of help from their friends."

"A C-130 brought in fifteen hundred rocket-propelled grenade launchers from the CIA last month. Against that you need some help."

"I guess."

"The real problem is the economic one. That's where they can blow us apart. The corporate governments have stolen and banked huge amounts of capital. They can stand the world on its head and shake the money out of its pockets any time they want. Every time the guys on the poor side of the tracks scramble to their feet— zap—they're upside down again. That's bad enough in Zimbabwe but pure death in Eastern Europe. This is the industrial base that has to show success and bankroll our other friends until they can succeed, too."

"So it's Poland."

"You've got it, Steve. The devil himself couldn't have done a better job. They couldn't get to the Poles' minds, so they got to their stomachs. They couldn't knock off the government, so they knocked off the economy. They couldn't make the people turn on the army, so they fixed it so the army would have to turn on the people. They fixed it so the lifeblood of the movement, the poor workers for whom the whole damned thing was put together, crippled the only system that can save them. Five combat divisions couldn't have done more damage to Poland than Solidarity."

"They've broken Solidarity. It's just a word now."

"But they haven't broken the Iron Fist. I tell you there's something like the PLO shaping up there. But against us. Nothing less than a rebel army behind the lines of the revolution."

"I think you're making too much of a splinter bunch."

"Bullshit! We may be stuck in the bushes in Salvador, but we get state-of-the-art info from our friends. No rumors—just hard facts. The kind of stuff they look at in the war room. And the word, Stevie boy, is that Uncle Sam is not going to let the Iron Fist make the mistakes Walesa made. Nothing's going to happen until the structure is in place, and it's going up fast. No amateurs this time. They're training in Utah, even in Poland, making the perfect model for export."

"How will it go?"

"A strike will begin it. In the mines, most likely. Those miners are the toughest. Crazy bastards. They'll come in fast. And that's where they can set the pattern for wrecking. Just imagine what fifty gifted, well-led men could have done with mine explosives during the Solidarity trouble. The economy would have vanished."

"But it didn't happen."

"Only because the bullets all flew one way. This time there'll be return mail. The army will slaughter, and that's just what they want. In a world of workers, when the workers become your enemy, it's all over. You can send in every gun in the Warsaw Pact and it won't help. They'll collect martyrs. The Poles are damned good at that."

"Listen to yourself, Ben. You sound like you're talking about people you hate."

"Heaven knows I don't mean it that way. But when they're too thick to figure out who loves them and where they should put their hatred—it drives me wacko."

There was a long silence. Somewhere, far off, the engine of an aging lawn mower coughed to a stop. Glasgow spoke first.

"What can I do, Ben?"

Eagles turned to check the empty church. "You can do more than any other man we have. We've got confirmed information that Stanislaw Kuzianik is coming here."

"I'm not surprised. His old man's been hinting at it."

"Kuzianik draws the best brains, the best hearts, the best fighters. The people have turned him into a Mohammed. Not just the miners and farmers, but the thinkers, too. Inside the government and inside the army. We've got to derail him before he picks up any more speed."

"Good luck."

"We've already got his itinerary. To Boston to speak at Concord and Bunker Hill rallies. Next, Washington to meet the President— then Pittsburgh to whip up the unions and on to the Czestochowa shrine in Doylestown to get to the Poles. After that, Steve, he's coming here for a tearful reunion with his old father. He'll hang around a few days and proclaim the great bond between our people and his. He'll finish up his stay in America right here in this church, at a High Mass seated next to his father. Roots, religion, small town. What a setting."

"For what?"

"For your speech, Steve. To counter the one Kuzianik's going to make at Doylestown. The one that to all purposes declares the workers of Poland at war with the Soviet Union. It will get back to Poland through the blackout. Then the blood will start."

"How can you know all that?"

"They turned one of Kuzianik's typists. I've got a rough draft of what he'll say right here in the pocket of my Don Ho Hawaiian shirt." He drew out a folded sheaf of papers and waved it under Glasgow's startled eyes. "Here, Stevie, is where you get to play in the Super Bowl."

"Yeah? Like how?"

"You call a press conference on your own. You do it fast—before the diocese can turn it off."

"You mean I take him apart?"

"Exactly. But with the greatest reluctance, with your heart breaking, with anguish written all over your face—the whole, beautiful thing in close-up and glorious color. You say you admire the brave people fighting in Poland. You mourn their setback and know what they feel. You say you'd rather cut your tongue out than speak out for a certain faction in the church without an okay from the diocese. But this is different. Certain things must be said at any cost."

Glasgow made a face. "Maybe you'd better get Laurence Olivier."

"Since you'll know pretty much what he's going to say, it should be easy. You'll have all these brilliant point-by-point comebacks. Your deep feeling will have given wings to your tongue."

Glasgow felt his breathing come faster. My God, he thought, is this it? The end of the long wait? "It's all written, then?"

"They'd like to do every word. In fact they did. It sounded like the instructions on a gas mask. Write this one yourself, Steve. They'll love it."

They? It might be just the bishops, Glasgow thought. Wouldn't that be sweet? After twenty-three long years, blowing his cover for the big one to do a favor for a half-mad old roommate.

He laughed to himself. The big one indeed. Chances are they'd thrown out his file years ago.

"I've got to think on it, Ben."

Eagles handed him the Kuzianik speech and went on as though he hadn't heard Glasgow's reluctance. "Just light a fire under the basics. In the long run, the Iron Fist would destroy the country and the workers just as Solidarity would have. It's an irresponsible group led by a clique of crazy hotheads, and Kuzianik is the worst of the bunch."

"That should go over big."

"The more uproar, the bigger the headlines. Make war the issue. Scare 'em witless, spitless and shitless!"

"Why not do it yourself, Ben?"

"No way. I'm a bad-smelling, wild-eyed lefty with a scruffy beard and the malaria trembles. I've never had a scrubbed-up American parish with Las Vegas nights. I have chosen to consort with brown-skinned geeks who do not watch the Perry Como Christmas Show and who would, our superiors believe, lend me the use of their titties faster than join me in a Hail Mary.

"But you, Stevie, are the voice of Yankee Doodle Dandy America. You haven't made a peep about politics in your entire life that could make the Sunday bulletin. When it comes from you, it comes from the heart of Grand Old Flagsville. Now, for the love of all that's merciful, say you'll do it so I can go get a beer."

"I've gotta think, Ben."

An edge crept into Bennett Eagles's cracked voice. "If you leave us hanging, Steve, I'll be forced to tell the archdiocese and the government certain things."

Glasgow tensed. "Such as?"

Eagles grabbed Glasgow by the front of his cassock and pulled him close. "Such as the name of the depraved young seminarian who was caught short during a High Mass being celebrated by the late Cardinal McEvoy. The one who slipped into a side office and in gross rupture of the laws of man and God did shit grandly into a U.S. mail bag and its contents. The loss to the students in cakes and socks alone turned a dozen souls from the priesthood. And, Stevie boy, I happen to know that that shit is still in a filing cabinet at the FBI and could be traced back to you with ease by those foul chili peppers you used to eat."

Glasgow's whoop filled the cavernous church. The old Bennett Eagles had gloriously returned, and the two old friends roared their long-stored laughter until their eyes streamed and their throats burned.

If it was one more gimmick, Glasgow thought, it was a good one. "Okay, Ben. Tell whoever sent you that you've found your sucker."

Eagles rubbed his eyes briskly and sighed. He'd wanted this one. "Since you're obviously dying to know, it's a certain Sister Mary

Augustine who's running this. It's her plan to slip a nun with an oak ruler into the war room. When the man reaches for the red button—whack! Knuckle purée and peace in our time!"

They talked for a while, but Glasgow could see that Eagles's thoughts had begun to move elsewhere.

"Stay a little longer, Ben."

"Can't. I'm behind schedule now." Slowly unfolding his long frame, Eagles stuck out his hand. "Listen, Stevie, I'm going to pray for you down there. Promise you won't laugh, but I've gotten real good at it. I go like two bastards, and I think someone hears me." He placed his hands gently on Glasgow's shoulders. "Goodbye, Steve. Keep it in your cassock, okay?"

Bennett Eagles walked slowly up the center aisle and never looked back. When he opened the big door to the brightness outside, the sudden flash dazzled Glasgow and made it seem that his old friend had become part of the light.

12

Sam Sandusky found Peter Keene seated in a spot of honor on the newsstand, waving his racing form as he held forth on the fine art of betting to his new friends from the Den. With his upper dentures removed and a fine growth of gray stubble going, he was the picture of the loud, gabby, retired civil servant he would surely have been had he not chosen the priesthood.

Keene had a special fondness for a fedora of beige polyethylene pressed in a pattern to look like straw, and a tee shirt two sizes too large that proclaimed *"No More Mister Nice Guy."* He had salvaged both items from a parish clothing drive to protect the needy from themselves, and wore them with much style.

"Petey, I gotta see you inside," Sandusky said. Keene followed the bookie through his store to a room at the back. "It don't always look so crummy. My wife is a great cleaner, but she's been with her sister for the last month. Laura had her plumbing took out and she's got nobody but the wife. Probably won't see the old girl for a while."

"I'd like to meet her sometime, Sam."

"You will. In the meantime, I have Jilly Jubcek making house calls. You keep doin' a good job for me, and I'll buy you a night you'll never forget." Sandusky looked at Keene's emaciated frame. "On the other hand, she might kill you."

"We'll see who kills who." Keene smiled. Marie's absence made the priest's work more difficult. He had counted on getting next to her for more details on Father Smead.

Sandusky spun the dial on a safe. "Go through the book and pull a list of everyone that's three weeks behind."

"Three weeks isn't much to carry."

"Used to give 'em more. But you, you old shit artist, changed that."

The book Sandusky lifted out of the safe was bigger than Keene would have expected for a town this size. It amused him that it was known to the world's bookies as the Bible. It contained a careful rundown of all betting action in the Lost Hessian area, most of it handled by Sandusky. In the back was a list of deadbeats sent in by bookies from surrounding towns. Sandusky, of course, returned the favor. "I tried working by phone a few times, but I'm no good at it and you can't control that bohunk Ivan Dinkova. If they didn't say they were comin' down with the bread in five minutes, Ivan wanted to run over and break their mothers' toes. Phone bugs are two cents a dozen now and they got lousy laws about threats on the wire. But soon as I heard your line of shit, Petey, I knew you were the man. A great thought I had."

"I believe the thought was mine, Sam."

"Yeah, but I knew it was great, right? What d'ya want, a friggin' patent?" Sandusky pointed toward the scarred wooden table in the center of the room. "Work there."

Knowing that bookies were not generally known for a blind trust in their fellow men, Keene was proud of how he had gained access to the Sandusky Bible. His charm had always served him best when it could be made to serve others. But he did not forget that Sam had made a point of having him meet Ivan Dinkova, a man built like a row of coffee machines and whose nose, though substantial in size, did not protrude as far as his brow.

Sam would sit at the table and sip coffee while Keene did his phone work. He now set down a large pot of coffee and two mugs. "Just love to hear you talk to 'em, Petey. 'How's your job? How's your mom? How's your cat? In any trouble? Any way I can help? I know a guy wants a car just like yours. Wanna sell? A friend of mine put a garage on his house by gettin' a loan on his insurance. You got insurance?' " Sam chuckled into his coffee. "The damned money's been flyin' in."

"Speaking of money flying in, Sam—"

"Yeah, yeah, yeah. Wanna take it in action?"

"Only half. I gotta live, too." Keene took twenty-five dollars from the bookie.

He had worked his way through a pot of coffee when the phone rang between his calls. Sandusky took it.

"It's Scranton," he said after hanging up. "They got some Syrian gun seller in Philly wants to go down on a soccer match in Austria. A five to one underdog and he wants to see all our cash before he bets. Christ, it's like amateur night. But the numbers are too big to say no."

Like many people who talked to Keene, he realized he had said too much only after he had said it. "I'll be luggin' the mint, so Dinkova will be with me and he'll be packin' his new Ingraham. About six million shots a second. Somebody comes after me, I'm gonna be real pissed at all the guys who knew."

Keene smelled his chance coming.

Sandusky started to reach for the Bible, then stopped. "Pull the behinds for next week, too. Then put the book back in the safe and spin the dial." He saw Keene look into the safe, and quickly pulled out several bound stacks of money and tumbled them into a scuffed briefcase. "I'm leavin' two grand in the safe. Exactly. And watch the counter outside. Don't let the kids hang around the stroke books—they leave greasy marks. I'll be back tomorrow morning and lay another half a C on ya."

It was not until Keene heard Sandusky's Lincoln pull away that he turned to the record of Father Alfred Smead.

Peter Keene had a special talent for looking into the financial affairs of priests with habits too costly for the life they had chosen. He had squirreled out drug habits, woman habits, drink habits and even chic French restaurant habits. Gambling habits were not so tough, because gamblers were big talkers and compulsive record keepers. They'd either tell you about it themselves or lead you to some piece of paper that told you. He was certain that somewhere in Smead's rectory room there was a copy of the information he now quickly transferred into a notebook.

It was evident that Smead was a thoroughly inept gambler. So seldom did he win that it took twice the money for him to stay in action than it would have taken a man with only average luck. His net loss to Sandusky was running at just over five hundred dollars a week. Allowing Smead two hundred fifty a month from the church and a hundred fifty from stipends, then figuring in his few wins and his likely take per person per month, Keene realized that the priest was extorting money from hundreds of people on a steady basis.

Without question he had enough to confront the priest right now, but that was not his way. He first had to know the man deeply. He had to judge the weakness against whatever value in him might be worth saving.

Father Smead didn't show up until Keene was pulling the newsstand inside the store. "Don't let the Polack get away, Pete. I got a nice hit."

"Too late, Father Al. Sam's gone to visit the kids at the orphan house."

"Hope they've got the money to pay him, or Dinkova will bust up their frisbees. Damn! Brett's hot as a hooker's ass. A little action on Kansas City's like stealing. I really should confess it."

"Sam's back in the morning. You can get on the game then."

"Yeah, but not tonight's. Damn. Want to do some cards?"

"Not till my check comes, Al. You've been cleaning my clock."

"Suppose I put you on the arm for a while? I feel like a beer and swapping some bull."

" 'Fraid not. Playing on the arm is bad for a man of my means. But I'll ride along with you. Wait while I toss a couple of Sammy's beers into a cooler bag."

Once in the car, Smead never let Keene get started. He was ready to go.

"It's got me, Pete. It's really got me. I thought of going to Glasgow. He's my pastor. Not a bad guy, but there's a streak of something in him that doesn't belong."

"Belong where?"

"Talking to God. don't think he connects upstairs. It's like he fills out a form and passes it on."

"What would you tell him?"

"That I don't want to be found dead in an eight-by-eight plywood room in some rectory where I was helping swab the toilets for my keep. That I don't want to go into the box without spending one day at the best Las Vegas casino—with five thousand in chips in my pocket and a deluxe room with a phone by the can for the Keno. I want to be served hand and foot and hear people laughing out in the hall during the night."

"Maybe if Brett keeps hitting—"

"Don't jiggle me along, Petey. I know what I sound like."

"Why don't you just quit?"

"I need the living."

"Yeah, I guess you do, Al." Keene made his first probe. "Sammy can really cost you."

Smead took his eyes from the road to study Keene for a moment. "You have any idea what it's like to spend your life seeing how much people enjoy sin? The lesson you learn best being a priest is that sin is the only thing worth getting up for."

"Well, pinching a little for Sammy keeps you in the game."

"Don't worry, I give them back plenty. But I tell you, Pete, I'll blow soon. That Glasgow. He's strong. He's smart. If I thought I could talk to him—"

"Praying is what you guys do, isn't it? Why don't you try some?"

"I keep ringing that phone, but nobody picks up. I thought it might be better when I got a job inside the altar rail. It's really why I joined up." Smead turned from the road again. "You getting a thing I'm saying, Pete?"

"Sure."

"You wouldn't tell any of this to those geeks at Sam's?"

"Hey, Al. We're friends."

"We're not. But I don't think you will."

"Why not tell this Glasgow what you've been doing at Sam's? Tell him you're going to stop—that you need him to understand."

"Maybe. Maybe."

"Why just maybe?"

"Because I think he's losing it himself. Something's gone out of him."

"You think he's losing God?"

"Maybe something worse, Pete. Losing God doesn't often upset a priest."

These words from this sour, turned-in soul struck Keene with their simple truth. He thought of the pain inside Alfred Smead that would cause him to spill out his torments to a drab little stranger who had crossed his path for only a moment.

Where there was pain there was still hope. Keene decided to spare Smead for one more week.

13

Georgi Bikoyan's sharp mind was not dying as fast as the rest of him. It struggled to find meaning in the wild swings of fortune that had tumbled his life over the past weeks.

He felt no fear of the end he knew was coming. He had not sought the miracle that had saved him the first time, and he would seek none now. Besides, he had done more good living in his forty years than most of the other two hundred fifty million souls living the gray life of the Soviet Union were likely to do in a hundred.

Grunting against the pain in his joints, he pushed down the stiff hospital sheets and raised his bed gown to examine his body. The black and blue splotches had grown frighteningly in the short time since he had last checked them. The doctors refused to discuss the mysterious disease and if they had reached any prognosis, it had not been made known to him.

Twenty-four hours ago, he had been as healthy as any man in the Soviet penal system could be. Now the life had all but fallen out of him. The doctors were good, too, not the bored hacks he had known during his earlier stay in prison. They had the look and manner of the best and came to check him at least once every hour. Clearly there was a very special interest in his case. Perhaps they feared he had some new form of plague that would spread to the cities. Maybe they would name it after him, he thought wryly. Bikoyan's Disease.

One thing was certain: He was not being treated. Not a shot, not a pill, not a knife. Either they didn't know how to help him or there was more interest at the moment in the progress of his ailment than there was in its arrest.

Bikoyan strove to focus his eyes on the spreading splotches on his legs and torso. Somewhere he had seen those marks before. Slowly it came to him. There had been a man killed at the plant in Odessa. He had been cleaning out a large solvent tank and was overcome by the fumes. His body lay undiscovered for hours. When a fellow worker came upon the tragedy, Bikoyan, as plant manager, had been one of the first into the tank. The man, clad only in shorts, was lying face down. When they turned him over the entire front of his body seemed soaked in this same blue-black wine stain. The plant doctors had later said that the man's blood, seeping out of vessels that had dissolved, simply followed the tug of gravity and lay in great dark splotches on the inside of the victim's skin.

Bikoyan now wondered if the grisly patches on his body were his own blood, leaking from his veins and pooling in his body while he still lived.

His Armenian mind, toughened by the endless business intrigues of Soviet Georgia, welled with distrust. If they wished to spill his blood, he thought, why had they not done it three weeks ago in the far more abrupt fashion they had planned?

He fumbled the sheets up around his neck again and closed his eyes, trying to rest. More and more his breathing took on the sound of a man struggling under water. Something was filling his lungs.

Still, he could not complain. Exactly one month ago, he had been living at the very top of the lively and rewarding world of state plant plundering in Odessa. Theft from the state came naturally to Bikoyan and his boyhood friends. They had risen as a group, bribing, muscling and pulling each other up.

Bikoyan had been the best. His endless guile, his reckless thrust, his oily blend of style and portly good looks had seen him become manager of the Red Banner Concrete Construction Allocation Plant before he was thirty-five. To be at the head of any state plant was a perfect dream of pillage, but the opportunities at Red Banner were the envy of the entire black market network in the southern Soviet Union.

Of all the things in short supply in the country's creaking industry, concrete and board lumber were certainly near the top of the list. With his command of Red Banner's vast supply of concrete and the board lumber sent along as pouring forms, Bikoyan stood at the head of a corrupt army.

Throughout the south, other plant managers, chronically short of basic building materials necessary to fulfill their part of the latest five-year plan, knew that a shipment of cash or favors to the Bikoyan group would bring a boxcar or two marked "Waste Bins" with enough of what they needed to meet the planners' demands. Those who were clearly entitled to what Red Banner produced met frequent and fatal delays in getting what they needed unless, of course, they offered certain things to a Bikoyan man.

Bikoyan smiled despite the pain. Ah, what times they were. Visits to the barber who had been the choice of the young Brezhnev. Brutish, carnal romance with the high-toned niece of a member of the Politburo itself.

Walking the edge? Perhaps. But what else was there in this huge, sad land?

When they had finally come for him, it happened much as he had always imagined it would. A manager to the east had talked a bit too much over wine with someone who wanted his job. Bikoyan had been quick to note that the dour commissions that appeared at least a dozen times a year to urge him forward now contained men with the special swagger of KGB. But there was just too much to cover up. He supposed he could have gotten himself and most of his fortune to Turkey, but he had been confident to the end that he could buy his way out of trouble. Those with worse crimes than his did so regularly. Besides, where in the world could he find people as easy to steal from as the Russians?

His arrest at the office in the middle of the day had surprised but not shaken him. He stood calmly through the long list of crimes against the state as they were read in a loud voice with the door open for the rest of the staff to hear. As they led him away, he bid a joking goodbye to the workers.

Having failed to squirm free despite his money and well-placed friends, and knowing too well the grave and widespread nature of his crimes, he fully expected that he and those accused with him would be shot immediately. In this he was only partly right.

He had to admire the bearing of all who stood trial with him. They exposed only those who would have been taken anyway, turning down every deal to give over the hundreds of others who were involved with them. When all six of the plant managers were sentenced to death, each accepted his fate as stoically as if asked to pay a small traffic fine. The two who did not have families to worry about were free and jocose in their abuse of the Russians who thought they had rights in the Republic of Georgia.

Having been allowed the shortest of farewells to those who cared for them, they had been whisked to an army base at the edge of the city. On the second evening, five of them had received a nine-millimeter pistol bullet in the back of the head. Only Georgi Bikoyan was spared.

He, who had seen no more than the bell tower of the Catholic Church since he was a boy, got as far as a final holy communion before they announced his stay of execution. But his relief had been cut short by the abrupt onset of his strange illness.

He now fell into a harsh, liquid cough, and every heave of his chest drained more strength from his body. He might have tried to sleep away the heavy hand that seemed to be crushing him, but he was too cold. With great effort he weakly sounded the bell left near his hand, to call the guard for a blanket. The two doctors entered the room.

"I'm sure I don't need all this genius to bring something to keep me warm."

"It is time for us to look at you."

"Well, kindly hold a match beneath the damned stethoscope before you clamp it on me." The bubbling had almost drowned his voice.

The doctor in military uniform took two folded blankets out of a metal locker and placed them at the foot of the bed. "We'll tuck you in nice and warm after we're done."

The civilian doctor took Bikoyan's hand and used a needle to draw blood from his thumb. "Are you in pain?"

Bikoyan nodded. "It's getting worse. Will you give me something?"

"Soon. Right now it could get in the way of what we're trying to do."

"A shoemaker could do more. I haven't had so much as an aspirin yet."

They pulled back the sheets and rolled him onto his stomach. From their murmurs of awe Bikoyan guessed that the other side of him was in even worse condition than the side he could see. They tapped him with fingers along the length of his spine and listened to his heart and lungs, passing the stethoscope back and forth. When they finished, they moved to a far corner of the room and talked in voices too low for the words to be made out. Freezing, Bikoyan tried to get over onto his back and go for the covers. He was amazed that he could not. He grew angry and tried to swear at the doctors, but the shift had spilled the fluids into new parts of his lungs and all he could do was cough and fight for air.

The two men rolled him over and peered into his eyes with a light. Neither seemed shocked by his sudden turn for the worse. The civilian doctor went out the door and returned with a man from the next room. Bikoyan strained his fast-blurring eyes and saw that it was the priest who had earlier heard his confession and given him communion.

"As bad as that, Father?" Bikoyan managed.

"There is always hope."

"I think it's time for the rest of your Catholic magic."

"Perhaps."

"I believe in getting all the edge I can. You saw that when you read my charges."

The priest smiled softly. "Think of all the fine days you've had. I enjoyed that long talk we had in your cell the other night. What stories! A bit strong for me once we passed your boyhood. But I really feel that I know you, Georgi."

Bikoyan could barely whisper now. "You look different out of black, Father." The man now wore a three-piece gray suit with a watch chain across his stomach.

"I must travel soon. It's better to dress this way." He exchanged a look with the doctors and smiled. "Godless Russia, you know."

"My mind is getting so thick. Your name, Father. I can't remember your name."

"It's Gorslev, Georgi. Zamlet Gorslev."

Georgi Bikoyan died so quickly that the doctors could not tell whether the final movement of his head had been a nod to Gorslev or just the falling away of life.

"A very strong man," Gorslev said.

The civilian doctor peered at the gums of the dead man. "He must have been in far worse pain than he let on. We must get to the autopsy right away."

"Did we give him too much?" the army doctor asked.

Gorslev shook his head. "No. That fast slide at the end is necessary."

"You could use less with someone smaller. Is the next one a big man?"

"The biggest," Gorslev answered.

The army doctor picked up the two unused blankets from the foot of the dead man's bed and returned them to the metal locker. Gorslev took a last, lingering look at the still form of Georgi Bikoyan, then started from the room.

"Have a safe trip, Doctor Gorslev," the army man said.

Zamlet Gorslev turned at the door. "Just one other thing. Before you release the body, put a bullet in the back of the head. And thank you for a nice stay."

14

They lay quietly, side by side, the green velveteen of the couch cover rumpled and sweaty beneath them. Claudette's dark eyes, focused on the ceiling, showed no emotion. She made no attempt to rise, so Glasgow could not do so without seeming to dismiss her. He rose up one elbow and kissed the tip of her nose. She turned away.

"What's wrong?"

"I suppose it's back to the rectory now for some wine and a snooze."

The words surprised and angered him. "That isn't fair."

She turned to face him. "I always thought waiting for a married man was some sort of special madness. Now I find myself waiting for a priest. I'm not just fighting a wife and a couple of kids, Steven, I'm fighting almighty God Himself, and I know I'm going to lose."

She tried to get up, but he held her. "Why have you waited until now to do this?"

She glared. "Because I thought I could make you take off that collar. Because it terrifies me that I'm losing God and screwing up my life—and you seem to be handling it all so nicely."

Claudette rose again, and this time he made no attempt to stop her. She walked to the bedroom and pushed the door half-closed behind her. He listened to her quiet sobs and thought of walking out and ending it. But, after a moment, he followed her inside.

She was sitting on the bed, staring at the handkerchief in her hands. He sat next to her.

"You know it tears me up, too. How can you think it doesn't?"

Her eyes found his. "I suppose I wouldn't stay with you for two minutes if I really believed it didn't. That's my only hope."

Glasgow put his arms around her and eased her back on the brightly flowered bedspread. He kissed her, gently at first, then harder. "Forgive me, Claudette," he whispered.

"Oh, Steven, it's just that I feel so guilty, so humiliated all the time."

"I'm sorry."

"Do you love me?"

"Yes. Yes, I do."

She kissed him about the throat. "Say the words. Say them with my name."

"I love you, Claudette. I love you, my darling Claudette."

"More than God?"

"As much, I think."

She reached down for him. "Before you leave here, Father Steven Glasgow, you'll know that no woman on earth could love you better."

When her thighs came around him, Glasgow opened his mouth to tell her once and for all that this perfect joy was soon to be theirs for all time. But beyond a whimper of bliss, not a sound came forth.

Steven Glasgow's days took on a low, steady fever. He fretted at the thought of leaving his parishioners in the hands of his two curates even for a moment. Perhaps he should leave a note for the new pastor, outlining the worst cases and advising how to handle them.

The countless details of a priest's day—the bills, the banks, the sermon writing, the committee meetings, the baptisms, the funerals—all became events to savor now that he was about to lose them.

The arcane movements of the Mass became the focus of his day. On the altar the bright vestments flowed gracefully around him as he whirled, knelt and strode between God and his children. He could feel the ancient chain of words and chants stretch two thousand years, rattling out of the legion of men who had chosen the torments of this lonely land of the mind and heart. Bored, exalted, venal, selfless, stupid, brilliant, cowards, martyrs, they had brought the Word. Glasgow knew that in that chain had been men who believed nothing, who would sooner have served a devil than a God. But through it all, the Word had come down, passed on by those who scorned it no less than by those who went into the fire for it. If these men had carried nothing, then nothing had never been carried so well.

He now stared hard at each face raised to him at the altar rail. Here, when he should have been starting to cut them away, he felt himself going out to them. He found himself wanting to shake the ones who took the wafer numbly. Men had died and been denied for it, had been bored and flogged and had their lives drained dry. He wanted them to know the soaring, blazing myth of the gentle man who had died in pain to raise the merest of them to peace. All the great ideas were in the end a tiny electric spark that passed from head to head. That so many of these ideas were rooted in nothing was not the point. The beauty was there in the spark, and that spark was in Steven Glasgow.

Somehow his people looked at him and saw clearly the outlines of the God that was not in him. More and more they blossomed in simple, happy belief at his touch and his words.

The pipe does not have to believe in the water to conduct it.

15

Even over the phone, Peter Keene could hear the swelling panic in Father Smead's voice. The words tumbled out so quickly that Keene had to close the phone booth door against the babble of the newsstand group in order to make them out.

"I've got an awful problem here, Pete. You're the only one in the world I can think of who'd help me."

"I've got about a hundred and ten bucks."

"No, no, it's not that. There's been an accident. A woman's hurt bad."

"Call a doctor."

"You don't understand, Pete. I can't get involved in this."

"Speak up, Al."

"I can't. Dizak's listening."

"Who?"

"Karl Dizak. I'm at his house. You remember it, the two-story yellow stucco at Berry and Oak. Can you come right away?"

"I've got no wheels."

The whisper became frantic. "Get some kid to loan you a bike. For Christ's sake, Pete, you can walk it in twenty minutes."

"Thought you said she's hurt bad."

"She'll keep for twenty minutes. Just leave now."

"I'm getting a nasty feeling," Keene said, "but I'll be there."

He hung up, thought for a moment, then threw a quarter into the phone. He gave the hospital the house's location, asked for immediate help and took off at the closest thing he could manage to a run.

By the time he knocked at the Dizaks' front door, his legs were trembling and his breath came in long wheezes. He'd made it in just under fifteen minutes.

Smead opened the door, his hair a tossed white haystack. "Get in here quick. There's a guy next door with a nose about two yards long."

As Keene entered the house, a foul-smelling hulk of an old man bore down on them. His worn robe hung open, and Keene could see he was sweating and naked beneath it. "Who is this bum in my house?" he rasped. "I want him out of here." The wild-looking man tried to push Keene toward the door, but Smead restrained him. "Easy now, Dizak. This is a good friend. He's here to help us."

"That's good, Father. Maybe he could help us carry her back upstairs."

As Keene's eyes took hold in the dark shadows, he made out a pale heap at the foot of a long staircase. "Good God," he gasped.

He quickly crossed to the sprawled body of a well-formed woman in her fifties. Her nightdress was raised above her breasts. The upper bone of her right arm was bent at a sharp angle where it had snapped. A deep gash in her forehead reached up into her scalp. Thick blood had run back into her hair and pooled on the polished wood of the floor. Blue-black bruises swelled at her shoulders, hips and knees. Keene spotted a slipper halfway up the long staircase. It was plain that the woman had tumbled most of the way down the metal-edged flight of stairs.

Her eyes flicked open, clear and dark, without pain. Keene could see that she was looking into a different time. "James, why are you home from school so soon? Snuck out on the teacher again, didn't you? Imagine a little boy like you walking alone through the Den! You could get stolen." With her good arm she caught Keene's hand in a strong grip and examined both sides. "Now you wash those hands and get up to your room 'til supper's ready. Your father will deal with you when he gets home. And don't forget to feed your fish." She released Keene's hand and patted his shoulder to dismiss him.

"Good Lord, she's knocked herself silly," Keene said.

"She never makes sense no more," Dizak grumbled.

"Alzheimer's," Smead said. "Pretty far gone."

Dizak gave a rattling chuckle. "She's still good as a woman, Father. Damn good." He turned to Smead. Part of the stench that rose from him, Keene realized, was whiskey. "Let's get her back upstairs now, okay?"

Keene pulled the woman's nightdress down to cover her. "You mean that's what's been taking care of her?" he muttered to Smead.

"She's got some kids, too. They drop over once in a while."

"That's not enough, Al. She needs full-time care, and I don't think he's far behind." Gently, Keene slipped a throw pillow beneath her head.

Father Smead grabbed Keene's sleeve and pulled him into the dining room, leaving Dizak to prowl around the fallen woman. "Look, here's how it is, Pete. I've sort of been looking after the old lady for an hour or so almost every day. The daughters know about it." He held up a key. "Even gave me this so I could let myself in when I stop by."

"And this is what you found when you came today?"

"Well, not exactly. Actually I was here when it happened." Keene saw that Smead's collar was sodden with sweat. "I was sitting in the living room, reading, when she tried to run down those stairs. Missed the first few and, wham, just bounced and tumbled the rest of the way."

"Why weren't you up there with her?"

"That's the whole point, Pete. That's what the daughters will want to know. I think the Church could be liable for this."

"Answer the question, Al."

"Well, Dizak likes to be—you know, alone with her once in a while. To talk with her. Things like that. But she doesn't want him, being off her head and all. So I sort of—talk to her. I've known Danya a long time and she trusts me. Always seems to know who I am. Anyway, I convince her to let Dizak come in. Believe me,

Pete, without my going into that bedroom first, she'd tear the joint apart. She can be a real wildcat."

"You mean she was trying to get away from him up there?"

"She might have been. I'm not sure."

Keene watched Dizak in the other room mumbling over his wife. "How do you want me to help, Al?"

"Dizak's real upset. Drunk. Practically off his rocker. There'll be cops here, and doctors. Maybe even reporters. He could say something real crazy and get our Lady of Jasna Gora in all kinds of trouble." Smead seemed to lose his breath. Wet streaks had appeared across his chest. "Jesus, Pete, who wants to listen to Glasgow?"

"Go on."

"I want you to say you were here with me. People know we ride together a lot. The way we tell it, we found her this way when we got here. It won't hurt a thing and could save a lot of trouble. What do you say?"

"I think you're making too big a thing out of it, but if that's what you want, okay."

Smead's sigh was interrupted by a squeal of pain from the injured Danya Dizak. The two men rushed back into the living room to find a grunting Dizak covering the woman with his body. She kicked and struggled with startling vigor as he tried with his hands to control her. "Hold still, damn you. I'm your husband," he shouted.

The woman got her teeth into the flesh at the base of her husband's thumb and bit down hard. Dizak reared back with a bellow of pain, and Smead and Keene were able to pull him off and topple him over backward. They tried to pin him to the floor, but the burly man fought to his feet, roaring, "I pay you, you stinking priest. Now you help me."

"Shut your mouth, you damned Polack," Smead shouted, attempting to bend the man's arm behind his body.

"Listen to me," Keene yelled. "Your wife needs help." Dizak's thick arm brushed him aside.

"She's mine and she will give me what's mine. You've poisoned her against me, damn you. Get out." Nearly out of control, Dizak fought his way back to the woman. "I love you, Danya. I love you."

With a violent whirl, he spun the two gasping men off him, dropped his robe and knelt naked above the woman.

Keene saw what he had to do. He snatched a two-foot brass statue of the Blessed Virgin off the console radio and swung it with his full, wiry strength into the soft flesh just below Dizak's ribs. A stream of whiskey poured out of the man's mouth as he collapsed sideways.

They dragged him limp and moaning to an armchair and wrestled him back into his robe. Dizak sobbed drunkenly, thrashing his huge head from side to side. "Don't take her from me. I need her so."

"Beg God to forgive you, you pig," Smead shouted.

Dizak's eyes rolled up into his head. "You dirty priest bastard. All you do is rob me." He gagged and with a final moan fell into a deep, drunken sleep.

The pain in Danya Dizak's broken arm focused her mind for a moment. "Please don't let him hurt me anymore, Father. Talk to God. Make God stop asking me to be with him. He hurts me so."

Keene rose to face Smead, his blue eyes no longer soft. "You let him do this to her? For money? You should be whipped through the streets."

"Just where in hell does a two-bit gambler get off . . ."

The siren of an approaching ambulance interrupted. Soon there was a squeal of brakes outside. Keene opened the door for a young doctor and two attendants.

"Sorry for the delay. Emergency across town."

Keene pointed to Mrs. Dizak. "She's had a nasty fall, Doctor. We found her that way. The husband is drunk."

The doctor worked over the injured woman. Smead, crushed and frightened, did not take his eyes off Keene. The medical team first treated Danya Dizak for shock, then carefully splinted her arm. A further examination indicated that her skull was not fractured and nothing else was broken.

Keene smoothly fielded all the questions and filled out several forms. He stuck to the story that Smead had proposed and promised to stay until the husband awakened.

It was fully ten minutes after the ambulance had departed before

Father Smead lifted his head to face Peter Keene's glare. The light-hearted newsstand bum was gone.

Smead squirmed. "All right. Who are you?"

"I'm a priest. Father Peter Keene. I was sent."

The color left Smead's face. "Sent? By the chancery?"

"No. The bishop. On his own. We try to keep these things to ourselves until we're sure we can't fix them."

"And you're sure you can't fix this one?"

"Damn sure."

Smead stared at the floor. "Who called you?"

"Sandusky's wife. She wrote a letter."

"Because a priest was having a little fun?"

"No, because a priest was stealing. From his church and his people."

Smead faced his accuser again. He shook his head sadly. "I really trusted you, Pete. For the first time since I took this lousy job I really believed that I'd found a friend. I honestly thought you liked me."

"I tried real hard, Al. If I could have found one thing in you to save, I swear I'd have gotten you out of this."

"And now?"

"You quit. We'll try to make it easy. Nothing will be said about the rest of it."

Smead's hand went to his throat, as though to keep Keene from tearing away his collar. "Isn't it the damnedest thing. I've been praying for the guts to get out for twenty years. Now that there's no choice, I don't want to go."

"You're not a lazy person. There's always a way to get money."

"It's not that so much. I guess I feel the way I did that first time my old man threw me out of the house. I knew I wasn't worth a damn and probably deserved exactly what I was getting, but I just never stopped hoping that suddenly he'd say he loved me."

Smead's eyes suddenly filled. Keene patted his hand. "Whatever you've done, Al, God won't stop loving you."

Smead's face slowly hardened. "Sure. Maybe he'll get me a job making beds in some Protestant mission flophouse. I certainly won't get a thing out of *this* loving Church."

"I'll talk to the bishop. He's got more contacts than a Philadephia alderman."

"Maybe for his Irish cronies and paroled dago drugstore robbers, but that's about it."

"I'll even look around for you myself," he said.

"I've got to get away fast. Even with a couple of hits, I still owe Sandusky three hundred bucks. He'll have Dinkova out looking for me."

"I'll square it with Sam."

"Hey, would you? That'd be terrific." Assistance with a gambling debt was one kindness that impressed Smead.

They were silent for a while. In the far room, Dizak mumbled in his sleep. Smead's mood turned dark again.

"You feeling a little guilty, Pete?"

"I thought that would be your job."

"You gumshoe guys are all the same. Just love to come after the little fish. Never the big sharks that might chew back. Never some guy who could make it tough for you."

"It's really all the same."

"Yeah? Then how come you're not checking out our saintly Father Glasgow and his fancy woman?"

Keene was careful not to react.

"Now there's a fine example for you," Smead continued. "Not only a breach of God's written law but the priest's unwritten one. *Nunca en la parroquia.* Never in the parish."

Keene's mind raced. The deal was suddenly very different. He probed cautiously.

"Now, now, Al. Lashing out with a lot of nonsense isn't going to change a thing."

Smead leaned closer. "Okay, Dick Tracy, what do you make of this? I took a call at the rectory last week. Some guy who runs a gas station way out of town says someone had left a wallet there a few hours before. Inside was a driver's license belonging to one Steven Glasgow. It had the church's address on it. The guy said he had to tow a panel truck to Lost Hessian later in the day and he'd be happy to drop it off."

Keene listened intently. It troubled him that the frightened Smead had turned smug and sure.

"So this guy turns up a few hours later while Glasgow was still out with the Pinto. Something about the name of the town on his tow truck struck me. Dunwood it was. I didn't quite connect it until later. Anyway, I took a couple of bucks from the wallet and gave it to the guy for his trouble. I said that Father Glasgow would be very grateful. '*Father Glasgow?*' the guy says, looking real surprised. 'The way he was dressed, I thought he was working on some road gang.' About half an hour after the guy left, Glasgow rolls up in the Pinto dressed as nice as you please in his collar and blacks. He seemed amazed that he'd left his wallet at the gas station. It was obvious he thought he'd left it somewhere else. Somewhere he could get it back real easy."

Keene shrugged. "Like a parishioner's house, maybe?"

"Exactly."

"Priests are always accepting money, Al. Who would know that better than you?"

"Then I realized why the name on that truck tickled my mind. Dunwood. The only parishioner who lives out that far is a foxy widow named Claudette West. She's had an eye on Glasgow from the start, and he's been damned glad of it. I know good old Father Steve. It's so rare he gets close to someone that it sticks out a mile when he does. They're thick, those two. No question about it."

Keene shrugged again. "This West lady is entitled to a visit from her pastor the same as those who live nearby. What's so unusual?"

"What's unusual is he visits her two or three times a week. Out of curiosity, I've been checking the mileage on the Pinto before and after he takes it. He's been driving out there a lot, I'd say."

"It proves nothing."

"Yeah, well what about his changing into work clothes? You suppose he digs out septic tanks as a special service to his flock?"

"Why not ask him about it?"

"Glasgow? Are you kidding?"

"Admit it, Al. It's pretty thin stuff at best."

"Ah, but here's the best." Smead allowed himself a full smile. "Guess what I found in the wallet?"

"You went through his wallet?"

"Just to check the I.D. That's when we spotted it. The gas station guy almost laughed out loud."

"Spotted what?"

"Well, you know how young guys are always breaking out a loose condom to keep in their wallet in case they get lucky."

"Yeah."

"And you know how sitting on it makes it show through the leather like it was embossed. Once my mother spotted mine, and my old man knocked the hell out of me."

"It could have been something else."

"Bullshit, Pete. There's only one shape in the world like that one. And there it was, big as life. The mark of sin on the sacred Steven Glasgow. Only a priest would be foolish enough to give himself away like that after the age of fifteen."

"Perhaps it's just wishful thinking," Keene said.

"It's you who's doing the wishful thinking. Face it, Pete, he's knocking her drawers off."

Keene watched as Smead's high spirits began to fall again. A hooked gambler, along in years, devoid of charm and fired by the Church, was not going to make it. No cheerful words were going to change that. Keene knew that the man would soon grow desperate. A dismissed, distraught Smead might invent a good story for anyone who would pay him. With the eyes of the world about to turn on Lost Hessian, the possibilities were terrifying.

Keene was sure Smead did not yet know the details of Stanislaw Kuzianik's visit. Keene himself had only been filled in by the bishop after a long evening of too much wine and old-country chatter. But he knew that as soon as word of that visit broke, Smead's gambler's wit would be quick to recognize that the odds had turned in his favor. The muckraking newspapers would spend brashly for the inside story of a sinning priest who would wash away the sins of a secular saint. Add to that the brutal ouster of the faifhful old curate who dared expose the truth, and the scandal could hold the headlines for a month.

The damage would not stop at red faces. Novices would be laughed at and lost. Young people standing at the crisis of faith would turn away forever. Bequests would slow for months.

Then there were the great enemies. The foes of the Church in the East would hold up for all to see the corrupt core of what pretended to be the last stronghold of ethical force. The thinly held line of the faithful would have to fall back when it had no ground to lose.

The defense of the Church was what drove Peter Keene's life. His mind dashed through all the possibilities: He could try to have Glasgow transferred immediately. Then, guilty or not, the pastor would be no further danger to the Church. But even with Glasgow replaced, Smead would still have his story. A nice scandal all the same.

Anyway, Keene thought, how could he accuse a man held in high and growing esteem of a thing so serious, based on the word of a proven thief and weakling? And would anyone believe the charges? Keene was known to be Bishop McCarthy's man, and the bishop's power was slipping badly with the inroads of health and age. It had become stylish to ignore him and his people.

Then Keene grew angry with himself. If he was such a great investigator, he could find his own way to the bottom of it. And the best way to handle Smead, he decided, was to make a deal now, before the old priest saw the strength of the cards he had been dealt.

"Look, Al. I see your beef real plain. A bookie's wife drops a letter and some old gumshoe is right on the job busting ass. And here you give me this big tip about Glasgow and you think I'm not going to follow it up because he's got purple coming and a good line of bull." He gave Smead's arm a squeeze. "Well, laddie, that's where you're wrong. I'm getting on this thing starting right now."

"A lot of good that'll do *me*."

"Wrong again. One of the Church's big problems is that too many curates are letting their bosses get away with too much. Why, hell, most of the time we come down harder on the whistle-blower than we do on the one who screwed up. And what's his reward for telling the truth? No one ever trusts him again."

Smead gave a series of angry nods.

"Well, I want to change all that, Al. You know how? I'm going to start by telling the bishop that you check out okay, but that this spot is wrong for you. Too hectic. Your nerves have let go. We've got to get you into a home for some rest. Six months maybe, while I check things. When you get out, you say you're feeling shipshape again and we shoot you into a nice soft spot. Out west maybe. I'll even fix it so you won't have to handle money. Being tempted like that could wear you down pretty fast."

There was just enough sting in the last remark to remind Smead that Keene's concern for justice had not caused him to forget that the straying priest was at his mercy.

"Would you do it, Pete? Honest? Jeez, that would be great. And I know you wouldn't do it for just anybody. All those days we spent together did mean something."

"Of course they did, Al."

"You're sure you can make it happen?"

"I'll be on the phone to the bishop before you're back in the rectory. Now you've got to understand, it'll take a bit of acting. Here's what you say: You knew you'd been slipping for a long time, but seeing Mrs. Dizak come bouncing down that staircase and watching her husband go around the bend because of it was suddenly too much. Tremble a lot. Cry. Stop shaving and eating. Drink heavier than usual. Take to your bed. Every time Glasgow tries to talk to you, start praying. Priests that never prayed in their lives do it when they crack up."

"I'll tell you one thing, Pete. I won't have to fake it much. With Sandusky watching me from one side and Glasgow from the other, my head feels like a bowl of Mrs. Sullivan's porridge."

"I figure three days should do it."

Keene felt the tension begin to release. The newspapers would find little value in the ramblings of an old priest speaking from a rubber room.

16

The new curate was an instant hit. After the dour plodding of Father Alfred Smead, Peter Keene came to Our Lady of Jasna Gora as a brisk, fresh breeze. His prickly humor, boundless vigor and high good spirits found immediate favor with the people of the parish. He almost challenged Father Glasgow, and left the dim person of Father Bolter in an even deeper limbo than before.

Keene himself was startled by his great success. In his days as a young priest, his antic humor and salty turn of phrase had again and again run afoul of the old-line pastors, men who believed that the sin of making friends among the mortals was surpassed only by the sin of having fun while working for God. So he had spent the better part of his ardent years shuttling between dying parishes, handling their deathwatch masses and preaching sermons to people whose English was a distant second tongue. His spirits smothered early and often, he had been only too glad to accept the bishop's rescue.

It was only now, with Glasgow, that he saw with a pang how he had been denied the use of his one great gift. With no particular talent for the twisting turns of deep religious thought, he held within him a genius for building bridges into the hearts of others.

With thoughtless ease, he made the most fallow minds in the parish catch the sense of a thrilling friendship with God.

It had taken Glasgow only minutes to free Keene of the stifling bonds that had been thrown around him through the early years of his priesthood. The pastor had been frank but not unkind in a recitation of the religious failings of Father Smead. Sensing the lively mind and wit in Keene, he had urged the new man to be himself and cut loose with what it took to open up the parish to a somewhat happier way of worship.

Glasgow thought it best to inform the parishioners that it was only because of the critical shortage of priests that the diocese had assigned Peter Keene, who was nearing retirement, to Our Lady of Jasna Gora. He would be replaced when a long-term man became available. The announcement that Keene's stay was likely to be brief prompted widespread expressions of regret throughout the parish.

Keene was always amazed at how well these bumbling deals set up by him and the bishop went down.

While he could see that Glasgow's affection for him seemed genuine, Keene's old charm could not fully work its way. There remained something austere and hidden in the pastor, and Keene's discreet, though persistent efforts to move closer to him came to nothing.

He was significantly more successful at wheedling information about Glasgow from the rest of the parish. As each detail was revealed to him, Keene became more and more impressed with the picture of the man that emerged. Recognizing that Glasgow was far from being a glad-hander or a sugar-coater, Keene found that the high regard in which the pastor was held came out of a solid respect for his work as a priest.

But Keene had to know more for himself. He had expressed a desire to see as much of the parish as possible and Glasgow was happy to oblige. For several weeks the old Pinto was seldom idle. After their duties in the church and rectory, Glasgow took Keene into dozens of homes and shared with him the counselings of scores of troubled parishioners. Each day that passed convinced Keene even more that Steven Glasgow was one in a thousand among Roman Catholic pastors.

Keene's quick mind absorbed the names and sorted out the parish cast of characters: the heads of troubled homes, the givers, the doers, the committee people, the hypocrites, the sick, the needy, those with callings, those who had to be helped every step of the way. But among all the names and during all the visits, he came across nothing of Claudette West.

Hoping he might hear something from her cousin, Michael Stassin, he brought his meager musical talent to the Mozart Society, a small amateur pianists' group of which Stassin was president, but the big man was obdurately close-mouthed.

With only five weeks remaining before Kuzianik's visit, Keene knew he would have to make things happen quickly. Lost Hessian was a small town. It would not be long before some of his former friends from the Den matched the scrubbed little Irish priest from the other side of town with the salty old dude who had just weeks ago left the employ of Sam Sandusky. He had already passed a few of them in the street while hidden behind his huge false teeth, large, silver-rimmed glasses and a fresh haircut. His clerical blacks and monkey collar alone served to turn aside the eyes of his old gambling buddies. But Keene knew he couldn't afford to work his luck too hard.

Peter Keene was always surprised by how easy it was to observe people without their realizing it. Not that he liked to depend on that. In this case, as in others, he was all care.

As part of his effort to get to know all the streets and roads in the parish, he carefully studied the local maps at the library. An old surveyor's chart indicated a road that cut behind Claudette West's property. Local hunters used it in the fall as a shortcut into the hills, but it was little traveled in the summer. The mayor, being president of the County Hunt Club, authorized county money for its maintenance, and it was possible to travel the road without a four-wheel-drive vehicle. Reading the topography off the map, Keene noticed that a short section of the road passed very close to Claudette's house and about two hundred feet above it. Take the high ground, he thought. Advice as good for snoops as it was for soldiers.

Having noticed that Michael Stassin seldom drove the smaller of his two business cars, an Omni, Keene was able to borrow it whenever he wanted. Then he had to equip himself. Spotting a birdwatcher's handbook among Mrs. Sullivan's possessions, he knew that a pair of binoculars could not be far off. Sure enough, the rectory housekeeper was happy to lend him the book and the glasses for as long as he liked. Her arthritis, she told him, had been keeping her out of the hills.

Finally, there was the matter of an electric drill. He bought the least expensive one he could find at a discount from Michael Stassin, explaining that he wished to put up some shelves in his room. With the drill he was able to use the skills taught him by a less than honest old friend who sold used cars. By clamping the Omni's odometer cable in the bit, he was able to turn back the mileage, thereby concealing his long trips to Claudette's.

The vantage point offered by the road above the house was ideal. There was a small grove short of the drop-off that conveniently hid the car from the few who drove by, and there was a fine, shady place where he could sprawl on the grass and observe both her back door and the curving front driveway through a break in the trees below.

When Claudette came out to tend her backyard clothesline, the powerful binoculars pulled her close enough for Keene to see the color of her eyes. Although it would have been difficult to spot him from below, in all the time he conducted his hilltop surveillance, she never once glanced in his direction.

Glasgow, he thought, was either very lucky or very careful. Keene could not follow the pastor every time he vanished with the car, but the old priest had worked out a pattern of random checks that he was confident would eventually catch him if he were guilty. Yet, after three weeks of careful observation, all he could show for his visits was a knowledge of the purple plots of a dozen paperback romances he had carried along.

He was surprised at how few people came to visit this vital young woman. There appeared to be no one friendly enough to drop in except her cousin, who turned up twice and stayed for less than an hour, despite the length of the drive out.

Keene considered that Glasgow might be visiting in the dead of night, when there was no easy way for a watcher to be there. Glasgow didn't strike him as one who shinnied down drainpipes after dark, but then, you never knew.

17

To Steven Glasgow, it all seemed to happen in a single morning. As sudden as a sunrise in the tropics, the great outside world rose on Lost Hessian. One day the pleasant streets flowed smoothly with the sparse traffic of a sleepy town in the Pennsylvania hills. The next, there was someone blocking the way wherever you turned.

The government security men didn't quite know how to play it. The size and placement of the town were all wrong for them. They could have slipped into a hamlet in Central America and done their work unseen for a month. They could swim unknown in the crowds of any large city for years. But here, they were undone.

Some of the agents wore dark Brooks Brothers suits of a style and color seen mostly at funeral parlors. Others, judging any spot west of New Jersey to be rural, appeared in outfits that would have been considered quaint in the heart of Kansas.

With their four identical black Ford LTDs parked side by side in the town center's one parking lot, it was well that there was no pressing need for them to be anonymous.

At any rate, they seemed happy enough poring over street maps and stomping through Our Lady of Jasna Gora and the surrounding buildings.

Experts at plotting lines of fire from high points, they were

vaguely annoyed to find that no structure on the route of the Kuzianik parade to the church rose higher than three stories. This,
coupled with their failure to turn up a single local left-leaning
marksman, made them content to regard with suspicion the town's
bearded young miners whose unions, after all, might shelter a Bol-
shie or two.

For all their faintly comic manners, Glasgow had a distinct feeling
that these intense young men with eyes that never seemed to blink
were expert at spotting trouble quickly and shooting it dead.

Lost Hessian's three small hotels quickly filled up. Homeowners
with an eye for a fast dollar bunched their families into one or two
rooms and turned the other space to rent. Not one mattress or
cushion remained for sale. The sporting goods store sold out of
sleeping bags and swimming floats. With Kuzianik's scheduled arrival still a week away, any informed visitor came to town in a
camper, or, at the very least, in a car with a couple of fold-down
seats.

Only in the matter of taverns was Lost Hessian fully equipped
to deal with the hordes. Like any town in a mining area, it had at
least two saloons on every block. These were soon filled with hard-
drinking TV technicians and newsmen, who quickly turned them
into noisy corners of New York or Los Angeles. Steady patrons
were uprooted from stools they had occupied half their lives.

The streets swarmed with TV network and news-service vans.
They never seemed to park, but prowled past each other, high-
backed beetles jostling for the best spot to begin gnawing some
woodland carcass.

Glasgow woke one morning to find a network TV van parked
in the church driveway. Mrs. Sullivan was confronting three technicians anxious to check out the power box in the rectory basement.
When he dressed quickly and came down to scatter them, they
knew very well who he was and how he might serve them.

A small man wearing a safari jacket, with a fifty-dollar haircut
and skin the color of a desert chieftain's, sprang from the van. He
had the air of a trapdoor spider ambushing a juicy stroller. He
removed his sunglasses, revealing eyes so inflamed that Glasgow
wondered how he managed to see.

"Father Glasgow, this is a great moment for me. I've heard such terrific things about you from our research guys in New York. The name's Artie Gordon. I head up this unit. What we bring back goes on the eleven o'clock news for the first anchor. We'll see that you get a major commentary."

"Mr. Gordon, tell your people to pull those cables back into the van and get out of here. I don't want you parked in front of the church either."

"Hey, that's going to make it real tough for you, Padre."

"How's that?"

"Means you'll have to travel to find us. For the one-hour taped dialogue with you and Diane Wallach."

"Diane Wallach?"

"Okay, she was just busted from co-anchor. But at least she's not the sports guy like one of my competitors has out here."

"Where, Mr. Gordon, did you get the idea that I was going to do a one-hour dialogue with anyone?"

"Doesn't your boss carbon you on the memos? Your archbishop, Mr. Doolin, called my archbishop, Mr. Cantrowitz, and set it all up. A nice shot of publicity for the views of the church."

What a break, Glasgow thought. Doolin wouldn't have the power to kill what was taped when it turned out to be not at all what he wanted.

"And what do you see as the subject of this dialogue?"

"Hey, they said you knew all the good things to say, Father. Kind of free-ranging, I'd think. You know, the American Church's view of Kuzianik and the Iron Fist. Backing up the Polish Church to the last drop of Polish blood. You'll be great, Father, being a native Pole and all that. The piece should have real clout."

"The politics of God."

"Good phrase. Use it. Hell, the Church, the Poles, the Russians and the Iron Fist might be shaping up the biggest battle between heaven and earth since the Thirty Years' War."

Ben Eagles was going to be a very happy man, Glasgow thought. Still, he wanted to annoy this sun-baked ass. "Forget it. I couldn't talk to my mother for an hour—and I like her."

"You know, I *told* them you wouldn't go for Wallach. Okay,

maybe we can do better. How about Arvel Pearson? New. Top drawer. The other networks are nosing around his contract even as we speak."

"I'd sound like a man reading out of the Shanghai phone book."

"C'mon, Padre. My research people told me you were a regular Patrick Henry in black." Gordon's eyes wandered up the side of the church. "Say, that steeple's a mess. You've got two different kinds of shingle on it."

"How perceptive of you, Mr. Gordon. It was hit in a storm a few years ago. They'd stopped making the old shingle."

"What kind of steeple you want, Padre?" Gordon said, lowering his voice a notch. "My job is making good things happen."

"I like that steeple. It reminds me how easy it is for God to break things in half."

Gordon laughed, then moved a step closer. "They told me you wouldn't be easy. Okay, I'll call the guys with the green eyeshades in New York. They'll come up with a lump figure. Nothing outrageous, mind you—"

"Get that van out of here, Mr. Gordon, and I mean right now."

Gordon stepped back and motioned for his men to gather up the cables. "Hey, no offense, friend. Suppose you just pray on it a while. I'll get back to you." Gordon turned to leave, then hesitated. "And listen, Padre, don't talk to those other networks. Ratings or not, we've still got the deepest pockets. Take my word for it."

18

Father Keene had it on good authority that Doctor James Yancey was a man who held himself to be "up front" about things—meaning that Keene would have to sort through a surfeit of loose chatter rather than pry information out of him. Being up front with your patients seemed to take a little longer than holding back, and Father Keene spent almost an hour in the waiting room even though there were only two patients ahead of him.

"Kindly old Doc Wendt was a goddamned butcher," Yancy was saying to a depressed-looking man as they emerged from the treatment room. "No question about it. We could have saved at least three of those molars if he'd had at least one foot in this century. And what he didn't tell you about treating your gums could cost you that whole side of your mouth."

"He was my father's dentist," the man said.

"How many teeth does your father have left?"

"None."

"Okay. And what about all the pain? Old Wendt was always so proud that he never gave shots. You think he did better work while you were jumping all over the place? You were a schmuck, Paul. Do what I told you and get back in here Friday. We'll see how those sockets are healing." He drove the man out the door with a series of slaps on the back, then turned to Keene.

"I know just what you're thinking, Father. In your day no dentist would ever say such things about a colleague. Well, that's why we get mouths like the one that just walked out of here. I spend half my day fixing up what that old chopper blew. I tell it the way I see it."

"I admire that," said Keene. In my day, he thought, it was known as having a big mouth.

"Looks like one of those old-timers got at you, too. Those are full uppers and lowers, right?"

"That they are, doctor, and they're sliding around inside my mouth like a handful of buckshot."

"Come on in. I know you don't see me around church, Father Keene, but I sure know all about you. Claudette West says you're worth an extra three hundred every Sunday."

"Three hundred souls, I hope."

"You can't buy that new parking lot with souls. Sorry, Father, but I think you guys have a bit too much of the venal in you. I just had to say it."

"That *is* your way, as you've said."

"Jump in the chair. How long since your last visit to a dentist?"

"Twenty-three years."

Yancey whistled. "No wonder these chompers are loose. I'm surprised you haven't swallowed them." He clipped a towel around Keene's neck and popped the dentures out of his mouth. He studied them for a moment, then rolled his eyes up into his head.

Soon Yancey was grinding a drill at the dentures in his hand. "Ah, Claudette is such a lovely girl," Keene said as though it were a vagrant thought. "I'm glad she knows young men like you, Doctor. She's my idea of what a Catholic woman should be."

"Mine, too," Yancey said with something of a smirk.

"I'm not sure I like the way you said that," Keene said.

Yancey smiled, his magazine-cover teeth showing bright and even. "Father Keene, it's all wishful thinking."

"Oh. She interests you then?"

"She interests me plenty. As a matter of fact, for the last six months, she's been about all I think about."

"Really. I find that surprising, Doctor. I've always thought you must have to take the bobby pins off the floor of that Corvette with a shovel."

"Just filling the time." There was a look of genuine sadness on Yancey's face. "There's no use mooning over what you'll probably never have."

"I can't believe you're a quitter, Doctor Yancey."

"As long as it's just between us, Father, I'll be real open with you. I can get whatever I want with girls I don't give a damn about. But with Claudette, it's different. I've never tried for someone so hard in my life. But nothing works. Not the old tricks, not the new. Not even being sincere, which, for Jim Yancey, is something *brand* new. I know what you're thinking, Father Keene. That I went after her like she was some pushover high school cheerleader and now she's giving me the freeze I deserve. Truthfully, I had that in mind the first time I saw Claudette. But I forgot all about it the first time I talked to her. Oh, I'll admit I made a few swipes, but just out of habit. It would have broken my heart if she'd taken me up."

"Well, well. Am I correct in thinking that this greyhound of the mattress is in love?"

"Ain't it a bitch? Crazy, nuts, schoolboy love. I call her three times a week trying to see her. If I'm real lucky, I get invited for drinks a couple of evenings a month. I sit there being real suave, telling her how rich and important and in demand I am. And she sits there pretending to enjoy herself. I never think about making a move, just about how lucky I am she hasn't thrown me out."

There it is again, Keene thought to himself. The soft center that undoes both the best and the worst of us. "Doctor Yancey, maybe you have some growing up to do."

"No maybes about it. How's this for a laugh? One night, I'm sitting there having a drink with her when who should come walking in but our own Father Glasgow. He was on his way back from someplace a far piece down the turnpike. It's the most natural thing in the world for him to stop by for a cup of coffee to break up the trip, right? Well, not for me, it wasn't. I was convinced that he was there to take a shot at her. Mind you, I'm talking about Steven Glasgow.

"In fact, I decided right there on the spot that he'd been getting at her all along. That the parish pastor was actually acing me out. In every look he gave her, every word he said, I saw some special meaning."

"Did you watch Claudette?"

"I watched her until my eyes almost fell out. On the outside I was being very cool, but underneath I sweated until my shirt actually stuck to the chair. If I'd thought I saw her sending any messages to him, I'm not sure what I'd have done. But he was just playing the friendly pastor.

"Later, she walked him outside to his car. Now get this. In this insane fever of mine, I crawled on my hands and knees to the window and peeked through the blinds like some goddamned voyeur hoping to see a little action. Am I nuts or what? I squirm just thinking about it."

"And of course you saw nothing."

Yancey laughed. "Can you imagine? Me thinking that the guy that invented straight is cutting my time."

Yancey shook his head back and forth, then returned to Keene's dentures.

"You think it's hopeless with Claudette, then?" Keene said.

"Father Keene, I do one hell of a root canal, and I don't have too many strong points after that. However, sticking to what I want is one of them. There's always another way. In fact, I'm giving one a shot today.

"I switched country clubs. The new one is out on the road just past her house. I told people it has a better golf course, which happens to be true. I told Claudette that the locker room is a disaster area, which is only half true. Well, after I angled around some, she, sweet, trusting soul that she is, suggested I come to her place and shower after I finished my round. It gets me a gin and tonic and a few hours to make some points."

Yancey seemed to drift into thought. He finished grinding the lower denture, sprayed it clean and pressed it back into Keene's mouth. "The uppers are pretty good now. How does this one feel?"

Keene worked his jaw around. "Feels like my tongue has the day off. I never realized how hard I was working to keep these things from falling out of the pulpit into the first pew. There's still a sharp corner, though. On the left, way back."

There were the makings of some useful mischief here, Keene thought.

They tried the teeth after Yancey had gone over them once more and they fitted just right. Yancey unclipped the neck cloth and spun the chair so Keene could climb out. "I've sure been babbling, Father. Thanks for the ear."

"Thanks for the teeth," Keene said. "And what do we owe?"

"Just say a little prayer to make Claudette see things my way."

"The good Lord has given you a Corvette for that purpose, Doctor, but if you're not ashamed to ask for more, neither am I."

"Tell you what," Yancey said, his face almost straight. "If I can convince Claudette to marry me, I swear I'll come back to that musty, dusty old church of yours."

There wasn't the slightest reason to believe him, Keene knew. But you could always judge the size of a man's feelings on any subject by the size of the lies he told.

19

Sitting at his desk in the rectory, Steven Glasgow considered how quickly he had come to enjoy the cheerful presence of Peter Keene. As he put some final touches to the notes he had worked up for his interview, he listened with amusement to the sounds of the old Irishman dueling with Mrs. Sullivan over what Sunday dinner should be. Keene was the only one Glasgow knew who could coax a laugh out of the sour housekeeper this side of a good, well-oiled wake. Certainly he was the only one who held even the slightest sway over her grim menus. As a result, the usual parade of nameless stews had begun to give way to some pasta and seafood.

As Glasgow keyed some notes into his writing, he heard Mrs. Sullivan concede in the matter of a fruit salad with such a gale of laughter that one might suppose Keene had touched her in a way not seemly to a priest. To cement his win, Keene began, somewhere back near the kitchen, to lead her through the words of an ancient Irish song, a spirited salute to the glories of grog.

Glasgow was setting up a list of tough questions that might come from Diane Wallach when Father Keene wandered in with his hands in his pockets and a dreamy smile that said he had no place to go and all day to get there.

One part of Glasgow welcomed a break, but the part of him that had been brought up to resist a good time as the robber of good work groaned. The other, smaller office he maintained in his room was stuffy, but it seemed the only place he could ever expect to get anything done.

"Peter, I expect to hear any day now that you and dear Mrs. Sullivan have eloped."

"Ah, the poor thing is mad about me. But how could I bear to have that proud beauty learn the dread secret of my war wound on our wedding night."

"I will lay a rosary on you for the fruit salad."

"Bless you, Steven. It took two of my own this morning to get her to agree." Keene peeked out the window. "There's a car blocking the driveway again. You'll have a hard time getting around it. Perhaps I should give Sergeant Luzzi a call."

"The town's just too crowded. We'd have to keep a cop there all day."

"Maybe if I took a bucket of yellow paint and marked out some limits?"

"Might be easier to keep the Pinto in one of the parking lots behind the courthouse. I'm sure they'd put it on the cuff."

"Good idea. We've got to have that car ready to go."

Glasgow scratched a few more notes, then turned the page. "Didn't I see you sail by in a little Omni the other day, Peter?"

"That you did. It's Stassin's company car. You were buzzing around in the Pinto and I had to get to the Kościuszko League to arrange a bus for the retreat. Stassin said I could use the thing now and then."

"I'm afraid I do hog the parish car."

"Never you mind. The way you fly around is what holds this parish together. But there is one trip I'd like to make."

"What's that?"

"Out to call on that sweet West girl."

"Oh?"

"You know I've been going to that space-age dentist with the toy car to have these loose biters taken in."

"Jim Yancey. Yes."

"Part of the man is fourteen years old, but the other part, from what I see and hear, is pretty dangerous."

"To whom?"

"In this case, Claudette."

Glasgow stopped writing. Keene now had his full interest. "Go on, Father."

"I need your word that you'll be discreet, Steven."

"You have my word."

Keene moved closer. "I drove out to see her once before, but it didn't come off."

"Why not?"

"As I came down the driveway, I spotted Jim Yancey's fancy yellow car parked out front. There was a bag of golf clubs on the seat."

Glasgow showed his annoyance. "Why should Yancey's being there stop you from going in?"

Keene was surprised at the force of Glasgow's words. "Come now, Steven. You never know what you're dropping in on these days. As it turned out, it was a good thing that I didn't just go sailing up to the front door. As I started down the hill to swing around, I got a glimpse of Yancey between the trees. I had to stop the car."

"What was he doing?"

"He was strolling out the side door and heading for the backyard clothesline to hang up some wash. Trouble is, the clothes he was lugging must have been the only ones he owned, because he was stark, staring naked. There he was, walking calm and easy in the sun, as though he owned the place."

"I don't have to ask what you make of it," Glasgow said.

"To a young priest like Bolter, what they're doing would be their own business. Maybe that's how you feel, Steven. But if you don't mind, I just can't leave this alone."

"Who else knows?"

"Can't say. But it's all there for anyone who visits the dentist. That Yancey just doesn't know how to keep his mouth shut. While I sat in his chair, he told me things about that girl that any decent man would keep to himself."

A rage was building in Glasgow. "About Claudette? What things?"

Keene shrugged and started to fidget. "Well, that he was dropping in on her every Thursday. It was a Thursday when I went by. He even changed country clubs to be closer to her house. To make it more convenient, he said."

The pastor stared in silence.

"I tell you, Steven, the man has an ego the size of the World Trade Center."

"Is she in love with him, do you think?"

"He's a good-looking lad. I don't think I'd bet against that."

"I think you're right." Glasgow's voice was now almost a whisper.

"I can't see a bit of good in this. He could hurt her terribly. Make her the local dirty joke."

Glasgow tried to slow his mind. He just wanted to scrub the vision of Yancey's naked body out of his head. "Maybe we're making too much of this, Peter."

"I'd like to believe that. Maybe it's just the way people find each other these days. And it wouldn't be the first time that the devil's path led to a happy ending at the altar."

"No, it wouldn't."

"But wishful thinking isn't our job, Steven. We must do something."

Suddenly, everything was coming apart. What this old priest had discovered was nothing new, Glasgow thought. Yancey must have been having her for weeks, perhaps months. It was sheer, willful blindness that he had refused to see it. Could her love for him have been all a lie?

He reviled himself for not having run off with her months ago. He knew he would do anything on earth to keep her. He had to find her and put an end to these dreadful uncertainties.

And Keene had to be kept out of the way. If she ever found out what Keene knew, the shame might drive her out of his life before he could sort things out.

"Peter, I'm as concerned as you are, but we must remember that this is not 1938. If Claudette asks for our help, well enough. But beyond that, we'll just have to let her work it through herself."

"I'm not sure, Steven. I'm not sure if that's right at all."

"I know Claudette. She's an intensely private woman. No matter how well we handle it, it's going to look as though we've been prying. And just think how she'd feel if she knew what you saw and that Yancey has been mouthing off about her."

"Okay, if that's what you want. But please let me try to keep Yancey quiet."

"Do it. He'll take it from you better than from me. You have a way with such things. I'm just too—"

"Too direct?"

"Yes, I guess that's it."

"And guys like Yancey don't like that," Keene said.

20

This time Glasgow did not change into his workman's clothes to visit Claudette. Nor did he take any of the side roads out of town. Instead, he drove the well-known Pinto right down Grand Army Avenue and nodded to those who waved at him.

He had raged inside himself at Claudette. A hundred times every hour, he had made up his mind to leave her to her faithless ways without a thought about what they had meant to each other. And a hundred times every hour he had changed his mind.

He had waged the battle to stay away from her for four days after Keene's idle concern had blown his life to bits. He had not answered the phone in those special hours when she sometimes called, and he had somehow not called her.

What had broken him was Thursday, the dreadful day when Yancey went to his new country club. With the cruel eye in his brain, Glasgow saw the dentist in his game of golf. He did not hurry the shots, but played them with great care, his tall, graceful athlete's body turning nicely into the ball and sending it straight to the pin. He was smiling because Claudette was waiting for him. The more slowly he played, the more eager she would be, and that boyish, slightly mean smile seldom left his face during the pleasant round.

He might even linger for a time in the locker room, soaping and cleaning his body with extra care, fondling himself in the shower in a tingling foretaste of what was to come. It would not be unlike him to trade man-talk with some of the other members, their big, slack bodies jiggling as they toweled off. He might wink and suggest that he really shouldn't have spent time showering because he had something nice lined up just down the road, and he was only going to get sweated up all over again.

Glasgow tried to stop the thoughts that wounded him, but the more he tried to make his mind as blank as the highway that rose up before the Pinto, the more new pain flooded in.

He saw them in bed, on the living room couch, on the kitchen counter. Although his own virility had been endless, the dentist would be fiercer and better. Huge and skillful, he would reach wells of feeling Claudette had never known.

Yancey was no foolish, bungling priest. He had improved his sexual skills and instincts with dozens of women. Claudette, at last freed from the need to teach and fake and hold back, would scream out her pleasure and quickly forget the pathetic fumblings of her poor pastor.

By the time Glasgow turned off the main highway, all his prepared speeches and strategies had fallen away into whirling indecision.

He had fallen low enough to call Yancey's club. Without saying who he was he had asked for the dentist, prepared to hang up if he came to the phone. Dr. Yancey was gone, he had been told. He had played nine holes, had a few drinks at the bar and left almost an hour before.

Nine holes. He couldn't even wait to play eighteen. He would be at Claudette's now. He might even be done and gone. That would be like him. A couple of tumblers of Scotch before steering her straight to the bed. In fast and out fast. That might be what she loved best. Who wanted to lie around later listening to the naive mutterings of a man feeling sorry for himself?

Although all he had learned told him it would be there, the sight of the yellow Corvette was like a fist in his eyes. From his brush with Julia Dean, he knew just what to do. He switched off the engine and coasted the Pinto off the road where he would not be seen by Yancey as he left.

The front windows open, he sat with his back against the door, his feet lifted onto the seat. His head was thrown back and his eyes shut tightly as he tried to steady his breathing. The breeze that blew through the cool woods swept across him, touching the sweat of love and fear that had soaked him through.

There would be no need to watch the house. Yancey's car was swift and loud, so he would know when the way was clear. Again and again, he looked at his watch. Always the hands had not moved, though it seemed years had passed. It came to him that for all the austere grayness of his life, he had never known a real hurt before. He had no defense, no callus. He recalled the words of comfort to a bishop of France who was about to be tortured and burned. "For you, hell will hold no mysteries."

The dark, green woods were loud with frogs and insects, echoing with the cries of swooping birds. Slanting toward autumn, the sun was flattening quickly. The turning leaves flamed as they caught the rays of brilliant orange. But for Steven Glasgow, it was all a dripping dungeon.

The abrupt roar of the Corvette's engine wrenched him back to high alarm. If he left the car and hurried through the trees, he could watch them taking leave, see her in a towel or blanket or nothing. He could watch Yancey's hands play over her body, lining up the next time, getting her ready now so he wouldn't have to fuss with a lot of phone calls next Thursday.

Glasgow gripped the steering wheel with both hands, holding himself in place until he heard the Corvette roar by in a clatter of gravel. When he heard the engine wind up on the highway far away, he let himself out of the car and began walking toward the house.

Claudette was nowhere in sight. At the driveway, he heard the screech of the backyard clothesline being pulled. How cool she was. The screw is over, now do the wash.

Glasgow could have walked around the outside of the house to find her, but he had to see what had gone on inside. Before she was there to close the doors and steer him away from the things he should not see.

The doorbell was a low chime. If she challenged him, he would say that he had pressed it. He walked inside. The sound of his breathing seemed to fill the house.

The living room was neat. There were two coasters on the coffee table, but no glasses and no ice bucket. The couch seemed rumpled, but the throw pillows were where they usually were, not gathered to cushion hips or knees. The liquor bottles stood in a straight line on the sideboard, except for the Scotch, which stood open in front of the others with its cap lying beside it.

The doors to both bedrooms were closed. He had to force his eyes to stay as he peered in. In each room, the beds were tautly made, the pillows fluffed and without a dent. He almost called aloud to her in his relief. His joy lasted until he reached the bathroom.

The shower had been recently used. There were still patches of steam on the corners of the mirror over the sink. The shower curtain, pulled back, was wet and the tile walls around the tub still glistened. A washcloth and a large bath towel had been used.

The eyes of a lover resolve like an eagle's. They see the small things first.

In the tub's soap dish sat a half bar of Ivory soap, used but still square and solid. In it were twisted pubic hairs, blond and coarse.

The wicker laundry basket next to the toilet mingled the damp, clumped clothing of Yancey and Claudette. They must have stood here, undressing, talking, showering together, preparing themselves.

Or maybe this was just the spot where the urge could not be denied for one more moment. She had been fixing her hair in the mirror and he had come up behind her, cupped his broad athlete's hand over her breast and begun to strip her. Her hands had gone to his clothing just as eagerly. The shower would have come later.

Glasgow squatted in front of the basket and went through the clothing. It smelled of the enclosed places of the body. Claudette wore the smallest, lightest underwear she could find. It had always excited him, but he had never attempted to remove it from her. She must always have wanted him to.

He brought her pants to his mouth and kissed them as honest priests kiss their holy vestments. There was a small tear near the crotch. He pictured one of Yancey's white, over-scrubbed dentist's fingers breaking through as he tugged in his heat.

He went through the dentist's clothing with icy disgust. A green golf shirt had a scorecard and pencil still stuffed into the breast pocket. A pair of red plaid slacks had a Saks Fifth Avenue label. He went into the pockets. A penciled note on a prescription blank read "Thank you." Cute. A little something to be found later.

The only male undergarment was a supporter. It was old, stretched, obscene. It hung from his fingers, sullen without the vast, compressed load that had risen into the woman he loved.

It was here that Claudette West caught him: as he squatted before the laundry basket, Dr. James Yancey's jockstrap held at arm's length.

She gave a frightened cry, startled by the bent, black mass of the priest crouched in her bathroom.

"Sweet Jesus. Steven. Steven, what—?"

Glasgow stood and faced her, the garment still in his hand. She started to step forward, but he stopped her by swinging the supporter in front of her face.

"How long have you been here?" She could not keep her voice steady.

"Outside for an hour and a half. Inside only a few minutes."

He watched as her mind pulled itself clear of the sudden shock. He knew that when she realized what he had done, how he had skulked into her home and into the private corners of her life, she would drive him away. It had been a violation worse than rape, because he had been driven not by a body out of control, but by a brain rotted with thwarted ego. She would flinch in horror at the thought that she had ever allowed this man to touch her.

"Oh, my poor love," she said softly. "What awful things must be in your mind. Please, Steven, put that thing down."

If she had torn into him, he might have walked out in tongue-tied rage, or he might have cringed and begged until she pushed him out. But at her first gentle words, he felt all the power of the righteous wronged well up in him.

He threw the supporter into the basket. "Do you want me to go? No questions asked?" For a cold instant, he was afraid he had played his weak cards too strongly.

She seemed to have composed herself, with the air of one who could not be shaken. She would not be swerved by rage, hers or his.

He had the feeling that this was his last chance to do and say all the right things. It was a moment of great danger, and he who had been so ready to sting her with his famous tongue was suddenly dumbstruck and helpless.

Claudette took his hands in hers and with her eyes closed kissed them. She drew him slowly to her and kissed him again, this time on the lips. He wanted to draw back to show his anger but could not. He let himself melt to the tongue drawn across his mouth. There seemed to be no tension, no hurry in her.

Before he had quite enough, she gently pushed herself free, picked up the basket of wash and slipped by him into the kitchen. "Steven, if you wish, you can shoot a million doubtful holes into what I'm about to tell you. I suppose I could make you believe me better by throwing in a few little lies. But I'm going to tell you the whole truth. If you believe me, you'll know there is nothing important between me and Jim Yancey." She turned and stared at him hard. "You'll also know how easily there could have been."

There was nothing he could say. He watched as she flipped open the washer and began loading the clothes. He now realized that her hair was dry and softly waved. Obviously, she had not showered with Yancey. She was fully and rather tidily dressed in jeans and a plaid shirt. Not the look of a woman after a lover had come to visit her bed.

Claudette threw in the laundry powder and turned on the washer. Then she jumped up to sit on top of the machine.

"First, you should know that Jim Yancey is in love with me."

"That's not much to be proud of."

"When he thought David had been dead long enough, he began making all the tired little moves. Phone calls, coy notes. Would I like to go to Great Gorge with him for a few golf lessons? How about Puerto Rico to get a jump on the summer? Then he began stopping by. For coffee, at first. Then for a drink. Pretty soon, one drink became two and more. That's what was going on the night you found us here. I knew how you felt, Steven, and I rather liked it. No, I loved it. It was nice that you were jealous and angry. I wanted you to see that I might not always be here. It did wrench my heart a bit to see you craving just a secret little smile or touch. But it did me good to know that you were feeling that same hopeless pain that I feel all the time."

The feeling in her words rocked him. "So you decided to lead him on?"

"Yes. Was that awful of me? Jim was suddenly useful. So I started answering his funny notes. Once in a while, I'd make the phone call myself and suggest we have a drink. I even let him set up a weekend in Quebec, then canceled out at the last minute. I wanted to set the hook good."

"And you were quite a success."

"I went too far. Jim had never worked so hard for so little. It began to hurt his feelings. So he tried still harder, and ended up falling in love with me."

"Wasn't it a little cruel?"

"Yes. Still, it's made him very happy. And I'm sure he really believes that someday I'll return his love."

"That's just a dream, I hope."

"I hope so, too. But, in all honesty, Steven, the distraction of James Yancey has been very nice, very flattering. And he's so available. Do you know how much that attracts me? On nights when the moon is full and I'm restless and you're tied up with a novena, it's good to have a handsome, willing friend sitting next to me. Every time I go for another drink, I can see the end of my bed peeking through the door, and I know I could fill that bed with the lift of an eyebrow."

He saw her cheeks had grown a little wet. "And will you lift that eyebrow someday?"

"I'm not sure. You know my strengths and weaknesses better than I do myself. Will I?"

The answer he found in himself was quick and clean enough to startle him. "Yes, I think you will. Probably very soon."

"Should I be angry with you for saying that?"

"It might make me feel better."

"If I do sleep with him, will you leave me?"

"Yes, I think so." After another minute he said, "No."

"I'd never sneak around about it. I'd tell you."

"The answer is still no."

"Suppose I told you that I don't want you coming here on Thursdays?" She studied his clouding face. "Now, that's got you."

"Tell me about Thursdays."

"It's another one of his games. He played golf at Piping Hollow a half-mile outside of Lost Hessian for years. Suddenly, he switched to Schweikert's Roost, thirty-five miles away. It takes him right by here once or twice a week. Anyway, it wangles a shower and a bunch of drinks out of me every Thursday. He even gets me to do his wash—throws it right in with mine. The next time Julia Dean passes through she'll have plenty to see on my clothesline."

"What if I asked you to stop seeing him?"

"What if I said I wouldn't?"

"Well, since there's nothing going on."

"Not screwing isn't the same as nothing going on. The high point of Jim's visit is his running about naked. Not in front of me, mind you. Not quite. He'll conveniently forget his fresh clothes and have to run out to the car for them. Or he'll zoom down the hallway to get a comb he left with his wallet on the end table. And he loves strolling in the sunshine au natural while I'm busy doing things inside. It's kid stuff, of course, but then I'm not supposed to be sneaking looks."

"And are you?"

She wrapped her legs round his waist and drew him to her on the washer. "I like watching him naked," she whispered. "It makes me tingle. It makes me miss you even more."

"Doesn't it tempt you?"

"If only I could tempt *you* that much."

He darkened and tried to back away, but she locked her legs around him more tightly and brought her arms about his neck so that she was suddenly suspended from him in the air. She nodded her head toward the back door. "Let's go outside, Steven."

"Be careful," he grumbled. "You've got these floors waxed like glass. I'll fall and kill us both."

"Out the door. Move."

Grinning at last, he eased them through the back door and into the startling brightness of the tree-ringed yard. The sun had just cleared the high hill behind the house; its blaze flooded his eyes. It was the same brilliance he felt inside when he was with Claudette. The rage and tension in him suddenly broke and he hugged and kissed her as if to draw the very life out of her. "Let's go to bed."

"No, Steven, it's time to talk." She slid her legs to the ground but kept her arms around his neck. "I notice we don't do much serious talking after we stop standing up."

"We could go in and sit."

"Sitting is halfway to lying down. Now speak to me. And you're going to have to do it all on your own this time. I'm not going to ask the questions. I'm not going to make the demands. Somehow you always slip around me. The only man I know who can pin down Steven Glasgow is Steven Glasgow. I'm listening." She lowered her head so that he could not see her face, and that somehow was worse than the iron in her gaze. He needed intense contact with her as much as she needed air.

He had not considered seriously enough how hard their love might make her. He thought of the things she had said to him in the house, and made himself feel again the bruising scourge of the last few days. Certainly she would not give up the potent weapon that Yancey had handed to her. Given time, if he did not say the things she had to hear, she would take Yancey into her bed in order to tear her priest out of his church. There was no choice left for him but to collapse and let her life into his.

"You know that I love you and will always love you more than anything on earth," he began.

"I know, my darling. It's what isn't on this earth that's been our problem."

"That won't be in our way any longer. I promise you. I'm going to leave it."

Claudette pressed her cheek against his chest. "I don't want you to leave at all. I couldn't live with that either. I want you to have your God. Believe in Him, pray to Him, adore Him, follow Him. But when you take off that collar for the last time, you'll have both Him and me. As it is now, you have nothing and neither do I."

"Can you wait until after Kuzianik comes? They're counting on me."

"Look at me, Steven Glasgow, and tell me this is not just one more stall."

"As soon as Kuzianik leaves, I'll tell them. It will happen very fast after that." And it would look as though the church had forced him out for what he'd said. Perfect.

The soul-crushing dimness and dampness of the church basement, the endless press of souls wanting his attention, the blessed societies and bingos, the novenas and paper drives started to fade as soon as he had spoken. He hardly dared think of that shining face and sweet smelling hair on the pillow next to him each morning for the rest of his life.

Claudette gave a little purr from deep in her throat. He felt her sag in his arms as if she had just run a thousand miles.

"So that's all there was to it," she said in a voice he could hardly make out. "It took all those months and all that agony to say just that little bit." The words were hardly out of her before she straightened up and looked at him, frightened. "I'm sorry, Steven. That came out all wrong. I know how much it's cost you. What could my little guilt be, compared to what you're feeling? Please, forgive me."

"My God, I can't believe what I've put you through, Claudette."

"You've given me more joy than I ever thought possible. I'll make you happy, Steven. I swear it to you. I swear before Almighty God that I'll make you happy."

Before he could say another word, Claudette covered his mouth with hers. It was not a kiss, but a devouring, a quest for the center of him. Her hands went under his jacket and his collar came off and fell to the ground. With a whimpering urgency, she began to undress him under the bright, hot sun. His jacket came away. Her fingers quickly tired of looking for buttons and dug into the cloth of his shirt. With a force that he never knew she had, she tore down to his naked chest and kissed the thick slabs of muscle running under the dark hair.

As the excitement rushed through him, he tried to steer her toward the house.

"Don't move," she whispered. "And if I catch you looking over your shoulder, I'll never forgive you."

Glasgow was shocked at the difference the priest's clothing made to him. Claudette had undressed him many times before, but never under an open sky. His unease, his sense of God betrayed and watching, amazed him. Was it possible to mourn the trampling of a belief he'd never held?

Her hands darted with the grace of small white birds. The shirt glided off her and the front catch on the bra unsnapped with a brisk crack. Full and broad-nippled, her breasts rolled out into his eager hands. There was the split-second rasp of a zipper and her jeans slid down the whiteness of her legs. Her slippers came off as she stepped out of the pants. The world dropped away.

Although he was taller, the length of her legs held her groin as high as his. She pressed onto him, squirmed and as before brought her legs up around him as she hung from his neck. But now she was naked and he pressed forward until none of him remained. He hardly knew that he held her as she moved against him, first quickly and then, as he rose near climax, slowly and with a teasing twist.

The joyous knot in his loins began to rise like the first note of a vast thunderclap. He fell to the ground with her. They clasped together as the great waves broke and rolled through their hearts and bodies.

Long into the afternoon, they lay naked on the grass, side by side, touching, laughing, planning amidst their scattered clothing. It was a long time before the heat of her body melted from him and he became aware of the first sharpness of the September evening. With that gradual loss of his heat came a tiny shiver caused not by a chilling touch of autumn, but by the cold hand of apprehension.

High above on the hilltop, Peter Keene turned away when he saw Glasgow's white collar tumble to the ground. He did not have to see any more. What was between them seemed to rise through the air and reach out to where he had lain watching them. How could they have hidden such feelings so well and for so long? Even at his advanced age, he felt stirred and shaken by the force of something he did not need binoculars to see.

He had always made a mighty striving to be more of a modern man, but now he felt that his beloved Church had been dirtied. He felt deceived. Too much of his liking and respect for Glasgow, he now realized, had come from the words of others. Keene reviled himself for not using his own eyes more.

That Claudette West had been dragged down by a priest filled him with a terrible coldness. One enemy inside the walls spread more fear than a thousand outside.

But could it have worked the other way around? Was it she who had taken the soul of the proud Glasgow? Keene had watched her riding him out of the house, a small girl in haughty command of a stallion a dozen times stronger. Every move had been hers. No matter what defenses God had helped Glasgow build inside, her attack, launched with sudden, subtle ferocity against someone who loved and trusted her, had to succeed.

Keene brought himself up short. In the end, a priest had to be judged strictly according to the plain laws of God. There was no way around it. With a leaden sadness, he realized that he must confront Steven Glasgow.

For the first time in his life, Peter Keene wished that his friend the bishop were a different man. Discipline within the Church, never really the changeless monolith it seemed, was enforced even more loosely in a modern church that was badly losing the battle to attract and retain its priests. Many times, in many dioceses, a stern warning might have been enough. But not in the diocese of Bishop Colin P. McCarthy.

There was never a doubt in the bishop's ancient heart that a fallen priest was worse than no priest at all. He truly believed that the rot of a soul could be spread to the faithful like a fatal disease. In many ways, he was a gentle, lenient man who loved his priests, and he had never been one to harass his people over small slips. But he punished severely those who broke the rules of God and the Church.

Keene realized that Steven Glasgow was not a borderline case. Still, his heart went out to Glasgow. Should he put the man's guilt before the bishop and plead for him, something he had never done before?

Hardly. When a priest began to make love out of doors in his own parish, the time was near when that whole parish would know about it. Any of the two dozen newsmen in town could have followed Glasgow to Claudette's looking for an interview or a peek into his daily life. The thought brought cold shivers to Peter Keene. His duty was clear.

21

The windows of Ed Gania's upstairs bedroom were wide open to the warm evening, and Keene heard his stifled cries before he and Glasgow were halfway up the front walk.

"Just watch, Peter. He'll hardly make a sound once he sees we're here, so as not to upset us. That's the kind of guy Ed is."

An hour after his return from Claudette's, Keene had met the pastor rushing from the rectory to Gania's bedside. Since both had helped the man through his long illness, the old priest had impulsively joined Glasgow on the sick call.

They had seen Gania only three days before, but in that short time it looked as if the cancer had cut his size in half. His soul seemed to be sucking the suffering flesh back into itself, gradually removing from the earth what could no longer live upon it. He had thrashed the covers to the floor, and his body had soaked a huge, wet circle on the mattress. Gania's housekeeper sat terrified in a corner chair.

"You can go now, Annie. You're a very brave woman," Glasgow said.

Gania's eyes fluttered open. "And that's no shit," he said in a voice that could scarcely collect enough breath. "You're the most beautiful woman I ever knew, Annie. I'd take you out dancing tonight, but it looks like I've got another date."

The woman broke into loud sobs and ran to him. As she leaned over the bed to hug and kiss him, tears welled in Gania's eyes. "Take care of yourself, Annie, O.K.? And thanks for everything." She ran from the room, not looking back. Keene guessed that they might have been lovers in the early stages of her stay. Ed Gania, tall, handsome and vigorous at forty-five, had never been an easy man to resist.

"Father Steve, if you ask me how I'm feeling, I'm going to get up out of this bed and lay one on you." He smiled at Keene. "Glad you're here, Father Pete. I've got sins enough for the two of you."

Glasgow sat by the bed. "We heard you from outside, Ed. If howling once in a while makes you feel better, just cut loose."

Keene looked at the jumble of drugs on the night table. "There's nothing here for heavy-duty pain. Why hasn't the doctor given him something?"

"Because Thicko here won't let one in the house," Glasgow said.

"That's crazy. Suppose I run over and bring back Doc Bruns?"

Glasgow shook his head. "I've seen this kind of pain enough to know that there's only one thing to do for it. And upright old Doc Bruns isn't going to use it."

Gania yelped like a dog run over and doubled himself into a fetal ball.

"We'd better get to it," Keene said.

When Gania became aware that they were getting ready to give him the last rites, he forced himself onto his back and straightened his arms and legs.

"Could you guys wait until I slip under?"

"It's best to do it while you're still conscious, Ed," Glasgow said. He knew the rites would make it easier on Gania's last fears. "You know, I'm not supposed to give this to people who have never known the temptation of sin. You do qualify?"

A laugh rattled in Gania's throat. "Qualify? I've got the friggin' post position."

Glasgow heard his confession and passed him the Eucharist. At the moment the wafer touched Gania's tongue, he seemed to find the courage to take the first step away from his burdened body. His eyes dimmed, and his hands, clenched and white, as though holding to the edge of the universe, began to relax.

Peter Keene prayed with fervor in a high sweet voice as Glasgow anointed Gania's forehead and upturned palms with the *oleum infirmorum* and said the ancient words.

"May the Lord in his love and mercy help you with the grace of the Holy Spirit. Amen. May the Lord who freed you from sin save and raise you up. Amen."

Keene sprinkled the room with holy water, recalling the first rite, baptism, with the last.

"I'll stay right here, Ed. Now try to sleep," Glasgow said.

Gania shuddered and whimpered as a long knife of pain drove up from the base of his spine. "Screw sleeping, Father. Just keep talking. I never knew I could feel so alone."

"Alone? Right now there are a thousand angels watching you. And I'll bet you know half of them, Ed. Your friends had a way of partying themselves right out of business."

"Wouldn't that be a hoot? To see a guy like Stutz Smith again with that big dumb smile on his face and a quart of Irish whiskey in each hand? You know he had a bottle clutched in his fingers the night they pried him out of the cab of his truck." Gania rasped a sort of laugh. "The medics had such a job wrenching that juice loose from him that they kept checking to see if he was still alive."

"It wouldn't be heaven if you couldn't enjoy some wicked company, Ed. Anyone else you should look up when you get there?"

"Yeah. I'd like to shake a few hands. Babe Ruth. Janis Joplin. Maybe I could scare a tennis lesson out of Big Bill Tilden."

"I'm sure everybody there can play just as well as Tilden simply by asking."

"Wouldn't care much for that, Father. Where's the challenge?"

"Well, you could be Tilden and look up some guy who wants to be Bjorn Borg. Might be a helluva match."

Gania's grin broadened, but his voice went higher at the touch of a hot iron to his back. "God, Steve, I must've had a thousand friends in my life. All those ballgames, all those beers, all those laughs. And all that loving. Of course I never imagined they'd be sitting in front of the house like it was Saint Peter's Square and the Pope was slipping, but I figured maybe there'd be somebody wanting to say goodbye."

"Nobody ever wants to say goodbye, Ed. I see it in hospitals all the time. You've got to drag the doctors to the ones that are going. Even the wives and husbands and children can't get away fast enough. You know why? Because they don't see *you* lying there, they see themselves. Not many can stand up to it. But I'll get anyone you want, Ed. Just tell me."

"No, I guess I don't want my friends watching. You know how it is, Father. The maiden lady who still wants to be asked."

"Some maiden lady."

"Hey, no dirty talking. I just took communion."

Glasgow could see that the troughs between Ed Gania's waves of pain were getting more shallow. He pressed the trembling white ruin of the once-strong hand to his own breast, as though he might transfer his heartbeat along with his terrible sorrow. From time to time they spoke, joining each other in a memory of the joyful banter they now so sadly parodied.

There was a heavy knock on the jamb of the open doorway. The priests turned to see a young man standing there. His eyes, burning black, were as old as the seas. He wore a heavy, high-necked cashmere sweater as though even the thick, damp heat of Indian summer could not reach a coldness that was in him always. Keene saw how much the slightly yellowed skin drawn tight over the elegant nose and cheekbones resembled what he saw on the face of the dying Gania.

"Hey, Father. I come right over like you told me." He could not have been more than eighteen, but the slow, rolling swagger with which he entered the room said that he knew some power. The crease in his expensive slacks had the sharpness of professional pressing. No shoes as fine as the ones he wore had ever been sold in Lost Hessian.

"Let's have it," Glasgow growled.

The youth shrugged and opened a tooled leather handbag. He

sat at the edge of the bed, pulled a wooden chair close to him and emptied the contents of the bag on it. There were only two items: a twenty-five-caliber pistol and a carefully rolled silk scarf. He glanced toward Peter Keene. "This old geek okay?"

"This is Father Keene. He's helping me. That's Ed Gania."

The young man smiled, showing large, mottled teeth. "Gania. Yeah. Ed Gania. I used to watch him play in the Industrial League. You hit some great shots, Ed baby."

"Ed, Peter," Glasgow said, "this is Paulie Rycovich. I asked him to come."

"You got no problem, Father," the youth said. He unrolled the scarf to reveal several disposable hypodermic needles still in their wrappings, a length of flexible plastic tubing and a number of glassine packets that contained a powder of startling whiteness. "I never fool around with God," Paulie said. "You got the best here."

"Isn't that heroin?" Keene asked softly.

"The same grade I use myself." Paulie added a spoon and a gold butane cigarette lighter to the items on the chair. "One pop and ol' Ed here's gonna think he'll live to be a hundred."

Glasgow saw Keene's troubled look. "It's the only thing that works at this stage."

"Have you done this before?"

"No, but I knew I'd have to someday."

Keene's voice grew cool. "So you've just kept in touch and allowed this person to walk around."

Paulie's hands flew as he prepared a needle. "Look, Keene, soon as I'm outta here you can call the friggin' Marines if you want and they won't get a thing on me. I'm only doing this 'cause Father Glasgow here was square with a couple o' my good buddies who got across Luzzi and the cops. So stay cool 'till I get myself clean. Shit, I put my ass on the line to make this connect."

"Okay," Keene said. "Steve, do you know how far out you're sticking *your* behind?"

"I do. And I hope someone does the same for me when it's my turn."

Paulie tied off Gania's withered arm with the plastic tube and picked up the needle. Keene was surprised at the gentleness of the young man's touch as he found the vein and guided the fine point into it. He took a long time to empty the barrel of the hypodermic. "That should be about right for a guy in his shape. Just above a nod. You can talk to him if you want, but he won't feel nothing bad. You watch me mix, Father? You got the dose?"

Glasgow nodded. "I think I can do it now."

"That's enough for a couple of days." He looked down at the dying man. "Plenty for him."

Gania's eyes opened wide as the jolt went through him, and then the pain-stretched muscles in his face began to relax. Soon he was smiling, and when he spoke dreamily it was once again the brave, firm voice that Keene remembered. "Steve," he said, fully aware of what had happened, "is it against the book to thank God for that?"

Glasgow forced a smile through his grief and turned to Paulie Rycovich. "I know this costs, Paulie." He pulled a roll of bills from his coat pocket.

"Holy Christ, Steve . . . ," Gania began.

"Am I going to have to confess you again, Ed?"

"Okay, cool it you two," Paulie said as he gathered his things back into the silk scarf. "This one's on me. Take the stuff with you, Gania, so no matter which way you go, you'll have a nice time. Father Glasgow, I expect a good word from you when I need it, which I think is gonna be real soon. I woke up from a hot spike twice. Can't expect things to come in threes. Have a nice day now." Paulie closed the bag, stuck it under his arm, and swaggered out with a backward wave of his hand.

The two priests didn't speak for a long time. Very soon Gania was in a deep, peaceful sleep.

"He might last until tomorrow," Glasgow said finally. "Go back and take care of things for me, will you, Peter? I'm going to stay here and see him out."

"I understand, Father."

Peter Keene wished with all his heart that he had not come to Gania's with Glasgow. Nothing, he thought, confounds us as much as finding that the enemies of all we stand for may see their way by a brighter light than our own.

Keene turned at the door before leaving. "Can I tell you something, Father Glasgow? You're the kind of priest I always wanted to be."

22

Stanislaw Kuzianik, who would have been shot in a cellar had he been taken in secret in Poland a week before, exploded upon the United States with the force of a nuclear missile. Shock waves of rebellion rolled out of his every word. If certain factions at the State Department had hoped that this visit could be held to a staid, guarded, handshaking tour, the glowering Pole quickly reduced those hopes to rubble.

The President of the United States had been begged by many not to greet Kuzianik at the airport in Washington. But this President was a tough, blunt man who saw the enemy as a changeless devil, and had ridden that horse into the White House.

During his long days in hiding, Kuzianik had acquired a direct, sturdy command of English. For all the passion of his views, his thinking was cool and precise, his words ringing with reason. He was the rarest of all media finds: a man of the people whose every fiery sentence had the power of a headline.

With peasant craft he knew from the first how foolish it was to throw away his words when the forum was not right. Only at the end of a dinner with a dozen senators, or at a press conference seated beside the Secretary of State or Defense did he let his views ring out. He quickly came to know the faces of the men from *The New York Times* and *The Washington Post* and saved his best for them.

By the time he left Washington, his name was the only one that counted in Georgetown. New invitations rolled in from governors, mayors, political groups of all kinds, but Kuzianik passed them by. His instincts told him that the base of his power had to be in the hearts of the sons and daughters of Poland. The people of Central Europe must not see him drifting to become just one more pro-Western exile. They had to know he would be first and always a Pole, leading his followers on Polish soil to meet their destiny.

If help was given, it was to be on the terms of the next government of Poland, the one he hoped he might live to form. If the West wanted more, then the West be damned. He had made that more than clear to the President of the United States and the director of the Central Intelligence Agency, and they had decided not to let him make a secret address to a paratroop unit of exiled Poles in special forces training in Utah.

No, they would not have his soul. He would take his fire where the Poles would be gathered thickest and let the centuries of yearning for freedom do their work.

As he rolled from city to city, the crowds grew in size and fervor. The count reached eighty-five thousand in Pittsburgh, and Soviet flags were burned in the streets. A petition one hundred yards long was sent to the President asking for military help in restoring to Poland a government that would serve only its own people.

On his last stop before Lost Hessian, Kuzianik brought in the full harvest of his American crusade. The sacred shrine of Our Lady of Czestochowa in Doylestown, Pennsylvania, was the sister shrine to the one that had been the holiest place in Poland for six hundred years. Each year numberless Poles traveled to kneel before the Black Madonna, a painted icon of the Holy Mother holding the Christ Child. It had been given credit for the miracle that turned back the long siege of the fortress monastery of Jasna Gora. The American shrine, with its own copy of the icon, had become the rallying point for twelve million Polish Americans.

Now they came in planes, cars, buses and trucks. Many came on foot over hundreds of miles to turn the day into a pilgrimage. The highways were jammed and the surrounding fields overrun. By the first light of dawn, the masses had poured through the grand entrance, swept over the huge parking field—filled almost before the sun had cleared the distant hills—and broke like a sea around the beautiful church with its soaring tower. From behind the church they surged past the Resurrection Monument, the Paderewski Monument and the Polish Veteran's Cemetery, swelling the faithful army to ever grander numbers.

Stanislaw Kuzianik did not disappoint them. Through scores of loudspeakers his guttural thunder lifted the mob to cheers that the press reported being heard two towns away.

For a full hour he took the crowd higher and higher, soaring beyond the best of the crowd-pleasing phrases he had perfected at other stops. Then he began to whipsaw them. First he dashed their hearts down with the vicious perfidy of the Soviet pawns; then he lifted them to the heavens with the hope of shining victories ripe to be won.

For the final ten minutes he wept unashamedly with the thousands, and his final words were a brilliant, throbbing call to a bloody revolt beneath his banner.

The dozens of Secret Service men dispatched by the President to protect Kuzianik were unusually relaxed for men of their intense breed. They were fully aware of another more certain guarantor of Kuzianik's safety: The open murder of this Polish hero while he stood in the eye of most of mankind, lifting the flag for his swelling army, would light the powder train to an explosion that the East might not survive. Indeed, the Secret Service had already received reliable information that the crowd contained agents of the other bloc, men prepared to throw their bodies in front of any attempt on the life of their mortal enemy.

23

The President of the United States sat with his big body tilted back in a favorite swivel chair and his feet propped on an upturned wastebasket. The sleeves of his white shirt were rolled up against the growing warmth of the Washington day. His back was turned to the three advisers who spoke to him from the other side of his desk so he could continue to look out through the wide-open French doors into the White House rose garden. Without malice, he lobbed paper clips from a rubber band at a wandering pigeon.

"What did you think of him, Mr. President?" said the man in the blue suit.

None of the men had to call him Mr. President. They had all known him for at least twenty years, shepherding him loyally through the perils of his early days in business and the labyrinth of America's western politics. The truth was the title made them feel important. When you already had your millions put away, little things meant a lot.

"I like him fine," the President said in his husky, commanding voice. "There's a very tough man under that twenty-three-dollar Polish suit. Not only would he not kiss my ass no matter how often I invited him to, but he said some damned snotty things about the feared intentions of this great republic."

The man in the gray suit grunted. "Afraid we're going to make Poland the fifty-first state?"

"Well, those guys have always had a problem convincing the soldiers who dropped in to go home," the President said.

"He's that sure we're going to send troops?"

"He's that sure he can hang on long enough for it to be a good idea."

"It'll never be a good idea," said the man in the checkered suit, with a great shake of his head.

The President made the pigeon hop with a clip whizzed beneath its breast. "Disagree. Remember the volunteers in Korea and Angola? All we could do was sulk and eat worms."

"I don't think we'd have let them do it in Canada," the checkered suit said.

"I can think of several presidents who would have. One, in particular, would have sent the Welcome Wagon."

"We just can't do it, sir."

"What do the Joint Chiefs say? Any change? Any update from Langley?"

"Everybody thinks it's do-able. Nobody thinks it's a good idea unless they can get through the first weeks, get hold of most of the army and establish good defense lines on the eastern rivers," said the blue suit.

The gray suit leaned forward. "Get maybe twelve thousand guys in there from the air at night. The best. Load them with the one-shot, one-kill weapons we haven't trotted out before now. Give air cover, but only fight offensively if they send air against us. They're so scared about that eighty-two to zero skunking against our stuff with the Syrians that they might go easy. But we can't stay."

"Of course we can't," the blue suit agreed. "We just want to be a trip wire that they might not want to touch off while we're giving the Poles time to decide if they're going to switch sides."

The gray suit handed the President another box of paper clips. "They might figure the Poles will fold in any case, and they know we couldn't last against them with just airborne. They know we'll be just looking to give the thing a head start and then get out."

A clip zipped across the pigeon's tail feathers. "The Joint Chiefs still feel we have to get out no matter what happens, huh?"

"Most of them."

"Disagree. I can see Poland making a fast commitment to NATO. Then we could station what troops we wanted."

The advisers exchanged frightened looks behind the President's back.

"We don't have the slightest hint that they'd join NATO," the checkered suit said.

The President reached for a heavier rubber band. "You don't think I was going to take all that crap from the Pole and maybe commit American lives without getting a pretty big promise."

The others were shocked.

"Is he going to announce it?"

"Not until we're on the ground and we've got the Polish army with us, but it gives us a way to stick around. It makes the deal worth doing."

The man in the checkered suit, aware that the President had a bad ear, raised his voice. "You've got only the unwritten, undisclosed word of one man."

"True, but it happens to be the one man who can sell it, and the one man I trust to do it."

"I talked to him, too, Mr. President. He's conning you. He'd never let you in like that. And suppose he would. What if they kill him before he could do it?"

The President turned a rugged face over his shoulder. "Without him I wouldn't drop a company clerk with a cap pistol into Poland. Meanwhile, let's start spooling things up."

He turned back to the pigeon, took careful aim, and let fly with the heavier rubber band at full stretch. The clip skimmed off the bird's neck and it fluttered sideways in a convulsion of feathers before flying off on an erratic course.

"Never mess with the power of the United States," the President called after it sportively.

The three advisers saw that his mood had improved. That always worried them.

24

Steven Glasgow always enjoyed working with Michael Stassin on the financial affairs of the parish. His homely friend usually loved to throw ideas into the air and beat them around for hours in spirited debates with the pastor. But whenever they sat down to labor on the endless paperwork of the church, Stassin was all business.

Ordinarily, when they were working, the only sound in the church basement came from the incessant clicking of the two old adding machines. But today that was augmented by the roar from the black and white television set that rested on wall brackets in one corner of the room. It was safe to say that every family in Lost Hessian was tuned to this taped rerun of Stanislaw Kuzianik's televised speech.

Glasgow had had his doubts about the power of the young Kuzianik to stand in the path of the socialist locomotive. But as he watched the ceremonies at Doylestown, he could see that this was the kind of pebble that could begin a great derailment. The task that Bennett Eagles had given him had at first seemed too small to pay for the terrible investment in years, but Glasgow now saw its importance.

The friends of peace were powerful in the media. Even a single voice could rally them in telling opposition if that voice came from just the right place at just the right moment.

His hand trembled as he punched out a column of figures on the adding machine. He tore off the tape and handed it to Stassin, who did not miss the tremor.

"Is our poor old parish budget in such bad shape?" asked Stassin gently, "Or has that Polish fireball reached your heart?"

Glasgow felt himself redden. "Sorry, Michael. I guess I'm still not over Gania's death."

Stassin grunted and transferred Glasgow's totals into his own work. "Almost through now," he said. "I'll have the final figure in just a minute."

As Glasgow began to clean up some papers, a playback of the great, rolling roar that had greeted the end of Kuzianik's speech filled the room.

Stassin nodded toward the television set. "What do you think of him, Steve?" It wasn't a casual question. The man had stopped working to wait for the answer.

"I admire him, of course. The courage, the drive, the fire, the intellect. He's hypnotic."

"Who's he most like? Roosevelt? Churchill? Hitler, perhaps?"

"That's pretty fast company. I haven't thought much about it."

"I have. I've read every one of his speeches in *The New York Times*. Even taken them apart for structure. I can't vouch for the voice or the delivery, but otherwise it's pure Lenin."

"Don't you have your sides mixed up?"

"That's what makes him so effective, damn it. He knows the old dialectic of the opposition. He knows it's been dribbled into every schoolchild in Eastern Europe for nearly forty years. It's the way they're trained to hear and reason. Listen to those catch phrases he uses. The reasoning, complete with the holes. The way he scratches at the scars until they become wounds again, and then pours in the salt. Pure Lenin turned upside down and used as a club."

Glasgow smiled his surprise. "I'm amazed, Michael. I thought your reading ran to snow shovel catalogs and your interest in politics ended with lobbying Mayor Djunjek to collect your garbage more often."

"Anyone who doesn't pay attention to someone like Kuzianik would have to be dead."

"Perhaps," said Glasgow, "but people who do pay attention to him *will* be dead if they're not careful. He's a menace to life. You've certainly heard me talk about this."

"Never that strongly. Go on."

Glasgow thought he'd be a bit cautious, even with his friend, and keep it in terms of humanity. "I think of it this way. Subtract maybe a dozen men from all of history and you've probably saved a hundred million lives. We all know who they are: Hitler, Napoleon, Genghis Khan, Kaiser Bill . . ."

"Stalin, Pol Pot . . . ," Stassin continued for him.

"Sure. And I really think Kuzianik could join that group. This country is very close to backing him. Just imagine the heart being torn out of the middle of Europe again. It's terrifying."

Stassin waved at the screen. "Seems there are a hundred thousand people right down the road who think the heart has already been torn out. And that Kuzianik's the one to put it back."

"Why do they always think that just a little more death is the answer?"

"They could be right, Steven."

"I'd give my life to prove they're wrong," Glasgow said. In fact, he thought to himself, I already have.

"You surprise me, Father. All I've ever heard from you on this has been at christenings and bingo nights. I'll admit you walked the edge a little on Flag Day, but it was a long way from getting them to march on the Winter Palace. A lot of priests are cutting loose down in Central America, and I'll bet most of them don't feel as strongly about it as you seem to. Are you planning to join them? To do something about what's eating you?"

Glasgow found himself stung. His courage and manhood had been challenged, however mildly. Against reason he wanted to tell Stassin all that he had endured for his cause. God, he thought wryly, was that what he had been suffering for all these years? Recognition?

Still, it was almost over. Why not share at least a bit of his final act as a buried man?

"Michael, I'm going to show you something, and I don't think you'll like it." He took his speech from a manila folder on the chair beside him and handed it to Stassin. "A man from a major network, a Mr. Gordon, has promised me a golden moment in the media sun after the Kuzianik mass. What you're holding in your hand is what I plan to say."

Stassin wiped his glasses with care before he picked up the pages and began to read. He proceeded slowly, going back to reread certain sections. When he had finished, the look he gave Glasgow was grim.

"I'll admit it's a beauty, Steve. It could really get in Kuzianik's way. Something for people to rally around."

"Thanks."

Stassin shook his head and folded the pages down the middle. "But you can't give it. I won't let you."

"I've given this a lot of thought, Michael. I know exactly what the costs are, and I'm ready to pay them."

"More than ready, from the sound of you."

Glasgow wondered if Stassin might have guessed about Claudette. He reached over and pulled the speech from his hands. "I shouldn't have let you see it."

"No, Steven, it was important for me to see. Now I know precisely what that fool Eagles was up to."

After the initial shock, a jolt of anger shot through Glasgow. "Okay, Michael. Who are you in with? Is it the archbishop?"

Stassin smiled weakly but said nothing.

"I'm very impressed. Central America to Pennsylvannia. That's quite a reach. They must have had someone on poor Eagles all the way up. The poor bastard trusted one priest too many." He returned the Eagles speech to its folder. "You can't stop me, Michael. I'm not going to play their little games. Disgrace doesn't frighten me. They can throw me out of here tomorrow and ship me to Zamboanga, but it won't work. The more they try to discredit me, the more people will listen. Tell that to the cardinal."

"Calm down, Steve."

"Does Claudette know about any of this?"

"I've never told Claudette a thing about you. You'd have known it from her in five minutes. These glasses may be thick, but I'm not blind."

"And what happens now?"

"I'm going to get this damned job finished." Stassin tore the tape out of the adding machine, wrote a number on the bottom with a felt-tipped pen and passed the paper to Glasgow. "I think we're at the bottom line at last."

Glasgow stared at the number and felt a violent tug inside. In startling detail, he recalled the day he had been told to memorize those seven digits.

Using the matches Stassin threw him, he destroyed the paper in his hand. Even before the flame took hold, the sheet felt like a glowing coal in his fingers. When the number had become a small wisp of ash, Glasgow knew the only place it was now recorded was in some guarded room in Moscow.

Moments later, as Michael Stassin watched, silent and expressionless, Steven Glasgow also burned the speech written at the urging of his old and dear friend Father Bennett Eagles.

25

The three priests from Our Lady of Jasna Gora were on the committee that welcomed Stanislaw Kuzianik to Lost Hessian. Word had been received that he, never in the best health, was ready to crack from the exhaustion of the past days. At his request, the planned parade, the speeches of welcome and the reception at Paderewski Hall were pushed back forty-eight hours.

The streets were mobbed, and there were cameras and reporters along every foot of Grand Army Avenue. Sergeant Luzzi's men led a line of state troopers on motorcycles who herded the caravan of limousines. The cheering people had hardly a chance to glimpse the tired wave and weary smile of the man who would free Poland.

The ceremony at the steps of City Hall was shortened to a one-minute speech by Mayor Djunjek and the presentation of a bouquet of roses by his four-year-old daughter, Wanda.

When Stanislaw Kuzianik and old Gustav caught sight of one another, the rest of the earth seemed to vanish for them. They met with joyful, sobbing roars in the middle of the steps, the defeated old fighter for Mother Poland reborn in the arms of the new. Each second they embraced drove the spirits of the people higher. And when the two turned to face them and lifted their twined hands, Lost Hessian suddenly became the capital of the West.

For a fleeting moment the grayness left the face of Stanislaw

Kuzianik. He seized little Wanda Djunjek and her huge bouquet and held her aloft, a living, laughing torch of flying red flowers, reaching up to freedom.

As soon as Kuzianik was away from the crowd, however, a bone-deep fatigue brought a slump to his massive shoulders, and the lines on his granite face seemed to become wounds. Glasgow saw far more gray in the great shock of hair and the thick mustache than there had been in pictures taken only a year ago.

Although Kuzianik was always polite and never lacked the proper response, the pastor could see that he had mastered the art of attending to his minor audiences with only the top sliver of his mind. No slouch at the trick himself, Glasgow admired the man's smoothness.

Yet, later, when the pleasantries were over and old Gustav had taken to the middle of the floor for one of his vodka-fired harangues, Kuzianik approached Glasgow with what seemed genuine interest.

"Ah, Father Glasgowicz. You are the one my father cannot stop talking about. He hates you and he loves you. There is no doubt that you drive him crazy when you two have your arguments. He wants you for Poland but fears the red devils already have you. He thinks we should speak."

"If it's the kind of speaking you did at Doylestown, I'm sure I'll be on my way to Poland this very night with an Iron Fist flag and a pocketful of grenades."

"No, no, Father. I have something more important for you in mind. There have been too many cheers. I'm growing flabby. I need an honest man with a strong mind to resist me." He smiled, and Glasgow realized he had never before seen a picture of him doing that. "Of course I must warn you that I shall quickly reduce all your views to ruins."

"Be careful, now, I can be as stubborn as old Gustav."

"That's fine, my friend. As long as you don't cuff me when I am winning, the way he does."

For several minutes they felt one another out, as playful as lion cubs and, to Glasgow's surprise, as easy in one another's company.

Finally the door opened and four burly young men in ill-fitting suits filed into the room. The largest and oldest of them spoke to

Kuzianik in Polish, glaring at the others in the room with a jealous protectiveness that only those who worship can project.

Kuzianik sighed. "These are my protectors, Father. All good men, but what a pleasure it is to leave them once in a while. They say I am tired and must go. And they are right."

"I hope we can talk again."

Kuzianik drew Glasgow away from the other priests. "You'll be sorry you said that. They'll let me sleep for a few hours and then be at me for a thousand things. Perhaps we can be alone later, and dispose of a bottle and a couple of full pipes."

This was not what Glasgow wanted. He had known even in these few minutes that he should have turned away from the man at once. Not that his resistance would have made a difference. Stanislaw Kuzianik seemed to go where he wished.

"I have a private number in my room at the rectory." Glasgow scrawled it on the back of a card and handed it to the Pole. "I'll look forward to your call."

Kuzianik smiled and nodded toward his bodyguards. "If you promise not to murder me, I'll leave the police dogs behind."

The aching knot at the back of Peter Keene's neck reached all the way to his shoulders and tightened with every breath. He had declined a ride back to the church with Glasgow and Bolter, preferring to burn off the clutch of his nerves with a long walk. He agonized over not being able to gather himself to do what he must with Glasgow.

He was sure he had caught some of his tenseness from Glasgow. No matter what went on inside the man, he knew that the pastor had the inbred calm and strength to master it quickly. Yet, just minutes ago, he had seen something change. The calm was still there, but it was different. Now Keene saw the silent, utter control of a stalking leopard.

The old priest's chronically tired feet took him where they would, and soon the sun of late September fell behind the trees. Dusk quickly deepened into a clear, cool night spangled by the lights of front rooms and haloed street lamps. When he came out of his thoughts long enough to see where he was, he found he had wandered onto Michael Stassin's block.

From the distance he saw that the gas lamp on Stassin's front lawn was lit, something Stassin did only when he was having guests. Then Keene remembered this was Thursday and the Mozart Society would be meeting. He saw there were three automobiles lined up in the driveway and four more at the front curb.

During the past weeks, Keene had come to know the disparate members of the Mozart Society as a fussy old bunch of perfect delights. He had continued to attend their sessions even though he had learned all that he was likely to about Claudette West.

Having had quite enough of business for this day, he could think of nothing nicer than a touch of piano, some nice people and a drop of that lovely Château du Cros Loupiac '76.

As he walked up to the house, Keene recognized each car and knew each owner exept one. The car parked last along the curb was a brown Pontiac with plates that showed it to be a rental.

Keene climbed the front steps and found a note taped to the door. It read: *Ring if you love Mozart. Walk right in if you're good looking.* He grinned, opened the door and entered. In the music room at the end of the hallway, the Bösendorfer piano was in full cry. It was the kind of piano, he had learned, upon which amateurs found it difficult to hold back.

Walking into the cheerful, brightly lit room, he found sweet old Mrs. Gegel, eyes closed and shoulders hunched, playing an intricate piece. Her husband, still touchingly in love with her, sat on the bench next to her turning the pages of music. The others—there were seven of them—had pulled the big, plush chairs around the piano and were curled up in various degrees of rapture. They roused themselves to send Keene a flurry of happy, silent greetings. He gestured for them to keep their places and waved Stassin back to the seat from which he had jumped. While the lengthy piece continued, Keene leaned an elbow on the mantle and scanned the room until he found the unknown face.

The man was seated with his jacket off, his sleeves rolled up and his vest thrown open over his wide peasant belly. With his eyes closed above a loving smile, he followed each note of the music with a wave of the thick glasses he held in one hand.

Mrs. Gegel finished with a grand flourish, and the room exploded with heartfelt applause. Everyone gathered about the glowing little woman and covered her with hugs and kisses. Stassin's friend, calling bravos in a strong accent, clamped his glasses back on his nose. Although he was far from old, it took real effort for him to rise from the low sofa on which he had been sprawled. He crossed to the others with a rolling limp.

The man kissed Mrs. Gegel's hand roughly but with feeling. "My dear Madame, what a thing of marvel. You undertake for us the Liszt *Legendes*. So very long and difficult, and cruel to its interpreters. How kind of you to invest so much time, and so much courage. But then, with a talent such as yours, one doesn't need so much courage." He kissed her hand again and the old woman beamed with pleasure.

"You're such a charming liar, Mr. Korbin. And you may continue those lies after we've heard you play."

"Oh, I couldn't inflict that upon you." He held up his hands and flexed them gingerly. "See the swelling at the joints. I fight it, but the weather in Budapest is chilly and very damp."

"Well, you're not in Hungary now, Mr. Korbin, and it's not yet October," Mrs. Gegel said.

"How true, and the company here is so much warmer. Perhaps I'll try, but first a bit of this nice wine."

During the brief break, Keene made his greetings and let Stassin guide him to the man.

"Father Keene, may I present Franz Korbin. He represents a fine line of European hardware. We've known each other for many years."

It was all Keene could do to look at the man as he shook his hand. The lenses of the glasses were so thick that the huge, distorted eyes seemed able to burn into his mind and take out his thoughts before they could be delivered. "I'm pleased to know you, Mr. Korbin. So you're from Hungary. I've read that your people have become quite the capitalists."

Korbin laughed. "Not nearly so much as we would like, but very good for a Communist state, yes? If our people could just come to America for a while, see all the goods, all the wealth—a system that works—they would certainly want to stay here, no? That is why they see to it that we travel so little."

"You've been to America before?"

"Never, I'm sad to say. I met with Michael twice in Europe some years ago. In Prague."

"Forgive me, but your accent doesn't sound Hungarian," Keene said.

"How perceptive of you, Father. Actually, it's Russian. My parents were Estonian. Very close to the Russian border, but it would have been a terrible mistake to tell my father he was Russian. He managed to get us all to Hungary when they took the Baltic states, but things were almost as bad there. Nineteen fifty-six broke my poor father's heart."

"Our pastor, Father Glasgow, left Europe just after that. I'm sure your experiences were similar."

"Is that so? How I would enjoy comparing memories with him, but unfortunately I must soon leave. I really should be working right now. But when I heard there was to be piano music at Michael's tonight—and upon a Bösendorfer, no less—I was obliged to, how you call it, barge right in."

"How long have you been here?" Keene asked.

"Just three days."

"Will you stay for our big moment on Sunday?"

"The Kuzianik ceremonies? Believe me, I would love to. It has become something of a world event. And I salute the man. But I must be off very early that morning."

"Give me your coat, Father," Stassin said. He slipped Keene out of his topcoat. "It'll be on the bed in the room at the head of the stairs." He turned to the others. "Okay, folks, let's persuade Mr. Korbin to play for us. He'll be the first foreign artist to perform before our Mozart Society."

To general cries of encouragement, Mr. and Mrs. Gegel took Korbin's arms and guided him to the Bösendorfer. With a huge sigh, he settled himself on the bench and loosened his fingers with several thundering runs. He was having a very good time.

"I wish, ladies and gentlemen, that I could subtract five years from these poor old hands, but I shall do my very best for you." He began to play.

The society members quickly saw that the top of his velocity was gone, but he made up for that with fine fluidity and suppleness. There was grandeur, breadth and vitality in his Schumann *Fantasy*. Then, without pause, he went into parts of Beethoven's Eighth. When he had completed his final flourish, he bowed his head and let a full minute of applause and bravos wash over him.

It would not have been possible for any of them to follow Korbin's grand performance with a serious piece, so Keene, making a great thing of a horse that had stepped on his hand, rolled through a thumping, three-fingered-bass Irish medley, which included "O'Reilly's Daughter," "Brennan on the Moor," and, at last, "Legion of the Rearguard."

It was not really in keeping with the habits of the Mozart Society, but Keene could not resist singing in his ruined tenor:

> Up the Republic, they raise their battle cry
> Pearse and MacDermott will pray for you on high
> Eager and ready, for love of you they die
> Proud march the soldiers of the Rearrrr-guard.

Keene's audience, upon whom the wine had begun to have more than a little effect, clapped in time and urged him on.

> Legion of the Reeeaaar-guaaaard
> Answering Ireland's caaall
> Hark, their martial tramp is heard
> From Cork to Donegaaaallll
> Wolfe Tone and Emmett guide you
> Though your task be haaaaard
> De Valera leeeeads you
> Soldiers of the Legion of the Reeeaaar-guaaard.

At this stage of the evening Keene's crude effort was received almost as warmly as Korbin's magnificent one.

When the priest had finished to rowdy applause, Korbin came

over and clapped him on the back. "Ah, Father, the songs of rebellion are the best, are they not? Love songs are nothing. After
the great classics there is only the music of revolution. The Mar-
seillaise, the Internationale. Not sophisticated, mind you, but they
have carried whole nations to greater destinies."

"All true, Mr. Korbin. But I have always preferred singing them
in a warm pub with nothing more dangerous coming my way than
a tall mug of stout."

"You chose to walk the path of peace, Father, so you could not
fully understand."

"My sainted brother Brian stopped a .303 with his thick Irish
head while hauling grenades for the army in Derry. I think I understand very well, Mr. Korbin."

"I'm sorry, but there must be losses. Are you not proud of your
brother's sacrifice?" The wine had taken hold of Korbin.

"No, just sad."

Stassin came over and put his arm around Korbin's shoulder.
He made a gesture as though to pinch his mouth closed. "There's
something of an unwritten rule here: We only discuss the weather
and music."

"We've done the music and I'm afraid I don't have time for the
weather," Keene said. "There's much to be done to get ready for
Sunday. I really must be on my way. Don't trouble yourself, Michael. I'll just grab my coat and stop back to say goodbye."

The light from a bulb in a hallway fixture filtered into the bedroom at the head of the stairs. Keene felt along the inside wall but
could not find the light switch. Making out a dark heap of coats
piled on the bed, he entered and began to sort through them. The
bed was wide, and his coat was not where he could put his hand
on it.

He circled around the footboard and entered the space between
the bed and the wall. As he moved quickly in his annoyance, his
foot struck something on the floor with great force. It fell over, and
he heard a sharp clink of metal. As he groped blindly for what he
had kicked, his shoulder brushed against a reading lamp that pivoted
from the wall. Some light at last.

Now he could see a man's black leather bag lying on its side.

There was a small padlock hanging open in the hasp that would have fastened it closed. Several shiny implements had spilled out, and Keene saw that they were surgical tools. He had long ago learned that much of what the world had to tell you was available only for seconds. If you let those seconds escape, you missed things you should know.

He quickly set the bag upright and pulled its mouth open wide. This was a doctor's bag, he saw, one that had been carried by its owner for many years by the tired look of it. It contained all the regular equipment for a standby bag, but there was a great deal in it that had nothing to do with the practice of medicine.

There was a stack of twenty handkerchiefs, several soiled socks in a plastic bag, and some notebooks wrapped in rubber bands. The writing on the corners was in Cyrillic script. There were also two copies of *Playboy* magazine and a small automatic pistol. The star and the CCP emblazoned on the grip told him that it had at one time been Soviet military issue. He sprung the clip and saw that it was fully loaded with eight bullets.

When he ran his fingers along a shallow paper-holder sewn along the side of the bag, he came up with several restaurant receipts, a leather folder holding business cards printed in the name of Dr. Zamlet Gorslev and a copy of the Sunday bulletin of Our Lady of Jasna Gora. A corner of the front page had been torn out, but Keene, who had edited this issue, knew very well what was on the missing piece: a photograph of Father Steven Glasgow.

Before he came down carrying his coat, Keene flushed the toilet in the upstairs bathroom—just in case someone had marked the length of time he had been gone.

He told Michael Stassin how much he had enjoyed himself and fussed through the other members of the Mozart Society with great charm. When the man known as Korbin came smiling to embrace him and bid him goodbye, the priest tried to read his eyes, but the distorting lenses once again turned them into blurred and wavering blue pools.

Peter Keene walked back to the rectory, feeling the earlier tension begin to settle back into his shoulders. As he fingered the business card of Dr. Zamlet Gorslev, his mind ran to a sandy-haired, middle-aged man who had written to him a couple of years before. He was a former altar boy who had heard where Keene could be reached and wished to bring him up to date on an old protégé and his now-grown family. The man's modest position with the FBI would come in very handy now.

26

Although he could not believe it, Steven Glasgow was quite drunk. What's more, he intended to get still drunker.

Stanislaw Kuzianik had slipped away from his bodyguards and made it unseen to the rectory. Since Mrs. Sullivan was out shopping, Glasgow had let him in and led him upstairs to his room. The Pole had carried with him an unopened bottle of good vodka and a big, curving meerschaum pipe.

To Glasgow's surprise and amusement, the first thing Kuzianik had done was go to sleep. With little more than a yawn to explain himself, he had stripped away his jacket, shirt and tie and curled himself into the room's big easy chair in his undershirt. Then, like an animal chased through the night who had momentarily shaken his pursuers, he fell into a deep, shallow-breathing sleep.

If it was true that the real character of a man stole onto his face while he slept, Kuzianik was even fiercer than the hard lines of his waking features suggested. A cruel spring wound tight inside seemed ready to explode him into a murderous fury at the slightest touch. As Glasgow watched, no muscle slackened for even a moment. The coiled, bunched sinews in his long arms and broad chest seemed poised for attack.

Yet, Glasgow had thought, all Kuzianik's finely tuned natural alarms had failed him. For the man who would kill him, who already, with a chill, saw him dead and rotted in the ground, sat within arm's reach. But even with the man asleep and unaware, Glasgow could feel in himself the glow of fear that this deadly fighter called up in his enemies.

Although he had been certain that Kuzianik would sleep long, the Pole had sprung awake before an hour had passed. There was no grogginess, no shaking of the head. He came erect in an instant, bright-eyed and fully alert. His hands went at once to the bottle of vodka.

"I don't apologize when I do that, Father," he had said. "It would take too much of my time. In Poland my pursuers were always so close behind that beds and long sleeps were pleasures I could not afford. Now, if you put me in a room alone with sheets, a mattress and an empty stretch of hours, I don't know what to do. So I prowl about like one of those small, voracious mammals. The ones with an inner fire so hot that they must hunt each hour to stay alive, and sleep only for a few moments between kills."

"What a sad way to live," Glasgow had remarked.

"No, Father," Kuzianik had said. "I think what you are doing is the sad way to live."

The first vodka had been poured, and they began a slow circling of one another, a cautious sparring meant to draw blood if it was taken too lightly.

Glasgow had known that he should make his answers flat, his questions and comments without interest, but there was a magnet in the Pole that drew him on.

He had also known that the vodka in his hand could be as dangerous as nitro. His tolerance for drink had always been high, and he tended to withdraw as he sank deeper, rather than open up. But there had never been so much packed into him under such pressure. It was something he should not have played with, but he had.

And now Kuzianik's pipe, packed full again and again, was filling the room with the friendly, biting haze of the old Polish taverns that Glasgow recalled so well. The drinks ate at them in small, steady bites. Their gestures become broader, their voices louder. For certain particularly heady exchanges they slipped into Polish.

Although there was nothing tender in anything they said, their hearts began to tumble together.

The Pole, through his father, knew all the leanings that Glasgow had ever permitted to show. His questions came crackling in bunches, each driving the priest to a different defense until those defenses became confused and tangled about themselves. Glasgow came back at him, whipping up the mind that had not been challenged so briskly in years.

To Kuzianik's taunts that the Church in the United States had turned into a red-loving cabal of homosexuals, welfare recipients in cassocks and golf-playing Irish drunks, Glasgow returned his views of the Polish Church. They were, he said, the unforgiving great-grandsons of land-owning peasant-whippers and pogrom-makers. They wanted to use the blood of those who would still be serfs except for socialist progress to restore that serfdom. When Kuzianik accused Glasgow of betraying his manhood by crouching in the Pennsylvania hills, Glasgow accused Kuzianik of betraying his nation and mankind by crouching in the Polish hills to lead a battle against the human dignity that a man's labor should guarantee.

As heated as their battle was, Glasgow found that both of them had quickly fallen into the high spirits that always accompany a good game against a good friend. For all his flinty toughness Stanislaw Kuzianik had a strong and sometimes antic sense of humor that he used with great effect. But through it all the steady eye of the Pole never stopped sizing up the man beneath the cassock.

Glasgow, liking the other more with each moment, didn't know whether to be proud or ashamed at how well he masked the deadly thing inside him.

"So, priest," Kuzianik said, blowing up a thick cloud of acrid tobacco, "before we both slide to the floor, there is something I must say to you. In fact, two things."

"I can't believe there are two things that we haven't already covered."

"First, I must tell you that I don't believe in your God."

"I thought I saw a picture of you kissing the Pope's ring. Did you mention that to him?"

"I didn't have to. He is a brilliant man who read it in me as we talked. But, like me, he recognized how badly we need one another. Our coming to the great stage at the same time was what you might call made in heaven."

For a reason he could not place, Glasgow found himself shocked at Kuzianik's disbelief. "I can now understand why I'm not Pope. You would have fooled me with ease."

"Perhaps, then, you have spotted my slight reservation."

"An atheist with a reservation is an agnostic."

"Here is my vow to your God who doesn't exist. If, in my lifetime, Poland throws off the Russian bear's hug so we can hang all her vile cubs who now pollute our government, I will proclaim, from the bottom of my soul, the divinity of Jesus Christ from every rooftop in Warsaw. I will take holy orders. I will crawl on my belly to Jerusalem with a cross strapped to my back and the flag of Poland flying from the crossbar. I will raise armies and lead a crusade to sweep away the last infidel. I will become not only the thirteenth apostle, but the first saint who knows how to build a tractor."

"I believe you actually mean it."

"I do. Now don't tell Jesus, but one great victory in just one of the big cities is all I'll need Him for. Then I can do the rest. One great victory and He'll have me. Heavy stuff, even for Him," he said with a laugh.

"What's the second thing you had to tell me?"

"That I am more of a communist than any man who ever marched across Red Square on May Day. If your president knew how total my commitment was to that ideal, your rectory would be surrounded by Marines."

"Forgive me, Stanislaw. I've had too much vodka. Make it simple."

"The capitalist system is the same as the devil's. Don't be fooled by my playing with you in our little debate. I was testing you. I would fight under the flag of the demon and his sister to bring the great dream of Mr. Marx to my people in the pure way he first dreamed it. But we must rid ourselves of the hyphen. Marxism-Leninism is a brutal joke, where the highest goal is not to become a great worker but a great jailer. In the system we hate, the ruling class brutalizes with money. But with the Lenin boys, the brutality is with the labor camp, the mental hospital, the water cannon. And, in cases like mine, the bullet. How can they call me an agent of the counterrevolution when the revolution that Marx foresaw has still not been allowed to happen? Not yet, not anywhere. I want my grandchildren to grow up under a government that will share with them not just the full wealth of the nation, but the full wealth of all its officials. A government that will weep for them when they are hungry the way I weep for them. At the same time I want them never to forget what their grandfather bled for. And in his memory, I want them to go out into the street every day and call their wonderful government vile names at the top of their voices. Then, if they are not harassed, or jailed, or shot for doing so, they will know that for at least one more day their country is as wonderful as they thought."

"And how long do you think you'd feel that way after you were in charge? When the enemies inside your country came after you with all their power, trying to pull down what you'd built?"

"It is not important how I would feel because I would be gone. At the very moment it became time to form a new government."

"You're telling me that after all you've gone through for Poland you wouldn't want to stay and lead it?"

"I want to lead my country from the bottom of my soul, but I must not. Great revolutions don't flower until they are rid of their Robespierres. The men who hated and bled and slaughtered cannot be changed. More than twenty years after they secured their little island, Castro and his thugs still strut around in battle uniforms. Every day they think that just a hundred more bullets in the head will guarantee their security.

"As soon as the last cannon of the revolution in Russia had been fired, Lenin should have wangled himself a pension and gone to take the sun on the Black Sea coast. With no Lenin, the bloody habits would have been prevented by the first laws, not promoted. There would never have been a Stalin. Russia today would be as benign and free as France. And far more prosperous, because the country's huge wealth and energy would flourish in a pure Marxist state. The only thing that could foul up Poland would be Stanislaw Kuzianik. And believe me, Father, I will not give him the chance."

A great horror began to steal over the priest. The man across from him was not the enemy of that to which he, Steven Glasgow, had given his life. He was its true voice. The vision of Stanislaw Kuzianik, he now saw, was a thousand times more pure than his own. This was the man for whom Marx had waited a hundred years. His vision rose beyond that of all those who now advanced against him. Why then must he die? He wanted to change a government, but the cause was not a government. Like Glasgow, he sacrificed himself so that every worker would stand as part of the same heart, the same mind, the same wealth in a world that would at last stop bleeding.

This fall from resolve had to be stopped, Glasgow told himself. The warnings from his long-ago training came rushing back. When the arguments of the enemy seemed better than your own, you were in greater danger than you would be from any knife or gun. And how could he, hidden away within the Church for so many years, pretend that his judgment in the matter was greater that that of the men whose great rebellion had become the first hope of most of mankind?

Kuzianik poured two more tumblers of vodka and handed one to Glasgow. "We are too drunk to talk further, Glasgowicz. Politics make me so tired."

The priest downed the liquor, wondering blurrily if he was trying to drink past his point of control so that he might let slip to Kuzianik some hint of his danger. He would never know the answer. By the time the Pole reached for the bottle to refill the glass, Glasgow was asleep.

27

A Federal Express messenger brought Peter Keene's answer from his former altar boy. Along with photos of his children, his pretty wife and a house with a teardrop-shaped swimming pool, there was a half-page printout of everything the FBI knew about Dr. Zamlet Gorslev.

His parents had both been heroes of the Battle of Leningrad during the German siege. This had opened doors for Gorslev, and he had been admitted to the medical school there. He had graduated high in his class and soon published a precocious paper on the nonsurgical control of circulatory blockages in the aftermath of traumatic arterial damage. It had been reprinted in several Western countries and gained him a small but sturdy reputation as a rising authority on circulation. Based mainly on that, he had been to London twice, Toronto once and New York City three times before he was thirty. The fact that those were the great agent centers for the Soviet Union at that time caused U.S. intelligence circles to consider that his famous paper might have been prepared by older and wiser doctors to open the way for the travels of a talented young operative. Hence the birth of the FBI file that Keene now read.

Gorslev had taken his medical travels back to Europe. He was well wired into the government and consulted with them on matters thought to relate to industrial safety. He had not been observed in the company of people known to be KGB, but it had been noted that the cities to which he shuttled almost always had events or locations that would be of interest to an agent.

The last entry on the printout had been included very recently. It showed that Doctor Gorslev had arrived in the United States just three weeks ago, not for a medical meeting, but as a guest of the Soviet Mission to the United Nations. They had allowed him the use of a rented brown Pontiac. At last knowledge he was still in New York City. The date he had given for his return to the Soviet Union was the coming Sunday.

The photograph of Zamlet Gorslev was old and blurred, taken, it would seem, with a very long lens, but there was no doubt it was the soulful pianist Franz Korbin.

While there had been plenty of lies, Keene realized that it might be nothing evil. He knew that Russian nationals could not travel freely everywhere in the country. Wasn't it simpler just to change one's name and history when coming a few miles to visit? There were surely no missile bases or sensitive factories in the area. There was only Stanislaw Kuzianik, and that was a tourist attraction that might draw anyone.

Keene thought about Kuzianik and the gun in Gorslev's bag. Would they send one of their own nationals, an arthritic, middle-aged doctor with glasses half an inch thick to fire a bullet from a Soviet-made pistol at an enemy who was the personal guest of the President of the United States? Hardly. And any prudent Russian who had ever read about the crime rate in New York City might well have borrowed a pistol from his hosts for his stay there.

The evening had closed down, and it was time to go to the church and empty the four donation boxes. Boys from the Den had been known to break in at night, and the boxes were their first target. Keene folded his letter away in a deep pocket, checked the ring of keys Glasgow had left hidden for him in a fruit bowl and went out the side door of the rectory.

This was the approach to Our Lady of Jasna Gora that Keene loved best, especially on these brisk autumn nights when the tree frogs and crickets filled the air with cries of farewell. Although the clouded moon offered little light, making the path too dark for comfort and a bit dangerous, the sky, where clear, blazed with stars. And, as always, the sweet scent of Father Glasgow's garden filled the soul. It was the one overt expression of tenderness that could be seen in the pastor. He had begun to plant and nurture these beautiful trees, shrubs and flowers, Keene had heard, almost from his first days at the church. What had been a near-desert of sparse grass was now a series of wooded trails where the foliage at places rose higher than the head of a tall man. While Glasgow would not accept personal gifts of substantial size, the local nursery people and garden clubbers knew he would never turn down a fine young tree or vigorous shrub.

Keene slipped into the empty church, savoring its hush and the dance of shadows thrown by the sloping banks of yellow-flaring candles. Gliding along the side aisles, he circled the pews, unlocking the donation boxes as he went and pouring the coins and bills into a leather pouch he had slung from his shoulder.

His last stop was the box near the baptismal font at the rear of the sacristy. As he drew close, he saw through wooden scrollwork that a light had been left burning. Squinting through one of the openings, he saw Steven Glasgow standing in profile before a table.

The pastor had already emptied the box from the font, and the money lay in a pile before him. Keene was about to walk straight in, but something in Glasgow's manner gave him pause. He had the same look that Keene had seen on the faces of children rehearsing for the Christmas pageant, in which expressions and gestures were still mostly inside and each movement seemed to come in a dream.

The sacristy was lighted only by a stand holding four large candles, and Keene could not at first see what Glasgow was practicing. But soon there was a clue.

The pastor's hands suddenly flurried at the empty air as though to catch an elusive something, and a coin bounced on the slate floor. After observing for a few more moments, Keene almost laughed aloud. His austere pastor seemed to be rehearsing sleight of hand with the coins from the donation box. He was attempting to manipulate two quarters at a time in his right hand.

He wasn't very good at it. Even in the poor light, Keene could see the clumsy folding of his thumb as he tried to hold both coins in his downturned palm.

There was no doubt that this was something Glasgow was serious about. Each time he failed, the look on his face was not just annoyance, but actual pain. Keene shook his head. There's a ham lurking inside the best of us, he thought.

The curate gave his money pouch a loud jangle and marched into the room. Glasgow's surprise caused him to lose control of one quarter and it jingled to the floor.

Keene caught the coin on the first bounce. With a twinkle in his eye, he thumb-flipped it high over his head and caught it behind his back. "To properly approach the black arts, dear Father, you must first approach the black magician. You are a very fortunate lad. I have brought home many an honest shilling from the county fair for the practice of skills I will now demonstrate for nothing more than the love of God and all apprentice performers. Please observe."

Keene saw the whiteness of Glasgow's face and vowed never to startle him that badly again. But this would loosen him up quick enough. Standing before Glasgow with his best get-a-load-of-this grin, Keene showed him a quarter in each of his palms and whipped into his act.

The coins seemed to vanish and migrate from palm to palm at his will. They multiplied, then fell from the air and suddenly appeared behind Glasgow's ears. The pastor lost his frozen look and began to enjoy Keene's performance.

"Peter, why am I running this parish? It seems that God has given you all the talent."

"And then, me bucko, he sent me to you so that such talent would pass forward. Now watch me and follow along. I'll tell you what to look for."

Glasgow still seemed terribly ill at ease, but Keene pressed ahead, showing the basic grips and the small side movements to distract the eye. Very quickly, Glasgow picked up the technique.

Finally, Keene clapped him on the shoulder. "That's a lot better,

Steven. Don't forget, it's a poor priest indeed who doesn't know how to make the parishioners' money vanish."

Keene swept the bills and coins from the table into his leather bag, grinned a goodnight and hurried back to the rectory. It wasn't until he had transferred the money into the safe in the office and climbed the stairs to his room that he realized he had not returned Glasgow's ring of keys. Rather than go back downstairs and put them on the dining room table, he decided to leave them outside the door of Glasgow's room.

Had the door been locked, Keene would not have gone in even though he held the key to that door in his hand. But he could see that the latch had not quite caught, and since the Almighty was in charge of details much smaller than this one, he took it as a sign that he might be required to have a look inside.

He had, in fact, no real idea of what he might be looking for, but the pastor's strained expression had coupled again with his own tight feeling. And there was the picture torn out of the bulletin that he'd seen in Korbin's bag. Korbin who was really Gorslev.

He vaguely recalled the words of a man for whom he had caddied as a boy. When the man would slam a ball into the deepest woods, where other golfers would simply drop a new one, he always made the young Keene go in for a ten-second look. He would say, "You never know what you may find sitting on top of a golden rock." Maybe that was where Keene found his own penchant for ten-second looks.

There was a *Time* magazine lying on the desk. It was the most recent issue, with Stanislaw Kuzianik on the cover. The painting had caught all the electric force of the man, and the Polish flag that flapped behind him blended into a stormy sky laced with lightning.

A letter opener marked one of the pages, and Keene flipped it open. Yes, it was the Kuzianik cover story. And why not?

The only other item on the desk was a vinyl folder containing some parish business letters. He tried the desk drawers and found only one locked. If there was anything to be seen, that's where it would be. It took him only the breadth of a sigh to decide to have his look.

The smallest key on the ring opened the drawer. The only thing in it was a long, brown manila letter file. He drew this up into his lap and let his fingers hurry through the documents inside without removing any. Only one caught his interest.

The plain, white envelope was sealed, and a piece of cellophane tape had been run across the flap. Since the envelope showed no signs of having been opened before, the tape had been put there by someone with great respect for what was inside. Keene turned on the desk lamp, removed the shade and held the envelope against the naked bulb. The light filtering through showed that there was no sheet in it. Off to one side, perhaps two-and-a-half inches square, lay something opaque. Keene felt it with care and decided it was a sandwich of light cardboard put in to protect what was inside. He guessed that its edges were sealed with the same tape that covered the outside flap. If he was lucky, he thought, only the top and bottom of the sandwich would be sealed. Then he just might be able, by holding the sandwich at its corner through the envelope, snap loose some hint of what was hidden.

He arranged his grip and snapped the envelope down sharply from his shoulder to his waist a half-dozen times. When he brought it back to the light a quarter-inch of something circular had begun to emerge from its cardboard sleeve. He decided not to shake it out any farther, now certain that Glasgow did not want this tampered with. But what was it?

Fully revealed, it would have been about the size of a coin, but it was far too light to be a coin. He looked closer. The edges of the arc were almost translucent. There was suddenly something very familiar about the object. Keene realized he was looking at a communion wafer.

There was no time to puzzle it out here. He replaced the envelope, refastened the file and locked the desk drawer. As he rose, the notion hit him to open again the *Time* magazine to the page marked by the letter opener. The spread was mostly pictures and he was able to read the text quickly. The longest paragraph dealt in some detail with Stanislaw Kuzianik's longtime heart condition. It told of his daily need for a very precise dosage of a blood thinner.

Keene realized that if Glasgow walked in there would be no way to explain his presence there, but something held him. He rubbed his forehead, drummed his fingers on the desktop, then idly picked up a quarter that lay near Glasgow's keys. His eyes focused on the coin as he deftly maneuvered it from finger to finger across the back of his hand. At that instant, far down in his mind, a switch began to close.

28

$\mathbf{B}$y Saturday afternoon, Steven Glasgow had come to recognize the horrifying irony of his situation. As he spoke to the scores of people who would be involved in the Kuzianik Mass the next morning, he realized that this moment to which he had pointed his life with selfless passion had become a baffling triple crossroads.

It should have been so easy. Tomorrow he would literally hold in his hand the way to three great fulfillments. He had only to choose among them: duty, love and—suddenly he had seen it—his Church. But each choice led as well to some betrayal.

Over and over he told himself that he must kill Stanislaw Kuzianik. The millions of men who had fallen on the blood-soaked earth at places like Stalingrad and Kursk must not be denied their victory. They had not beaten the demon only to lose to a craven priest and his wretched doubts.

Yet, even if these doubts were to drop away and he slew the Pole as the mortal threat he probably was, how could he go to his love covered with the stink of deceit and death? He thought with a shudder of Claudette's disgust should she ever discover what he had done. Could he bring himself to defile her for a lifetime with hands that had murdered in stealth?

A new agony had come to him, too. He loved Claudette to the point that there could never again be a happy hour in his life without her. But now, for the first time, he wondered if he was prepared to trade his soul for her. Or for anything else. Had he lived in his world of mirrors for so long that he had lost the image of Stefan Glasgowicz among those of Father Glasgow?

One thing was certain. He could deny all these doubts at tomorrow's Mass with the final beat of Stanislaw Kuzianik's heart.

His mind would not stop. What if he should decide to sidestep this mission after all? What would Stassin do? Perhaps nothing himself, but he might have others close by. Still, he told himself, these people were pragmatic. They must be accustomed to the occasional failure of even the greatest scheme. He could be wrong, but he felt they might be content to leave their former buried man to his present life. Or a new life. One with Claudette.

He looked at his watch. Three o'clock. In just twenty hours he would be facing Kuzianik at the altar rail.

Although it was chilly in the church as the sun sank, he found himself wiping his sweating brow on the sleeve of his cassock as he went over the music with the choir. As they squabbled over endless details, Glasgow, distracted by his own thoughts, failed to notice Father Keene standing among the group. When they surged back to their loft, the old curate was left standing alone before him.

There was something different about him, Glasgow saw. The ever-friendly twinkle in his eye was now a glint of steel.

"Peter. You've got a face as long as the Stations of the Cross."

Keene did not return the banter. "I know you have a desperate day in front of you, Father, but you must make some time for me. It's something that can't be put off."

Artie Gordon and his network crew had been waiting for their chance, too. They came roaring up on Glasgow like a convoy of eighteen-wheelers in high gear.

"She's here, Father Steve," Gordon said, neatly getting his shoulder between Glasgow and Keene. When Keene tried to regain his position Gordon shut him out completely by pulling in front of him a pretty woman in her middle thirties. "Father, this is Diane Wallach, as if you didn't know. She's all yours after Mass tomorrow. Di, shake hands with a real winner, Father Steven Glasgow. Give me thirteen half-hours and I'd make him another Bishop Sheen."

"Mr. Gordon, Miss Wallach," Glasgow said as he firmly pressed them aside, "the gentleman you broke in on is Father Peter Keene."

The woman, quick and cool, saw that Glasgow was annoyed. She took Keene's hand and let him see her stern but friendly six-hundred-thousand-dollar smile. "You can bet we're not going to forget you, Father Keene. We do our homework back at the store. We know what a neat one-two punch you two have become. There's quite a timely angle here." She turned to Gordon without letting go of Keene's hand. "A priest who looks like one of the old-guard geezers is really a cutting edge of the new Church. We could work it in."

"Wrong," Gordon said. "This is going to be an arrow, not a shotgun. We stick to the Church and Poland, just as we agreed. No sidebars."

A small lift of her eye, which Glasgow did not miss, told Gordon that it was all butter anyhow.

"Maybe I'll shoot a tag and use it later in the week. The Church should be hot for a while," Gordon added.

"I have not the slightest need to be on your television," Keene said icily. "But I would appreciate your patience and a bit of Father Glasgow's time."

Gordon put on his look of greatest pain and waved a hand heavy with jewelry at Diane Wallach and the two fretting producers who had arrived with them. "Would you mind bearing with us a bit, Father Pete? Steve here stood us up yesterday and again this morning. We really should be doing this back at the hotel so I can stay close to my phone lines from New York and the other media centers. But I said, what the hell, the poor pastor's got the whole Polish nation hanging on his can today. So I push six, maybe seven hundred thousand bucks worth of talent to this drafty bingo basement. To suit me? Not a chance. Three phones and a pitcher of cold beer would suit me. To suit the pastor here. Now I know God's waiting on what you've got to say, Pete. But with all deference, God's got an eternity to get it done while I've got to be on the air at ten o'clock in the morning. So how about it? Gimme an hour, an hour and a half and we'll disappear—poof—out of your diocese forever."

"I'm afraid Father Keene was here first," Glasgow said.

Gordon was almost able to keep the anger out of his voice. "Look, Padre, we sure as hell don't want to push. We'll just hang out for a while. Come on, Pete. Do it." He clapped his hands as though hurrying the cat into the house.

Glasgow started to lead Keene away from the network people, but the curate stopped him.

"It's too important to do this way, Steven. Just tell me when and where. And then don't fail me."

"It's a real mess today. How about tonight? Right after the evening Mass. In the sacristy. Can it wait until then?"

Keene's gaze was unblinking. "It will have to."

There was little doubt that something had gone terribly wrong for Glasgow. And the old priest wasn't going to tell him what it was until he was ready.

Peter Keene had hardly taken two steps away before Gordon led the second charge on the pastor. It was several minutes before Glasgow got the chance to look up from the clipboards they held in front of him. Between their swiveling heads he saw Keene, stonily calm, arms folded, watching him. Their eyes met and Glasgow found it impossible to disengage the contact.

As though to break the tension, Keene held up a quarter. He gave it a fast flip, caught it backhanded behind his hip and marched it magically across his fingers. Then, with a grand flourish, it was gone, absent from the extended palms which were held out and rotated so that both sides of the hand could be seen.

As Glasgow started to smile, Keene folded his hands as in prayer, closed his eyes and tilted his head slightly upward. Then his mouth opened and his tongue slid out, the perfect picture of a man at the altar rail waiting to receive Holy Communion. Steven Glasgow felt a sudden chill. There, perched neatly on the end of Keene's tongue, was the missing quarter.

29

As Glasgow tried through the afternoon to reach Stassin by phone, he had time to think about the man. It astounded him how little Stassin had changed since he had come into the open. He continued to twit Glasgow and his seriousness as before. And he could still speak for a solid hour about the great, almost unknown trout lake near the western state line that a lawyer friend had told him about.

His life for the cause, as he had told it, had been pretty much like Glasgow's, an interminable wait with little to show for it. His mission had been the same as that of most low-order agents assigned to ethnic areas. He was to look for people with strong European ties who might be willing to trade information and assistance for favors to relatives still living in the old country. Or people whose politics still leaned to the worker's state, and who might have passed them on to children now working in "interesting" areas. Stassin estimated he might have picked up four or five men in the past twenty years. He had also realized that what they had delivered could almost certainly be found by any good researcher in the Lost Hessian library.

Of course, Stassin said, it had been very sobering for him to be chosen as the contact for this mission, but he did not delude himself about the importance of his part in it. He had told Glasgow that he would never have had the stomach for it himself. Even the little he had already done in the matter of Stanislaw Kuzianik was causing him some sleepless nights. The cause was first and final, of course, but the death of a man, even one so dangerous to that cause, would weigh on him forever. Glasgow now wondered whether Stassin wasn't as ready as he was to give it all up.

The hardware dealer sounded very calm when Glasgow finally reached him by phone. "I understand your concerns, Steve. But backing out now? That's an awfully big move."

"Believe me, Michael, if Peter Keene knows what I think he does—"

"If they bust this, all they get is you. That's the way it's set up. Then you'll say you did it for the Church. You did it for peace."

"To make them believe that I'd have to use a pistol, cyanide. But when they find out about the Coumadin thing, they'll know I had the whole Red Army Chorus behind me."

"If they've been tipped they'll never let Kuzianik get to the altar rail. Oh, they could make their move right there and try to nail the wafer before you pass it, but that's not likely. It would make the Church look too bad. They don't want that, and neither does Kuzianik. If they're on to you, they'll stop you without a ripple."

"You haven't spent much time with his bodyguards."

"No, but I have a file on every one of them. And you're right. They're very short on politics and very long on blowing your brains all over the altar."

"I say we should call it no go."

Stassin sounded merely thoughtful. "That's not at all irrational. And knowing, or guessing, about you and Claudette, I understand. But, Steve, this is too big for a couple of little guys to decide to screw up. What's kept us going is the hundreds of millions of poor slobs all over the map getting the shit kicked out of them. And now that the moment is here for us to do something about it, we're looking to save our cans. Is that right?"

"The whole point is that I'm not sure we're getting the right guy."

"What are you talking about?"

"I mean, Michael, he's not the devil. He believes in everything we do. He doesn't want to blow out the system, he just wants to blow out the Russians."

"And without the Russians there to protect it, how long do you think that system would last? Pan Am wouldn't have enough 747s to fly all the CIA men into Poland."

"If Kuzianik can beat the bear, and I truly believe he can, then he can beat the eagle. You should talk to the man the way I have, Michael. In fact, I can arrange that. See for yourself. They're asking us to kill the very man we've been waiting for."

"Steve, Steve, Steve. Don't you think the people above us know what Kuzianik thinks better than we do? Don't you think they've analyzed every word he's written and spoken to the last degree? I know them better than you do, and they're not any more blood-thirsty than I am or you are. If they really believed they could save this man for the system, they'd move the world to do it. But they know you can't just look into a man's heart. Kuzianik's motives may be as pure and honest as Abe Lincoln's, but that's just the kind of man the bad guys can use. In less than a year there'd be carbon copies in Yugoslavia, Hungary, East Germany. 'Look at me,' they'd shout, 'I'm another Kuzianik. Now grab a gun and we'll get rid of the tyrants.' What's taken since nineteen-seventeen to build could be gone in five years."

"I've thought a lot about that."

"Okay, then let's both calm down and think this thing through. Have you any hint that Keene may be more than a priest?"

"No, but his showing up when he did was just too perfect to be a coincidence."

"And we don't have time to check him out."

"Michael, I'm certain he knows everything."

Stassin thought for a moment. "Look, we can't turn into a couple of old maids hearing things under the bed. Let's let it hang until Keene talks to you tonight. If it looks like he knows too much, we'll drop it."

Glasgow felt a sudden rush, the first happiness he had known in months. Was that all there was to it? Stassin, it seemed, was no more eager to press on than he was. Although he didn't know who

Peter Keene really was, Glasgow could have kissed him. "All right, Michael, that's a deal."

"Just keep hoping it turns out to be nothing," Stassin said.

"Priests don't hope. They pray."

Stassin tried to chuckle. "Then say one for me, too. Remember what they taught us: Learn to use the enemy's weapons."

Somehow Glasgow struggled through the afternoon. He was too strong for an attack of nerves, but a fatigue so great that he could scarcely stay on his feet came over him. Like a marathon runner who had mistimed his final surge and burned himself out a hundred yards too soon, he found himself doubting that any amount of will could carry him across the finish line.

He had not wanted to see Kuzianik again, but Archbishop Doolin and the State Department had been talking. They wanted pictures. They wanted stories. So the photographers and the reporters came boiling in.

Glasgow did not have to be so close-mouthed now. The interview tomorrow would be no bombshell after all. Just the diocese line, holding back nothing in his praise of Kuzianik. Strange, he thought, how deeply sincere he would be in these words that would serve to cover the tracks of an assassin.

Kuzianik had grown more quiet. Everything he said from here on would be anticlimax. Now he wished only to visit with his old father and gather his strength for what was ahead.

From the thousands around him, Stanislaw Kuzianik had selected Steven Glasgow as the one man with whom he could rest his battered trust. In the time they stole between questions and pictures he let Glasgow see some of the fear and loneliness that his enemies never guessed at.

"I will tell you this, Father Glasgow," he said just before they parted. "If I should weaken and allow myself to be alone, holding the warm breast of a woman who loved me for just one hour— perhaps one minute—I would move into my father's house and armies could not drag me back to Poland." He cupped his hand behind Glasgow's neck. "When we meet at the altar rail tomorrow morning, pray that I may receive some peace at last from that God you say is there."

"I will pray for that, my friend," Glasgow said. "Until tomorrow, then."

30

Glasgow said the Saturday evening service, aware of Father Keene hurrying in and out of the church. At one point he saw him carrying an armload of folded Polish flags down the side aisle. Later, he was in the sacristy drilling the altar boys for the Kuzianik Mass. The old priest might have caught his pastor's eye with a grin or wink, as was his way. But tonight he was all business, and Glasgow had no doubt that their appointment was as much on Keene's mind as on his own.

The final lingering note of the organ died away as the last parishioner filed out. Glasgow, quickly out of his vestments, saw that Keene was making an unusually rapid tour of the donation boxes, emptying those at the rear of the church into the leather shoulder pouch. Since he always came into the sacristy last for the box at the baptismal font, Glasgow opened it with his own key and emptied the money onto the table for him.

When the sober-faced curate walked in he barely nodded to the pastor. He didn't seem angry or nervous, just terribly sad. He brushed the money into the pouch. "We'll probably be here for a while, Steven. I should let Mrs. Sullivan know so she won't hold supper, and I'd best get this money into the safe. I won't be long."

As the door slammed behind Keene, Glasgow knew he should be planning answers to whatever accusations might be thrown his way, but it just didn't seem to matter anymore. He no longer felt the need to throw Keene off the trail. If what the man knew was dangerous, the operation would simply be canceled. Nobody knew about the sealed envelope. Simple, baffled denial would take care of anything.

He now considered a new thought. Even if Keene wanted to talk about nothing more important than an unwed pregnancy in the parish, Stassin need never know that. There was a clear way out for him no matter which way the Keene meeting turned. Glasgow probed for the sense of shame that should have been filling him and found it sweetly missing.

He had barely time to let this settle in his mind before Mrs. Sullivan, somewhere outside, began a shrill screaming.

Glasgow was out the sacristy door in an instant, running blindly through the darkness toward the sound of the housekeeper's moaning sobs. He cursed the thick shrubbery he had planted as it slowed him down and hid her from his view. "Mrs. Sullivan," he shouted. "Mrs. Sullivan."

"This way, Father," she gibbered, "the path by the dogwoods."

When Glasgow found her she ran into his arms, her eyes staring wildly through the bloody fingers she pressed to her face.

"My God, you're hurt. What happened?"

"It's not me, Father." Shuddering, she pointed to the path behind her. Through the darkness, Glasgow saw a sprawled pile on the gray flagstones.

He rolled the body onto its back. Only the bristling shock of grizzled hair told him it was Peter Keene. Whatever had hit his face had struck with immense force. Blood was splattered several yards from the spot where he had fallen. Glasgow began to wipe the wrecked features clean but saw that he could not. From the right eye socket, across the nose to beneath the left cheek, the bone structure had collapsed and crumbled randomly inward. Through the blood that bubbled out of the torn flesh he could make out several white, shattered edges. "Oh, Peter," Glasgow moaned. "My poor, poor friend."

"Was it a fall, Father?" Mrs. Sullivan quavered.

Glasgow saw that the shoulder bag with the donation box money was gone. "No, it was something else. He left me only a minute ago. You must have come along just as it happened."

"I was holding supper for him and it was getting cold. I came to see if the poor dear man was going to be long." She began to sob uncontrollably.

"Mrs. Sullivan, listen to me. Did you see or hear anything?"

"I thought I heard someone going off fast down the path, but I thought nothing of it—the kids are always sneaking into the bushes for a bit of kissing. Then I almost fell over poor Father."

When Glasgow slid around to feel for the pulse in Keene's wrist, his foot struck a chain lying in the path. It led his eye to the weapon.

The chain had been strung at knee level along the flower beds bordering the path. One of the three-foot iron guide bars through which the links ran had been disengaged and wrenched from the ground. After it was used it had been flung into a heap of drifted leaves beneath a withered rose bush. Glasgow saw the abrupt bend two-thirds of the way down the sturdy bar.

He held Keene's pale wrist between his fingers, trying to separate the thin thread of life that might remain there from his own pounding pulse.

"Sweet Jesus," said the voice of Michael Stassin, "is he dead?"

He had emerged from the darkness so quietly that Mrs. Sullivan yelped.

"I can't tell," Glasgow said numbly. "Mrs. Sullivan, call the hospital and then the police. Tell them how bad it is."

"Father Bolter heard the ruckus out front," Stassin said. "I'm sure he's doing that."

"Go now, Mrs. Sullivan, and do as I say," Glasgow said, holding Stassin with his eyes.

As the housekeeper hurried off, Stassin started to kneel over Keene. "Let me have a look."

As big as Stassin was, the priest's sudden, powerful shove against his chest jolted him backward. His legs came up against a standing section of the chain and he went grunting on his back into the ruined flowerbed.

"No one touches Peter until the doctors get here," Glasgow said, his voice level.

Stassin sat up slowly. "Better get hold of yourself, Steve. I know this is an awful shock, but they'll get the kid who did it."

"What kid?"

"Even these tanktown cops can't blow this one. Not with a witness."

"Who? Bolter?"

Stassin almost seemed to smile. "No, me. When I heard Mrs. Sullivan, I came flying through the bushes from down the street. There's a place along the outside path where the trees separate and the street light cuts through. That's where I spotted the kid. Just for a second. When he saw me he veered off the path and was gone like a squirrel."

"Did you recognize him?"

Stassin nodded. "He even hissed something at me in Polish. If I hadn't seen him I could still make a pretty good case against that trouble-making little hunkie. The one Luzzi is always running in. He had the money pouch, too."

"You mean Eddie Sadowski?"

"That's the one."

"Did he have a weapon?" Glasgow asked tightly.

Almost without looking, Stassin reached from where he sat and picked up the bent metal rod. "He probably used this. And from the looks of it poor old Keene won't be needing any help." He threw the bar aside. "Why don't you go inside and check on Mrs. Sullivan? I'll look after things here."

Glasgow folded his arms and settled his broad body between Stassin and the fallen Father Keene.

The phone shook in Glasgow's hand and his eyes burned as though he had been awake for a thousand hours. He had gone halfway through a bottle of Canadian Club that Father Smead had left behind, but couldn't feel its effects.

Doctor Weintraub sounded exhausted and discouraged. "I'm sorry, Father, but you saw the injuries. And with his age . . ."

"There's no chance at all?"

There was a glum sigh at the other end of the line. "I try never to say that. Father Keene got a bit of a break, if you could call it that. I figure whoever did it was trying to catch him high, but either Keene moved on him or the attacker misjudged in the dark. The facial bones and cavities caved in and absorbed a lot of the blow. There's a serious cranial fracture but, fortunately, nothing is displaced against the brain. He's lost an eye. And, of course, there's no need to talk about the shock."

Glasgow was unable to blot out the vision of the enormous Stassin delivering that blow to the frail Irishman.

"Do you think he'll make it through the night, doctor?"

"If you want the truth, I seriously doubt it."

"Father Keene's tough. He's stubborn."

"I found that out. While we were trying to figure out whether he was dead or alive, he yelled your name and scared the hell out of us."

"He was conscious then?"

"More like a reflex. It lasted only a few seconds."

"May I come over and see him?"

"Father Bolter is here, and there's nothing you can do."

"You'll call if there's any change?"

"Sure."

Glasgow hung up the phone and it rang again. It was Kuzianik. "Father, I have heard of this terrible thing. What can I do?"

"Nothing. It's with the doctors now. They tell me he hasn't much time."

"Such a tragedy. I will send my friend Sandor Holros. He is a remarkable man with prayer. He will go see the priest. He will lay his hands on him."

"I'm afraid he won't be allowed in."

"Sandor Holros is a man who does not know what it means not to be allowed. He will go, Father."

"Thank you, Stanislaw."

Glasgow hung up and wandered restlessly downstairs to find Mrs. Sullivan opening the front door to Sergeant Luzzi.

"I stopped by to let you know we've got an arrest. Doesn't do much for poor Father Keene, but it sure as hell does something for the rest of us." Luzzi was a short young man with the face of a bulldog, a tough cop completely devoted to his town. "I've been making some calls, and this is one kid that's not going to slip through the system. I just wish he was a couple years older so we could go for the cooker."

Glasgow had not thought that his heart could fall any farther. "Who was it, Sergeant?" he asked, knowing the answer.

"I thought Stassin told you. It's the Sadowski kid. We found him sitting home alone watching a rerun of "M*A*S*H" as cool as you please."

"You get a confession?"

"Not yet, but his eyes sure bugged out when we showed him that money pouch he hid under the doghouse."

"How fast did you get to him?"

"Not as fast as we should have. I was out when Mrs. Sullivan called, and so were the other cars. A double-hitch jackknifed into a Volkswagen bus on the pike—a mess and a half—so we couldn't nail him on the street. He had plenty of time to get home and hide the bag."

And so had Stassin, Glasgow thought. "Any witnesses for Sadowski?"

"Not a one. His folks were at the Pulaski Society all evening, and his sisters were out. Probably trying to peddle the hub caps he stole."

"Has he got a lawyer?"

"They'll appoint one."

"This town isn't overrun with great public defenders."

Luzzi broke a smile. "Yeah. Maybe all the breaks aren't going against us. We had to hang on to the bag for evidence, Father, but it's all logged in and you'll get it back with every nickel. My personal guarantee." He squeezed Glasgow's elbow as he left. "I'll be at Mass tomorrow, for a change, and not just for Kuzianik. Father Keene needs all the help he can get."

Because Keene had been assigned to him for only a short stay, Glasgow had never gotten his family information. Wearily, he climbed to the old man's tiny room and let himself in with a master key. He thought there might be an old brother or sister he could pick out of an address book. It would be a lot more personal than a cold telegram from the diocese.

The room was a smaller version of his own and, with the exception of not having an armchair, it was furnished exactly the same way.

Like Glasgow, Peter Keene was not one for having his personal effects in sight. But for a near-antique portable typewriter sitting at the side of the small desk, the room might well have been unoccupied.

The locks on the desk's drawers had given up long ago, and Glasgow sat down to begin his search. A crumbling leather address book sitting at the front of the center drawer came to his hand at once. He opened it and read the flyleaf inscription: *To Peter. Remember us always in your prayers, our blessed and beloved son. From Mom and Dad. Roscommon, May 4, 1939.* This was almost certainly an ordination gift.

In the pages of the book Glasgow found the names and addresses of three Keene women, one living in Chicago and the other two together in Kerry. While he copied these out he wondered why the name of Sam Sandusky was listed along with the number of the General MacClellan Hotel.

It was time to find out how much more Keene was than he seemed.

In the third drawer he looked into, Glasgow found a vinyl correspondence case of the kind sold in dime stores. He opened it and discovered that one side was divided into three pockets. Each pocket was filled with white bond paper.

The first sheaf, typed and worded with surprising skill, was a copy of a full report on the investigation of Father Alfred Smead. It was addressed to His Excellency Bishop Colin McCarthy. Glasgow read it and understood where Keene had come from and what he had to do with Sandusky.

The report was long and carefully balanced. Glasgow was impressed with the care Keene had taken in judging the thoroughly unworthy and unlikable Smead. Part of the report had to do with an evaluation of the pastor, and he was pleased at how well Keene had liked him.

The final paragraph confirmed Smead's guilt and recommended his instant removal. Glasgow was surprised that he, as pastor, had not been told of the investigation and its outcome once it had been completed. And the lenient treatment given to Smead was certainly not like McCarthy. Smead might actually have had a breakdown as reported to him, but Glasgow doubted it. The several times he had called Smead at the rest home the man had been composed almost to the point of being smug.

There had been more to this than now showed.

At the bottom of the last drawer Glasgow found a small chest of oak. The hinges and catch were polished brass that showed brightly against the rich color of the scarred and smooth-worn wood. The brass letters sunken into the top read P.V.K.

All the mementos of Peter Keene's long life did not even cover the small blotter on the desk. There was a picture of Keene as a baby, laughing so hard in the arms of his beautiful mother that the woman had been forced to laugh with him even though it was a serious studio portrait. He was no more serious in a snapshot with, if the sameness of look told anything, a slightly older brother and two younger sisters. Their strong, cheerful faces said that you could expect a bit of hell when the Keene kids were around. A shot of their fine-featured parents in a playful but hearty embrace by the sea showed that the Keene children came by their bubbling spirits honestly.

In Keene's First Communion photo Glasgow could see that a serious hand had at last begun to touch the laughing heart. There was already something priestly in the expression, as though the youngster had chosen to model his manner after some serene old pastor instead of the local rugby star.

The last studio photo had been taken on the day of his ordination. The proud, somber face was strikingly handsome, but the greatest gift, his laughter, was nowhere to be seen. Glasgow was glad that the old priest had finally found it again.

Other than a small, worn wedding ring of gold and a set of crystal rosary beads, last memories of his dead mother, he guessed, there was nothing else but letters.

Going back almost fifty years Peter Keene had saved the special letters sent to thank him for help he had given in desperate moments. While a few were eloquent and filled with detail, most were simple outpourings of gratitude for the remarkable love and care given to them by their funny scarecrow of a priest. The most recent letter was dated more than ten years before. We all burn out, Glasgow thought.

So the entire life of this good man and his good works could be fitted into one small, sad box. As pitiful as that life was, it was now to be taken from him as a minor precaution.

He didn't phone Stassin until he had been building his anger for more than an hour.

The deep voice at the other end was thick with sleep. "Is he dead, Steve?"

"Not yet."

Stassin sounded annoyed. "Damn that Mrs. Sullivan. One more swing would have done it."

"You make me want to vomit."

"That kind of stuff isn't our business. We're amateurs. We make mistakes."

"I called because I want to be certain we don't make another one."

Stassin's voice was clear now. "Forget about Keene. He's out of it."

"I want Sadowski out of it, too."

"Now hold on. That's the only part of this we got right. As long as Luzzi can put it on the kid, Keene's case stays closed. I know it's tough on the boy, but let's face it, Steve, he's not worth a damn. He'd be going up sooner or later."

"Have you given the police a statement?"

"Nothing on paper. Luzzi told me to come down in the morning when he's got a stenographer."

"Good. Then here's what you tell them. After thinking it over you realize that the light was lousy and you really can't be sure of what you saw. Confuse them. Tell them you forgot all about the beard and the red sneakers. Got the idea?"

Stassin was silent for a time. When he finally spoke, his voice seemed softer, more resigned. "I'm in bad shape, Steve. I think I'm coming apart. Frankly, if something out of my control makes this thing go away I couldn't be happier. I'd forget my number, put a new wing on the hardware store and give you and Claudette the biggest, most shocking wedding this town has ever seen. I'm no pro at this bogie man stuff. Without you with me, I'm finished. The whole thing goes down the crapper if you want. It's as simple as that."

"I'll ask you again, Michael. Do you know what to say about Eddie Sadowski?"

"I'll go along to a degree. I won't fuzz up the statement enough so they'll release the kid—finding that pouch in the yard means they'll hang on to him anyway. But I'll leave enough things up in the air so I can go back on my statement at the trial. I'll be the lousiest witness the D.A. ever saw. That I can promise you."

"And why should I accept that promise?"

"Because we'll have all we want out of Sadowski. With him on the outside there won't be anyone nosing around trying to open up the case again."

"Okay, we'll leave it that way," Glasgow said.

Stassin cleared his throat. "However this whole thing goes, Steve, I hope that someday you'll be able to forgive me for what had to be done. Now get some rest."

"Yeah."

31

Glasgow sensed that the phone had been ringing for a long time. He had fallen asleep with his head resting on his desk, the instrument only inches from his ear. He had been dreaming that he was swimming an endless ocean, his arms aching and leaden, when the sound of the bell came to him as though from deep under water. Claudette spoke his name before she knew who had answered the phone. Dangerous, he thought.

"Steven. Oh, Steven, my darling. I just heard about poor Peter." She was not hysterical, but he could hear that she was choking back tears. "I'm coming right in. Will you be at the rectory, or should I go straight to the hospital?"

The sound of her voice lifted him and blew the fog out of his mind. "Who called you? Michael?"

"Jim Yancey, as soon as he heard. He knows how much I love Peter."

So her cousin was leaving her out of it. Good. "I would have called you myself, but I thought you might face it better after a good night's sleep."

"I've got to see him, Steven. And you, too."

"You can't. Peter's dying, and this place is a madhouse. Someone's on me every way I turn."

"Then come to me. Oh, God, I need you so much. Why must I always come last?" Her voice was breaking.

Glasgow knew too well how she felt. He was ready to give his life just to touch her. "All right, but I can't come all the way out there and it mustn't be for long. Meet me at the boathouse at Moccasin Lake. The road going in looks closed, but the barrier isn't locked down. Just get out and give it a shove. There won't be anybody there and it's halfway between us. Start now."

"I have the car keys in my hand."

"See you in thirty minutes."

"I love you, Steven."

"Watch how you drive."

As the headlights of the speeding Pinto picked up the glistening wet leaves on the turn, Glasgow heard his own warning ringing in his ears. He was going too fast to swing clear, but got in a little braking before the rear end broke loose and he felt the car plunge backward into a cleared field. When it had slowed to a stop, he sat cursing himself. But he had been lucky: no ditch, no concrete stanchions, no heavy trees. And if he had gone in sideways, the car would have tumbled for half a mile.

The stalled engine started easily, and he put the Pinto into low gear, trying to ease it out of the field without sinking too far into the rain-softened earth. He had made about five yards when he hit a soft spot. The car stopped and the wheels dug in. He tried to gun his way out but only dug himself deeper. His attempts to rock the wheels out of their rut with alternate forward and reverse thrusts did not work.

Stupid moves made stupid problems. Here he was almost fifteen miles outside town on a road that went nowhere. Claudette would be waiting for him, half crazy. In three hours it would be dawn and Father Bolter would be knocking on his door.

Then he remembered something Bolter had said to him two weeks before. The young priest had been towed out of snowdrifts four times during the last winter. Next time he would be ready, he'd said. He was going to put a shovel, a bag of sand and a hand winch in the trunk. But had he done it yet?

Glasgow fumbled a flashlight out of the glove compartment and went back to the trunk. It was all there. He knew the shovel and sand would do him no good, but the hand winch would be perfect if he could find a place to secure it. In the glare of the headlights, which were facing the road, he could see no trees, no post, no rock heavy enough to hold the cable.

Frantically he scrambled up to the road and searched on both sides with the flashlight. It took almost ten minutes to find something that might work.

A culvert ran under the road almost in a direct line with the car. There was nothing to cinch the cable around, but the lip of the corrugated spill pipe on the far side would accept the open bill hook. The metal looked old and rusted, but he thought it might hold.

After fastening the winch to the front bumper and walking the steel cable to the pipe, Glasgow started to pump the handle. The car inched forward.

He had hoped that when the wheels came up out of the hole he had spun into the ground he would be able to drive the rest of the way onto the road, but the soft spot was wide and the mired wheels just sloughed through instead of climbing out. As he pumped, inch by inch, the bumper on the battered Pinto bulged outward and creaked at its tired moorings.

The bumper held, but when the car was halfway to the road the hook sliced through the rusted pipe and flew back almost to where he was standing. Using words he had only read, he slacked off the winch and ran back to reset the hook.

Twice more the pipe gave way under the strain, but finally the car was back on the road. He threw the hand winch into the trunk and looked at his watch. He had lost almost forty-five minutes.

The gate to the Moccasin Lake road was raised. He couldn't go too fast, because the leaves hid deep ruts that could jerk the wheels of a fast-moving vehicle into a tree.

Even in the closed car Glasgow could hear a heavy autumn wind whipping through the half-naked branches above him. The cloud-covered moon cast no useful light, and the only world that existed was the one caught in the headlights. Why had he asked Claudette to meet him in this terrifying place? What hideous tricks her mind must be playing during her long wait.

As soon as he had cleared the trees and turned toward the boathouse parking lot nearly a hundred yards away, he spotted her car. The headlights were on. Not a very good thing to do if you wanted to stay out of sight, but it must have been reassuring to her. He thought about touching the horn to tell her it was him, but then thought better of it.

He rolled closer, but couldn't spot her. By the time he stopped the Pinto behind her car, he knew it was empty. His heart began to turn inside him.

The motor of Claudette's car was running. The heater fan was set on the first position. All the windows were rolled up against the cold night, but the one on the driver's side was broken. Not cracked, but pulverized. It had been hit with brutal force by something hard and heavy.

The latch on the driver's door stood in the up position. All the other doors were locked. It was plain that the window had been broken to lift the latch and remove her from the car.

"Claudette," he shouted with all his lungs could deliver. "Claudette." The wind and the hissing rustle of the hard-blown leaves covered his words. He pulled open the door and looked inside.

Claudette's purse had been partially emptied onto the front seat. Her wallet and a sheaf of loose bills, some of them twenties, lay in the clutter. Whoever had done it wasn't after the money.

Then he saw the shiny steel comb pushed partway down between the back of the seat and the cushion. It was hers. He had watched her slowly pull it through her beautiful hair after they had made love. It was a rat-tail comb, big and well made. The pointed end, almost as good as a dagger, was bent sideways and there was blood on its tip. Claudette had emptied the purse while searching desperately for something to use as a weapon.

There wasn't enough blood to indicate that she had slowed her assailant in any way, but it also meant he hadn't torn into her body. At least not here.

Glasgow took the flashlight out of his pocket and searched around the car in widening circles, calling as he went. At every step he expected to find her, lifeless, face down in the shallows of the lapping water or hanging like a broken doll in the thick brush beyond the edge of the trees.

In the empty, echoing boathouse he kept waiting for his feet to brush against something soft and still, fearing his shoes would slide in the blood that had run out of his only reason to remain on this earth.

A soul-chilling half hour later, Glasgow started back toward the Pinto knowing that he could not call the police.

Although the dawn had not yet begun to streak the black sky, there were lights on in Michael Stassin's house. Had it not been for the steps and high porch, Glasgow might have driven straight into the front room. He took the stairs in two leaps and leaned on the doorbell. When no one came after a full minute, he looked through one of the living room windows.

The lights were burning in the music room. Through its open door he could see Stassin's bald head showing above the top of a chair turned away. Glasglow pressed the bell again, but Stassin did not move. The priest ran for the back door.

The key was under the doormat where Claudette had warned Stassin a hundred times not to leave it. It stuck in the lock momentarily, but then the door came open.

Stassin's eyes swung to Glasgow as he stepped inside, but they didn't seem to see him. The beating hadn't been professional or meant to kill—Glasgow had seen enough of those in the Den to know what they looked like. Stassin appeared to have been hit, probably twice, by someone who might have just lost his temper. The lesser blow had split both the man's lips and left the jaw swollen and abraded. The other, the one that had blasted the senses out of him, had landed at the turn of the temple and forehead. The eyebrow had been opened up and blood, now beginning to clot, had run down Stassin's face and onto his yellow pajamas. His eye was almost closed and a big black bruise, showing every knuckle clearly, was spreading outward.

"You bastard, you called them," Glasgow shouted.

Struggling to collect his mind, Stassin managed to nod.

Hurrying to the kitchen for a towel and some ice, Glasgow saw that the center of the keyboard of the Bösendorfer had been smashed. There was a litter of splintered ivory keys and polished wood on the piano bench and on the floor about the pedals. The demolishing tool, a plaster bust of Mozart, lay in two widely separated pieces beneath the piano. Whoever had beaten Stassin knew him well enough to destroy what he loved most.

As Glasgow pressed the ice down on his brow, Stassin winced and twisted. But five minutes later he was out of his stupor and again making sense.

"Where did they get her?" Stassin moaned.

"Moccasin Lake. She went out there to meet me."

"Oh, what an ass I am. What a four-star ass."

"It's my fault, too," Glasgow said dully. "Bringing her out into the open at a time like this."

Taking the towel-wrapped ice out of Glasgow's hand, Stassin waved him away and held the soothing coldness to his head himself. "I'm sure they were watching her. Probably just minutes away from breaking in when she left her house. You just made it more convenient for them."

"Any idea where she might be?"

"None."

"Will they send her back? After tomorrow, I mean?"

"The minute Kuzianik goes down. I'm sure of it."

"The whole thing could be a bluff."

Stassin dropped his eyes. "I don't think so. I heard them mention Vilna."

"Vilna? What does it mean?"

"It's a Baltic city where they captured three women a couple of years ago. They'd been passing information on movements of nuclear subs. They were almost to Sweden when a Russian patrol boat caught up with them."

"And?"

Stassin squirmed noticeably. "After they confessed everything, they were executed in front of the city officials. They ran a hot poker into their . . ."

"That's enough!" Glasgow snapped. "They're just stories, meant for people like us. Russian fairy tales."

Stassin's big shoulders sagged. "Perhaps."

"You need some stitches."

"Oh, I'll get my stitches." Stassin pointed to his battered face. "One of the gentlemen who visited me is a doctor, and I'm sure he'll be back. He'll want to be certain I look nice for tomorrow's Mass."

32

The crisp, crystal-clear autumn day that broke over Lost Hessian was seen by early risers as the personal handcraft of God. The brilliant orange fire flooding up from the successive ranges of gray-blue hills was the spirit of Poland rising.

Well before dawn, bedroom and kitchen lights came winking on all over town. Young children sensed not only the Christmas-morning brightness of the day, but also its special solemnity. They submitted quietly to the buttoning of stiffly pressed shirts and the fastening of neckties seen only at communions and funerals.

The high officers of the town's army of Polish organizations were first into the streets. Looking strangely shorn in their fresh haircuts, they appeared in uniforms flapping with the medals of assorted wars and testimonial dinners. Their cars trailing the white exhaust plumes of the deepening fall, they crisscrossed in the streets, calling to friends they had known through a lifetime of parades.

These leaders went to their firehouse or legion hall, their Kosciuszko League clubhouse or scout troop headquarters and became the nuclei around which the magnificent day began to build.

To accommodate all those who wanted to march, the parade had been programmed to pass through almost every street in Lost Hessian. Even the inhabitants of the underworld, like Sam Sandusky, pulled themselves from their beds to hang the stars and stripes next to the brave colors of Poland.

There was no way for Our Lady of Jasna Gora to hold all those who wished to attend the Kuzianik High Mass, one they would be talking about for as long as there was a Lost Hessian. Yet there was no reason to distribute tickets or jockey for position.

The regulars at Father Glasgow's Sunday High Mass knew who they were and so did everyone else in the decent part of town. They had attended that same Mass, sitting in virtually the same seats for a thousand Sundays, and there was not the faintest doubt in any mind that they would occupy those precious places today. Certain community pillars whose habits of sleep brought them to earlier Masses had unspoken priority for standing room at the rear, down the side aisles and around the edges of the choir loft. The rest would stand outside, surrounding the church on the streets and grounds. They would hear the service over speakers and watch it on TV monitors. Father Bolter, in a rare moment of enterprise, had extracted these from the network in exchange for the pastor's permission for a camera unit to be placed on a scaffold above a side aisle.

The press and the networks had staked out their positions. The color men, the bottom of the pecking order, were strung out with their minicam people along Grand Army Avenue, the main street that ran by Our Lady of Jasna Gora

The lordly anchors and their sprawling entourages were looking seriously out of place in the heart of the Den. They were clustered about a big, forbidding clapboard house, added to over the years with no regard for the laws of architecture, where the Gustav Kuzianiks had lived since their first days in Lost Hessian. Old Gustav was inside with his son, and Stanislaw's legion of hulking bodyguards had turned the house into a fortress that even the American press could not penetrate. All those heartbreakingly beautiful suits, haircuts and desert boots simply had to wait outside.

Of the heavyweights, only Artie Gordon and Diane Wallach were in place at the church. Gordon had found that the payoff in the network news business came in playing position, not following the action. Mrs. Sullivan now had a new wolfskin jacket, and the TV van was at last safe in the church driveway, tied by cables looped discreetly through a rear window to the power boxes in the rectory basement.

By nine o'clock the town police and state troopers had stopped the entry of all outside automobiles into the town to prevent the streets from strangling in traffic. Hundreds of motorists left their cars where they had been halted and walked into Lost Hessian on foot. One old priest in the crowd likened the sober procession to those he had seen on the road to Lourdes.

Long before the crush hit its peak, the security men had their positions staked out. On rooftops, at windows, in the streets, in the church, they stood by the dozens in a constant search for the face that might draw their fire. Beneath their unbuttoned topcoats were hung submachine guns hardly longer than a pistol and three-pound automatics crammed with thirteen-shot clips. But the main security had come from Poland.

When Stanislaw and Gustav Kuzianik stepped out of the old house at the stroke of ten, a watchful wall of thick-shouldered men formed around them. The flat expressions of the bodyguards were those formed in fields, mines and factories. Their hair was cut in crude, bristling shocks, probably by a wife or mother, and their suits were worn and shapeless. But their eyes promised they could crumple the attack of an infantry platoon.

The young Kuzianik held his proud father's hand as they talked briefly with the pressing mass of network faces. The professional pursuit, the artful question intended to trip or confuse, to ignite a headline, met a wall of ice. This was a changed Kuzianik.

The rabblerousing leader, the playful bear full of peasant wit, had vanished. As though a disguise long worn had outlived its usefulness, he now presented the hidden man. His answers were returned with the old intensity, but the words were reasoned and statesmanlike. His position seemed to take on nuance, cunning recognition of reality in the larger universe into which he was rising.

In the short time they faced him, the newsmen caught a glimpse of a Kuzianik who would be a tougher and more sophisticated foe than even the worst of his enemies could suspect. For this unsmiling man the mountains would soon be moving.

An armored limousine took the Kuzianiks to the athletic field at the edge of town where the parade was forming, and the crowd began to string out along the route.

People with second-story windows overlooking the line of march found themselves visited by friends and relatives they had not seen in years. The swarming streets blared, tinkled and thumped with the sounds of band instruments tuning for the big parade. The blazing leaves of the streets struggled to hold their own with the flap and flutter of a thousand flags and banners. Most often the days that mark great turns in the lives of men dawn like any other day. In Lost Hessian, this was not to be the case.

Father Glasgow had not touched his bed. He was terrified by the visions he saw when he closed his eyes. In his exhaustion, the faces of Claudette, Keene and Kuzianik whirled in his mind. For whole minutes he could not remember whether they were living or dead. And then he would realize it was something he could not know until after the Mass had ended.

His attempts to reach the hospital by phone were unsuccessful. The victims of the highway accident Sergeant Luzzi had described were from large families in the area, and they had flooded the hospital switchboard with their calls. Keene had probably been dead for hours, Glasgow thought.

He knew Claudette must be dead, too. They hadn't been able to take her by surprise. She must have seen them. No matter what he did they couldn't let her live.

But they also knew that he must seize on any hope.

How long had they known of his love, he wondered. While he had been worrying about an old Irish priest who just might suspect something, they must have been watching his visits for months. He hadn't made it very difficult for them, he thought bitterly.

He shaved and showered as if in an awful dream. Without quite knowing when he had begun, he found himself praying, first slowly and quietly, then loudly and convulsively, as though standing in front of the altar at Mass. This was not the praying he had done to quiet the pain of a grieving parishioner or to share great emotion with a dying friend. This was between himself and a God that had never been. It was as though he had stood too long, too close to the banks of a vast river that came into sudden flood and drew him in before he could turn away.

Glasgow never thought to ask for the lives of the three people he had brought to the lip of the grave. With no soul of his own, he could not be heard. He called out for that soul, pouring the words from his memory.

> I come sick to the doctor of life
> unclean to the fountain of mercy
> blind to the radiance of eternal light. . . .

Bolter, rushing by, knocked on the door to call him out. The rush of prayer did not stop as Glasgow finished dressing.

> . . . heal my sickness and wash away my defilement
> enlighten my blindness, enrich my poverty. . . .

Just before he left the room, Glasgow came upon one of Claudette's handkerchiefs among his own. There was still a hint of her perfume on it. He held it to his cheek and felt even this small ghost of her reach into the marrow of him.

> I pray that this Holy Communion
> may not bring me condemnation and punishment
> but forgiveness and salvation. . . .

The parade came up Grand Army Avenue in slow march. The crowd was not cheering now, but hushed, venerating. The older men held their hats over their hearts for Stanislaw Kuzianik and the flags floating above him. The young men, even the tough and uncaring from the Den, were grim and respectful as they held aloft their closed and gloved hands in the symbol of the Iron Fist.

The girls who wept over rock stars now wept over Kuzianik with the same fervor. Their mothers' eyes grew wet as he made them remember the handsome tigers their own men had been.

Father Glasgow, terribly pale, stood in the open doorway of Our Lady of Jasna Gora in a magnificently ornamented chasuble of green.

Waiting with Father Bolter and a platoon of washed and scrubbed altar boys bearing candles, Glasgow watched the grand marchers of Lost Hessian come to a halt in a fan before the church. The bands finished together in a stirring flourish, and the marchers behind brought themselves up to attention and then back to parade rest. The limousine rounded slowly to the curb and stopped.

The Kuzianiks left their limousine and stepped through the door held open for them by Mayor Djunjek. Gustav was the same as always, beaming aggressively over his flaring mustache and waving to friends. But Glasgow immediately saw the change in Stanislaw. He held the pastor's eyes as he mounted the steps of the church, but it was as though they had never met. Something had called him to a sphere that no longer included Steven Glasgow. The arrogance of fresh power? No, the priest thought. There was new rage, new pain in the Pole's eyes. Glasgow wondered what was filling his thoughts.

"Good morning, Stanislaw. Good morning, Gustav. God be with you." They returned his greeting with just a nod, but Stanislaw held onto his handshake for a second longer than he had to. A small sign for a special friend after all. Glasgow reached up impulsively with his left hand to squeeze the hard shoulder. As the sleeve fell back, Kuzianik noticed the turns of gauze around the priest's wrist.

"You hurt yourself, Father."

"Nothing serious."

Glasgow turned. Inside, the organ rang an opening peal, and the procession began up the center aisle. As the colorfully robed line stepped into the great vault of the church, Glasgow could see that Our Lady of Jasna Gora had never been more beautiful. Garlands of flowers that had somehow survived the bite of the harsh hill-country autumn were strung along the walls everywhere, as if the glowing presence of Kuzianik had sprung the blooms magically from the stones.

The altar boys held the candles high, and the organ boomed the choir and congregation through "Jesus Shall Reign."

> . . . Blessings abound where'er he reigns
> The prisoner leaps to lose his chains
> The weary find eternal rest
> And all the sons of want are blest. . . .

Behind the priest, the Kuzianiks and their bodyguards slipped into the pews held open for them. When Glasgow passed through the altar rail and turned to give the greeting, they were all seated facing him, their eyes the muzzles of a firing squad.

In the same row with the Kuzianiks sat Stassin, his lips swollen, the left side of his face a massive bruise slashed by a white patch of adhesive over the eyebrow. His expression was as blank and unchanging as that on the statue of Saint Anthony above him. He had told Bolter of his fall down the attic stairs while carrying some storm windows.

"In the name of the Father, and of the Son, and of the Holy Spirit," Glasgow intoned.

"Amen," responded the people.

"The grace and peace of God our Father and the Lord Jesus Christ be with you."

"Blessed be God, the Father of our Lord Jesus Christ." The responses were thunderous, heard out on the street and reechoed through the open door.

Glasgow felt a distortion, a subtle slowing of the time that was marching him to his fearful appointment. The ageless words and motions seemed to float in eternity.

He was surprised that the power and steadiness of his voice had not deserted him.

> I confess to Almighty God
> and to you my brothers and sisters
> that I have sinned through my own fault
> in my thoughts and in my words,

in what I have done,
and in what I have failed to do.

Through the Kyrie, the Gloria and the Opening Prayer he went
in a not unpeaceful dream. Through the Readings and the Homily
he seemed to be standing beside himself listening to the faraway
words of another man.

In the fervent voices of the deeply moved Poles, he heard a force
of spirit that struck him like a blow. In the flow of his movements,
in the swirl of his glittering chasuble, in the pulsating songs and
blazing banks of candles he felt centuries of strength and tradition
passing through his soul. To Glasgow it seemed that the enchanted
ceremony might go on through all of time.

But then the offertory song rose behind him and he found himself
moving into the liturgy of the Eucharist.

> How bless'd we are who share this Bread, the
> Flesh and Blood of Christ our Lord. May
> love unite us gratefully, as
> sons of God who live in Peace.

The prayers reminded him that these ancient rites were founded
in blood and death. The bandage on his wrist seemed to glow.

> . . . If you do not eat the flesh of the Son of Man
> and drink his blood
> you have no life in you.
> . . . so the man who feeds on me
> will have life because of me.
> The man who feeds on this bread will live forever.

From where he stood he thought he could feel the weight of
Stanislaw Kuzianik's eyes upon his back and hear the labored beat
of the heart he was soon to stop.

As though it were any ordinary Sunday, he sang with the people.
"Lamb of God, you take away the sins of the world: have mercy
on us. Lamb of God, you take away the sins of the world: have

mercy on us. Lamb of God, you take away the sins of the world: grant us peace."

He broke the host over the paten and placed a small piece in the chalice. He said quietly, "May this mingling of the body and blood of our Lord Jesus Christ bring eternal life to us who receive it."

Then, facing the altar, his back to the people, he used an index finger to slide the host hidden loosely in the bandage on his wrist into the palm of his right hand. With all his practice he was able to retain it easily in the fold of his thumb without hindering the hand's use. And, of course, he no longer had to fear the sharp eye of Peter Keene.

A deadly fever surged through him as the communicants filed forward. Beneath his chasuble the sweat soaked through the amice about his neck and ran down into the length of the alb until he felt drenched to the knees.

The choir sang beautifully.

> O Lord, I am not worthy
> That thou should come to me,
> But speak the word of comfort
> My spirit healed shall be.

The congregation joined in powerfully.

> And humbly I'll receive thee,
> The bridegroom of my soul,
> No more by sin to grieve thee
> Or fly thy sweet control.

The Kuzianiks were not to be first. Out of respect for the older members they hung back. Stanislaw and Gustav stood shoulder to shoulder in the second rank, lined up along the altar rail behind those now kneeling.

Towering above the tiny altar boy who held the paten beneath the chin of each communicant, Glasgow began to deliver the wafer and its sacrament. In Our Lady of Jasna Gora the people did not take the host into their own hands in the new way, but let the priest deliver it to their tongue.

The prayers reverberated within him. "This is the Lamb of God who takes away the sins of the world. Happy are those who are called to his supper."

Two bodyguards with restless eyes stood on each side of the Kuzianiks, and two more directly behind them. Out of the corner of his eye Glasgow was aware of the red light on the big, gray TV camera on the scaffold above the side aisle. Scattered everywhere were press cameras with lenses as long as rifles, and even the powerful singing could not fully drown the whirring of their motors. And then there was Stassin standing close by the elbow of a Pole even bigger than he was. He would be kneeling not five feet from Glasgow's hand at the moment of truth. Of all the witnesses beyond numbering he would be the only one who would know what he had seen.

As the first rank of communicants mumbled a prayer and rose, the second came forward to kneel in their place. Glasgow moved down the line, his voice staying steady with prayer, his hand moving easily from the chalice to the parted lips.

At last he came to Michael Stassin. The challenge Glasgow might have expected to find in the mangled face was not there. The swollen features were drawn and anxious, and the priest felt the man's pain for Claudette melt in with his own.

The Polish bodyguards almost snapped the wafer from his fingers. Glasgow had no doubt that if they had suspected what he held in the hollow of his thumb they would have torn off his hand with their teeth.

Old Gustav, scowling, never opening his eyes, was snarling his prayers under his breath as though he meant to blow down the walls of the church. But the passing of the wafer seemed to calm his prowling spirit in an instant. His head bowed into his hands and he was quickly silent.

Stassin rose from the rail and joined the slow, rumbling shuffle back to the pews. His eye caught Glasgow's just as the priest stopped before Stanislaw Kuzianik.

The singing thundered in Glasgow's heightened senses.

> O Sacrament most holy,
> O Sacrament divine,
> All praise and all thanksgiving
> Be every moment Thine.

The black storms in the eyes that gazed up at Glasgow almost rocked the pastor backward. Yet there was the slightest hint of tears. The kneeling man who professed no need of God was moved despite all his talk. With the weight of a great nation on his shoulders he could not stand alone. He reached out for a strength he had never understood or needed.

Glasgow's hand went slowly into the ciborium and a wafer appeared in his fingers. "The Body of Christ," he said.

Kuzianik's lips parted. As Glasgow swiftly placed the wafer on the tip of the tongue, his fingers brushed those lips. Had he trembled, the Pole, now praying quietly with his head bowed into his hands, would surely have felt it.

Steven Glasgow did not remember when the Mass ended.

33

Half unconscious from what was running through him, Glasgow went numbly to his television interview with Diane Wallach. He was able to bring sense and a bit of fire to what he had prepared, but all the vaulted barbs and beartrap questions of the clever anchorwoman could not draw him far beyond the platitudes of a small-town priest.

The frustrated Wallach, finally goaded by the off-camera signals of Artie Gordon, turned off her razor-toothed smile and snapped at Glasgow. "Father, let me be perfectly frank. The Steven Glasgow I'm talking to now isn't the man that we invited here several days ago. That person was an outspoken priest known to have certain ideas not exactly harmonious with Church thinking. Frankly, we expected that you would air those views before our cameras. Instead, we've gotten a conservative, old-Church party line that is slightly to the right of the Pope himself. Father Glasgow, have your views suddenly changed, or did somebody get to you? Someone in the Church or out of it?" She pointed into the camera. "Those people out there are waiting for an honest answer, Father. Did somebody get to you?"

It was the kind of on-camera bullying that had taken Diane Wallach high and, more recently, begun to bring her down. Coarse, unlikable, effective. He had watched her do it time and again on the air. Shooting blind, but with a brilliant sense of where the target was hidden in the dark.

What a glorious chance to make Bennett Eagles's life count for a moment. Or to call the justice of the world down upon his own head and Stassin's.

But Claudette was out there, somewhere.

Glasgow smiled at the coiled anchorwoman. "You asked me to be honest, Miss Wallach, and I will. Someone *has* gotten to me." He rose. "You have." Glasgow held out his hand to her. She took it out of reflex and went white through her TV makeup.

Gordon howled for the cameras to be cut and restrained Glasgow at the door with both arms. "A hundred miles out of line, she was. But no harm, Padre. We're on tape here. We just chop out the question, sit you down in that chair again and get a nice, clean goodbye for the people. The Archbishop will love you for it and my ayatollah will love me. This isn't much of a year for controversy anyway. Tradition is in again. Take my old man: a big honker in the ILGWU, and he voted Republican. Now just come over and . . ."

Glasgow squeezed Gordon's wrists so hard as he removed his embrace that the man whimpered. "Excuse me, Mr. Gordon. I'm late to a communion breakfast."

"We'll get something sent in," Gordon called weakly as Glasgow shouldered his way into the sunshine.

He hurried toward the church, trying to keep his mind empty for fear that one more emotion might cause his skull to crack. He met Father Bolter half running from the rectory.

"Was it the hospital?" Glasgow asked tightly.

The young priest nodded. "He made it through the night. Can you imagine? He even called out. So loud they heard him in the corridor."

"What did he say?"

"Nothing you could make out. There was only a nurse and Kuzianik's guy, the one who never stops praying. She ran for the doctor. Then Peter slipped under again."

"What do they think?"

"Weintraub still says he won't make it through the day. I'm sorry, Father."

"Thanks. I'll go to him right after the breakfast."

"Go now if you'd like. I can handle it."

"I'd best look after Kuzianik."

"He's gone already. Left before I got called to the phone."

"To where?"

"Back to his old man's house. He wasn't at all himself. Didn't say a word to anyone and couldn't seem to eat anything. It almost broke Mrs. Sullivan's heart. She stayed up half the night getting things ready."

"Did you talk to him before he left?"

Bolter shook his head. "I tried, but one of his guys said he wasn't feeling good. And he looked like hell. Walked out under his own steam, though. Maybe just a bit of the autumn flu. When you're that run down it can get you quick."

"Yes, I think you're right, Father. It must be that."

Glasgow spent the rest of the endless afternoon sitting in a hard chair at Peter Keene's bedside, but the tubed, shrunken mound of white sheets and bandages never stirred or made a sound of its own. The metronomic whistle of the respirator was in contrast to the wandering, almost random blip of the heartbeat on the oscilloscope.

There was only a nurse in the room now. When she went off duty she gave Keene an injection and told Glasgow that there was no way he would be conscious before morning. She suggested he come back then, and he nodded. He walked slowly back to the rectory and dragged himself up to his room.

Without removing his coat, Glasgow lowered himself to the bed. He had a notion to lock the door to keep out the well-meaning prowlings of Bolter and Mrs. Sullivan, but fell sound asleep before a muscle could stir.

In a long dream that he couldn't end, he saw Claudette, bloody and naked, hanging from a chain that lowered her slowly toward a mound of glowing coals. He could see her flesh begin to blister, shrivel and char. Each time he reached for the control that would lift her clear, the metal handle burned into his palm until the bones showed through. When he at last screamed through the pain and moved the control, he moved it the wrong way. She fell into the coals, howling his name, and vanished forever in a flash of whirling sparks.

Glasgow was wide awake then, but his hell didn't stop. The terror of his dream only grew more intense in a real world gone out of control. His eyes were wide open, he knew, but he saw nothing. Slowly, he understood that he had slept through the daylight.

He began to make out features in the darkened room. When he rolled his head toward the shaded window, he saw that the faint light was interrupted by the shape of a large man standing at the center of the room.

The voice, hard and low, spoke to him in Polish. "Father Glasgow. You must come to us now."

Glasgow blinked in the light of the small reading lamp he turned on. He knew the man, tall and red-bearded, as one of Kuzianik's bodyguards. The jacket on his undersized suit could not be closed across the broad expanse of his belly, and the butt of a large revolver in his waistband showed plainly.

A second man was waiting for them in the darkness of the driveway. When it became apparent that they had misjudged the long distance from the Kuzianik house and walked to the church, Glasgow gestured toward the Pinto and the red-bearded man grunted agreement.

During the drive to the Den, Glasgow saw that the tidal wave that had broken on Lost Hessian had receded in the short hours of his terrible sleep. The streets and sidewalks, still awash in the litter of the milling thousands, were now empty of cars and the sounds of excited people. Through the windows of the bars the lights seemed dimmer and only a few heads could be seen leaning over their drinks. The banners that had been hung everywhere now drooped sadly in the glow of the street lights. The same exhaustion that had drained Steven Glasgow so miserably had also drained his town.

Deep in the Den, the home of Gustav Kuzianik stood nearly dark. Only the windows of the rooms Glasgow knew to be the kitchen at the side of the house and the front bedroom showed light.

Glasgow parked behind the row of shiny black cars at the curb. Neither the man standing half-hidden in the doorway at the top of the front steps nor the man in the shadows alongside made any move to greet them as they walked around to the side door. He imagined that each had his hand resting on a weapon.

The side door led into the kind of kitchen that Glasgow had entered a thousand times in Lost Hessian. It was large and the smells of an eternity of strong Polish cooking had gone into the countless layers of flowered wallpaper. Doleful pictures of Jesus and the Virgin Mother commanded the key views of the stove and table, while votive candles flickered timeless adoration from atop an old refrigerator.

Gustav was there, seated at the table with five of Stanislaw's old aunts and uncles. Two bodyguards, stripped of their jackets now and showing automatics in shoulder holsters, stood with their arms folded and their backs resting against the porcelain sink.

To Glasgow's nod they returned only stares of cold iron. He climbed the stairs with one guard in front of him and one just behind. He could hear their rage in the way their heavy shoes kicked at the stair treads. But he had let go. He was past caring or hoping.

One of the men opened the door to the front bedroom and motioned him forward. Once he had stepped inside, the door clicked shut behind him.

He faced a large brass bed covered with a starkly white, heavily embroidered bedspread. The single overhead light was projected almost straight downward in a tight circle by a dark, conical shade. Upon nightstands on each side of the bed there flickered candles in red glass containers. From the wall behind, a large picture of the Black Madonna of Jasna Gora glared down.

In the center of the bed lay Stanislaw Kuzianik. He was neatly dressed in the same dark suit and tie he had worn to Mass in the morning. His eyes were closed and he was stretched out stiffly, his hand folded across his waist.

Glasgow moved slowly forward and stopped at the bedside, staring down glassily at Kuzianik's still, white face.

The Pole's dark eyes opened slowly and held Glasgow. "You must excuse me if I don't rise, Father. I am tired almost to death."

"I understand."

"I dislike bringing you here this way, but I promise I won't keep you long."

"Why am I here?"

"For an awful reason, I'm afraid. You know my man Sandor Holros, the one I sent to pray for your poor Father Keene."

"I know him."

"He was there when the Father was awake for an instant last night. While the nurse went to bring the doctor, Sandor spoke to him and your priest knew he was one of us. How much in his head he was, no one can say, and Sandor's English is very, very weak. But he grasped Sandor's hand with all his strength and tried terribly hard to make him understand something."

"And did he?"

"Sandor was able to make out only two words for sure. Sacrament was one. Poison was the other."

"I see."

"When I was told this, my first thought was to go to you, to question you, perhaps to confront you. But then I would never have known if you would . . . or wouldn't."

Glasgow only stared in silence.

"For a time I thought I might swallow the host without questions to show my faith in you. But they wouldn't let me—quite properly. So, when I bent to pray I took the sacrament back into my hands. And we returned here and located a man we could rely on to examine it.

It took some time, but he's finished now. Only he knows, Father. He's waiting in the next room. I wanted you to be here."

"Of course. I understand."

They gazed into one another's eyes in silence. Each man thought he had never seen such pain.

Kuzianik raised his arm to the wall behind him and pounded loudly with his fist. "Sandor," he called sharply.

It was the red-bearded bodyguard who guided a bald little man into the room. This time the bodyguard did not leave. He closed the door, lifted the revolver out of his belt and placed it gently on a sideboard next to him. Perhaps it was to relieve the tension of his bulging waistband, and perhaps it was not.

The bald man sniffed what was in the air, and his voice rose to a strained squeak. As Glasgow might have suspected, the accent was Polish.

"I'm sorry I took so long, sir, but I haven't had the pharmacy for a long time and it took a while to find an old colleague who would allow me to work in his store on a Sunday. Professional courtesy certainly is not what it was, I can tell you." His eyes fluttered above thick glasses, and the loose skin that flowed over the collar of his plaid shirt moved in a flowing quiver. Glasgow could see that the palm in which he held the small, corked flask was wet. The bits of a communion wafer lying at the bottom of the flask were barely whiter than his hand.

"Tell us what you found, Mr. Danzig," Kuzianik said.

"I found absolutely nothing, sir. I tested for hours. And I can tell you without a question that this is nothing more than unleavened wheat flour and water. The most standard communion wafer. I would hope that my children would take a hundred like it every year."

Kuzianik closed his eyes for a long time. When he spoke at last his voice was low and almost sweet. "Thank you, Mr. Danzig. I am most grateful to you. Father Glasgow will give you his blessing and you, of course, will always have mine. Sandor, drive this gentleman home and give him one of the pictures I have signed." He turned again to Danzig. "You will never speak of what has happened here, I am sure."

"Oh, yes, you can be sure of that, Mr. Kuzianik. It's been the greatest honor." He ran forward to embrace the reclining Pole and kissed his hand. Sandor, now finally smiling, came up to pry him gently away and lead him bubbling with pride out the door.

Kuzianik swung his legs slowly to the floor and sat on the edge of the bed. With an impossibly weary grin he drew Glasgow to him, circled his waist with his arms and rested his head against the priest's chest. "Steven, do you forgive people as readily as this God of yours is said to?"

Glasgow patted Kuzianik's back. "Not always, my friend. Not always."

"Please, go downstairs now. My father will fix you something."

"No, I have far to go tonight."

Kuzianik dropped back on the bed again and closed his eyes. "Then go with your God."

"May He protect you always," Glasgow said.

The priest saw that Sandor had left his revolver on the sideboard. He scooped it into his pocket as he left.

Sitting in the parked Pinto in front of the Kuzianik house, Glasgow twice lifted the gun to his temple, but in the end could not bear the thought of leaving a world where Claudette might still live. If they found her body—when they found her body—there would be time.

He looked at the hand that had failed to pass the wafer as though it were part of another body. He thought about returning to the room he had just left and killing Kuzianik where he slept. If he thought it would have saved Claudette he might have.

Glasgow let his forehead sag down to rest against the top of the steering wheel. Something had stolen into him over twenty-three years and turned his strength in upon itself.

There was a light tap on the windshield. One of Kuzianik's men was peering through, trying to determine if he was all right. He sat back, raised a thumb to the Pole and started the car. As he moved out, driving down the street beneath all the forlorn banners, he knew that he could not return to the purgatory waiting in his room at the rectory. He headed down the long highway out of town.

34

There were lights burning in Claudette's house when he rolled out of the trees at the end of the driveway. He had to fight for his next breath. My God, he thought, clawing for one more straw of hope, she's back. He tried to believe that they had realized that whether or not he had done his job she was no longer useful to them. They had driven her home, told her to forget everything.

He braked the car well back from the house and stepped out. Now he spotted Michael Stassin's station wagon at the side. The rear door of the wagon had been raised. When Glasgow slipped by he saw that the back of the second seat had been lowered and several neatly tied boxes had been shoved against the front seat. The car was being loaded. But with what?

He circled behind the house, moving through the same grass where he and Claudette had rolled in the bright sun.

The back door was open, and he let himself in quietly. There was nothing out of place in the kitchen, but through the doorway he could see that a closet in the hall stood open and most of the clothing that had hung in it had been removed. He peered into the living room and found it empty and untouched. In Claudette's bedroom, he heard someone pull open a drawer.

Michael Stassin did not see Glasgow come into the room behind him. His suit jacket hung neatly from the top of the door on a hanger and he stood at the bed, using its surface as a worktable. Half a dozen beautifully folded dresses were laid out in front of him. There were packing cartons on the floor, lined up to be sealed, their contents as perfectly arranged as any work of art. Other cartons had been placed along the back of the bed.

"What are you doing, Michael?"

Stassin started a little but did not turn around. He continued folding the dresses. "What I'm doing, Steven, is helping Claudette disappear from Lost Hessian. Poor girl. She has become the victim of an impossible love affair. Friends will learn she went back to Cleveland for the present. With plans to settle somewhere out West later. I'll say that she asked me to send along the remainder of her things and to look after the house."

"Do you think anyone will believe that?"

"Oh, there'll be letters for a while with all the right postmarks. Even a few phone calls. To Julia Dean especially."

Stassin seemed to be enjoying himself. Glasgow felt the rage building inside him. With a single motion, he took Sandor's pistol from his pocket, cocked it and held it against Stassin's ear. "All right, you bastard. I want to know if Claudette's alive."

"That you'll know in due time," Stassin said gently. "Things have to settle a bit."

Glasgow flung the gun aside and walked to the open window. A cool night breeze rustled the tall trees.

Stassin packed the last of the dresses into a carton. "Don't feel too bad, Steven. I never did see one of these hurry-up operations go right. We were lucky to have the time we did. Our guy in the Vatican had his finger on Kuzianik and Lost Hessian on the same day they hatched the plan. Not bad. And all it cost me was one pretty good piano and a fat lip from that phony beating I had my doctor friend give me."

Stassin sealed the final carton, placed it with the others, then picked up Sandor's pistol from the floor. He pointed it at the priest. "Now, if you'll sit in that easy chair, Father Glasgow, we can get on with business."

Glasgow turned and stared dully at the gun.

"Sit, please."

Glasgow sat and Stassin approached. "Believe me, they would have gotten around to this, but you've made it so convenient for me. Even brought your own gun."

Stassin raised the pistol to Glasgow's temple. "I really do hate this, Steven, but what have you got left?"

With a sudden thrust, Glasgow tumbled the chair sideways into Stassin, sending the huge man crashing down. The great bald head thudded into the metal base of a floor lamp. Stassin's scalp split bloodily and his eyes rolled into his head. But somehow he did not lose his grip on the pistol.

With no clear shot at the gun, Glasgow scrambled to his feet and burst for the nearest window, crossing the living room in three flying strides. He dove through the screen into the night, hit the ground rolling and came to his feet in an instant.

Stassin's station wagon protruded beyond the opposite end of the house. The keys glinted where they hung in the lock of the raised rear door.

Glasgow had taken one explosive stride toward the car when Claudette suddenly appeared beyond it, framed in the light from the bedroom. *My God, Claudette,*" he shouted, *"the car! Hurry!*"

Closer to the car than he was, she hesitated for just a second, then started to run. Stassin had yet to appear. They just might do it, Glasgow thought.

He drove his legs with all his strength, and the distance to the station wagon closed quickly. One of Claudette's shoes flew off and, half-stumbling, she struggled out of the other and kept running.

Claudette reached the tailgate a few strides before he did and tore the keys from the lock. Glasgow held out his hands for them, but she turned and flung them far into the night.

Glasgow never moved after that. He stood there frozen in place, staring at the eyes that had always invited him in, and finding only a hard wall. He felt around inside himself for rage but found none. Instead, there was only a sadness so great that all the night around him seemed to sift into his soul.

"You," he said.

There was a sound far behind them. A door being fumbled open. Then Stassin's footsteps, slow, staggering.

Claudette looked toward Stassin. Her hand rose to her throat. The wall in her eyes seemed to crack. A tear trembled through. She took a step to the side and tried to guide his eyes into the darkness lying open before him. But he just stood, letting her see what she had done.

The scuffling footsteps wobbled closer, shuffling once to regain balance.

Claudette backed away from him, slowly at first, then more rapidly, growing less distinct as she moved from the light. She sank to her knees and her hands began to move through the grass with a growing desperation. He heard her crying, a primal, frantic moaning as she crawled madly about in lurching circles.

Abruptly she stopped, and he heard her long gasp of relief.

She rose and stumbled toward him, the keys tinkling in her outstretched fingertips.

Glasgow heard the crunch of gravel at his side but still did not move. An instant later, just above his ear, he felt a brush of metal. The last earthly sound he heard was Claudette screaming his name.

35

The view from Piazzale Garibaldi at the top of the Juniculum Hill was always best at sunset. Peter Keene had come here every evening for the past two weeks to enjoy the magnificent panorama of old Rome and the surrounding towns lying in the mist of the green hills.

It had been two years since he had felt this well. He had at last stopped trying to make the glass eye work and had given in to a black patch that made him look positively rakish. His nose didn't work as well as it had, but it was certainly smaller and perhaps a bit prettier.

This was the first time in thirty years that Keene had traveled more than fifty miles from his assigned parish or the chancery. How like Colin McCarthy to have presented his old friend with the only gift that had any meaning this close to the end of his life. Keene had been alone with the bishop on the night he died. He had entrusted Keene with a handful of envelopes to be distributed to a few relatives and still fewer personal friends. McCarthy was well known for his canny ways with a dollar, and there had been some pleasantly surprised people who had always thought that the ways of the cross passed only through poverty.

Keene's envelope contained airline tickets to Rome, prepaid reservations at a charming hotel near the Spanish Steps for one month and a generous sheaf of money. Getting away was no problem, of course. The bishop had put him into a fine little parish outside of Boston where the young pastor was kind enough to respect an old curate.

The spiritual and emotional renewal he had found in Rome made him feel like a boy again even as it prepared him to leave this world. The doubts, the pain and the heartbreak of the past two years had mercifully left his dreams.

Then, as the sun slipped behind the distant Italian hills, he turned on the bench for a better look at the magnificent dome of St. Peter's and saw Claudette West.

She was standing perhaps fifty feet away, wearing a dark, graceful dress of high-fashion European cut. She held a dramatically large white purse of glistening leather, and her face was framed by an attractive white hat whose wide brim wavered in the evening breeze.

She had changed little. There was no doubt that she was looking straight at him, and it dawned on him that he might have been seeing her out of the corner of his eye for several days. But the clothes, the stately bearing, the sombre manner, all so unlike the Claudette of Lost Hessian, had put him off.

He didn't know whether to flee or pursue her. She held the answer to a thousand torturing questions, but he was not sure he wanted those answers.

Nevertheless, he nodded to her and she came forward, a beautiful woman who drew the eyes of all those on the terrace.

He rose and she took him into her arms and held him. The sensual playfulness he had always felt in her embrace was gone. Now he felt only loneliness, longing, regret. "I've missed you very much," she said, and he knew she meant it. Claudette drew back to look at his altered face with its eyepatch. Her eyes moistened. "I'm so sorry, Peter."

Keene raised his hand for her to stop and drew her down to the bench. "I'm just fine. I thought I would never see you again in this life."

"You weren't supposed to. Dear Sergeant Luzzi wouldn't even

let me go to Steven's funeral. I don't think I could have lived through it anyway."

"It wasn't just Luzzi," Keene said. "The diocese was in it with both feet. Bad enough their most respected pastor had apparently taken his life. They weren't about to have it known there was a woman involved. They called it the tragic result of a priest's lonely existence, coupled with the pressure of the Kuzianik visit. Luzzi even tore up that touching farewell note you left."

Claudette's eyes fell. "Stassin insisted." She was done being cautious, but Keene probed no further.

She looked so devastated that the priest eased the pressure. "You heard about Kuzianik?"

She nodded. "I read about it. Such a small, sad way for such a fighter to go. His heart giving out because he tried to climb too steep a mountain with too big a pack. It just didn't make him enough of a martyr."

"When that kind of heart stops it should always be because of a bullet," Keene said wryly. "It was smart of the government not to interfere with the big funeral. They even sent flowers."

"And danced in their offices, I'm sure," she said.

Keene watched her carefully. "After that the Iron Fist slowly dried up. I'm sure the government was relieved about that."

"I was, too. It would have been a terrible war."

Keene waited for a moment, then spoke again. "Where did you go? After."

"First to Canada, then to Paris. They wanted me in Czechoslovakia, but I couldn't do it anymore. I stayed in Paris . . . just got out of everything. I worked for a while as an interpreter and met a nice man I'd known years ago in school. We're married now, Peter. I'm expecting his child."

He took her hand. "That makes me very happy, Claudette. God bless you." Then his look darkened. "And Stassin?"

"I keep in touch with some old friends I served with. I heard he's somewhere in New Mexico. Out of it, too. They told me you were going to Rome and how to find you."

"Was that so important, Claudette?"

Her eyes suddenly filled. "I had to tell the only person on earth who would care that I loved Steven Glasgow more than anyone will ever know. I'll love him always, Peter. And I'll carry what I did for the rest of my life."

They sat quietly for a long time while Keene pondered the question he finally asked. "Could you have saved him?"

She thought about it and at last shook her head. "Even if I could have stopped Stassin's bullet, Steven was already dead inside. As it turned out, there was just too little in the things he believed in and too much in the things he didn't."

"I'm sure you're right," Keene said.

"God came so close to winning him, Peter. I often wonder how He's treating him now."

"A priest is the last man to ask about the mind of God. We're stuck between heaven and earth as a hard-used tool in His hand. And when the tool breaks, He just holds out that hand for a new one."

"Can you ever forgive me, Father?"

Peter Keene looked out over the ageless city through which the faith had flowed outward in a great river for centuries. The last rays caught the dome of St. Peter's and sent up a flash of gold that promised there would be hot sun and hope tomorrow. He knew that the Power that built the heart to serve so fiercely must understand all the terrible services into which that heart falls.

Finding his throat too tight to say another word, he opened his wallet and removed a picture of Steven Glasgow. The look on the fierce, handsome face seemed somehow gentler than he remembered. He passed the photo to Claudette. She seemed to vanish into it at once and didn't look up when he gently touched her shoulder in farewell.

When he had walked far across the terrace, Peter Keene turned back one last time. Claudette was standing alone, eyes frozen on the picture in her hand, fixed to the spot as though the man in the image still held her in his strong arms.